WITCH HUNTER

INTO THE OUTSIDE

J.Z. FOSTER

J.Z. Foster

Dedicated to:

My wife, Hanna.
Without you, I could not have
written this book.

Added for later edition:

Guys, you don't get it.
This woman puts up with a lot of shit.

ACKNOWLEDGMENTS

Frank Haar
Shelby Hostager
David Sorensen
Jason Talley
Maria Townsley

1

RICHARD'S HEART THUMPED WITH A HEAVY BEAT THAT threatened to break through his chest. "I didn't do it!" He slammed his fists on the table in the cold interrogation room. Two men stared him down from across the room, their faces icy and unflinching.

Richard ran his hands over his scratched, bruised face and into his blood-caked hair, wondering whether he had gone insane. He fought to focus, but desperation crawled its way up his spine and into his bones, making him shake just as his fingers found a wet spot on his scalp. He pulled his hands back to find them red. A tremor in his hands tapped out a rhythmic pattern against the table that left beads of red as he breathed slowly and painfully.

"Listen," he said, before taking another breath, "I didn't do it. I didn't."

"Really?" The rough voice belonged to a man twice Richard's size. Despite the chill of the room, the man was dressed in a shirt and tie with the sleeves rolled up to his elbows. Pulling away from the wall and closing the distance between them, he leaned in close enough for Richard to smell the coffee on his breath. "Because that lunatic about to have an axe party on the poor woman sure looks a hell of a lot like a fat bastard." Drawing up a nicotine-stained finger, he pointed at the blurry image on the paused TV screen.

The flickering frame held a man with an axe looming over a woman, ready to plunge it down into her skull.

Beth! Oh God no! She has to be okay. I didn't hurt Beth! This is all a mistake!

His mind shook with fear for her, and he took short, rapid breaths. But the gears in Richard's brain were turning more slowly than usual; lack of sleep and the confusion of the night had taken its toll. And there was the head wound, wasn't there? He hadn't processed quite everything the detective was saying. Not until he recognized the bag.

The walls closed in on him, choking the air from the room. This was a cage of stone and brick built around him. His instincts told him to run, run from this lie that he killed her.

But that was his face on the video. That was his smile.

"I... I don't know! Oh my God..." With trembling hands, he grabbed fistfuls of hair again. He gripped tightly and pulled hard, hoping that it was all a bad dream. But the pain wouldn't lie.

"Listen, you piece of shit," the larger detective said, thumping a fist down on the metal table. "What were you doing here in Bridgedale? Why did you waddle over here to murder someone? How many more have you killed?"

The words choked in Richard's throat, crawling back to where they came from like insects caught in the light. Before he could mumble something, the seated man, a graying detective, spoke. "Listen Dick, we found all the other shit in your van. The voodoo shit, the candles, the powders. Clearly, this is some kind of weird occult sex thing."

"Sex...? Wait, what? No! Beth was a reporter traveling with me! She was going to do a story on me," he protested and then hesitated, before the words squeaked from his mouth: "I'm a Witch Hunter."

"A what?" the gray-haired detective asked.

"A witch hunter. Listen, she was doing a story on me and there was a lead here in Bridgedale about some kind of witch presence."

The larger detective spoke again. "Bridgedale has a witch problem? Our small suburban community, which cancelled a fall festival because you axed a woman, has a witch problem? You're a *lunatic*. You need to get this night done with. Tell us where her body is, and we can get you the help you need. Give Beth some peace."

Richard drew in a troubled breath before he bellowed, "Bridgedale has a witch! The witch did this! I was onto him, and... and Beth was going to report on all of it! The witch, he, he... He did all this!" He forced his gaze to the TV, knowing somehow that it would have changed, that it couldn't possibly have been him—but he was wrong—it hadn't. His own familiar face still stared back at him, twisted into a madness he didn't know he possessed.

"There any more of you lunatics? You have a club of *Witch Hunters* that are going to be coming to Bridgedale and axing pretty girls that won't put out? We want the names of everyone. Right now." A notepad was placed on the table in front of Richard and the large detective thumped a fat finger onto it. "Now."

"Can I just—can I tell you the whole story?" He was boiling on the inside, the words hot in his mouth and wanting to spill out. He knew how insane he looked with his wide eyes and bruised face, and the disgust in their eyes confirmed it.

His head, again too heavy to hold up, slid down to the cold metal table. All the muscles in his body lost the will to move, to do anything but give up. He had challenged the witch, and lost. And now Beth was dead.

Dead.

"Fine. Tell us *everything.*" The detective reached over and pressed a red button on a recorder. It hummed to life.

Richard drew in another breath and squeezed his hands together. "Okay… So my sensei was—"

"Sensei? You study martial arts?"

"No, we're just..." Richard didn't look up from the table. "We're just really into Asian culture, okay? Feng shui and centering your chi you know? So I call my master *sensei.*"

The two detectives exchanged a glance. "Okay, go on."

"So my sensei, through his occult contacts, heard that there was a lot of black energy in Bridgedale. He sent me to investigate, but I didn't know it was real!" Richard drew his head back up again to meet their eyes. "Oh my God, I didn't know any of it was real. I don't believe in witches! I mean, I *didn't* believe in witches before tonight. I thought it was just like a role-playing club we were all in! And then someone contacted the news, or the news contacted us, I don't remember. Next thing I know, there's a reporter calling me saying she wants to go with me, and, and...."

Beth is dead and it's my fault.

There was nothing he could do now to change that.

She's dead.

"And what...?" The larger detective crossed his heavy arms. His attention was unwavering, and Richard felt the weight of the man's gaze piercing him, judging, waiting for him to break. It was all he could do to hold himself together and not completely fall apart. Beth was dead, but this was still important. He needed them to hear. But they wouldn't believe him. How could they?

I wouldn't believe me.

"Listen to me," Richard said, leaning forward in his seat. "This isn't a game. He killed Beth, he killed Ted, and he almost killed me. But it's hard to say exactly what happened." He bit his lip and clenched his eyes shut, trying to pull his memory through the fog. Only bits and pieces came back.

The witch. Sharp black things. Teeth. Fingers with hooks. Blood, so much blood. Death.

The detective scribbled away on a notepad. "Who the hell is Ted?"

"No dammit, you're not listening to me! Listen! We tried to kill a witch, but we failed. He killed everyone, and he's still out there. He's going to come here. He's going to kill everyone. He's going to kill everyone!"

"*...BRING out your jackets, and make sure you bundle up, because we are expecting an unusual cold front to move in with a chance of rain throughout the night. Our meteorologists are saying that temperatures could dip into the low—*" Beth clicked the radio off.

She couldn't believe how the events had unfolded; it was as though the universe were conspiring against her. She had gone to school for journalism to report on news abroad, cover what *really* mattered. Syria, Iraq, Israel—these were the places she wanted to be. Instead, she was off to some suburban autumn festival to interview and record a "Witch Hunter."

"Can you believe this, Ted?" Beth asked as she was fixing her hair in the mirror. "Why are we covering this? Why do I always get stuck with the crap stories when some plastic blonde on CNN is on her third trip to Syria?" She had nearly finished fluffing her hair to camera-ready perfection.

"Because you work for WB19 and not CNN? Besides, they're not hauntings," Ted said from behind the wheel. "Witches don't haunt things."

"That right, genius? Then what do witches do if they don't haunt places?"

He shrugged without taking his eyes off the road. "Hell if I know. Question number one for the Witch Hunter right?"

She rolled her eyes. It wasn't long before they were pulling into a Happy Burger to meet with Richard, their supposed expert in witchcraft. Beth knew better though; he sounded like a thirty-something that hadn't quite grown up yet. Probably moved out of his parent's house only a year or so ago, likely lives with two or three buddies that play more video games than a reasonable adult should.

Beth stepped out of the van and the cool air breathed onto her. A chill ran down her back that made the hairs on her neck stand on end; she pulled her jacket up around her neck. It was cooling down faster than usual, and the orange fall leaves already filled nearby parking lots. Someone spoke from around the corner of her van, making Beth yelp.

"Witches can drive the seasons faster."

A man an inch or two shorter than Beth and a few pounds overweight rounded the van. He had stubble across his chin and he was clearly trying to make his voice deeper as he spoke. "You're here for the witching?" He had a red hat pulled down over his face, casting his eyes into shadow.

Ted snapped his fingers, "See! I told you they don't haunt! Witches *witch* things."

Beth glanced once from Ted to Richard, and pulled on a rehearsed smile. "Yeah, I'm Beth." A few seconds ticked by before she reached out to shake Richard's hand.

"Oh good!" His deep voice was gone. He took her hand and shook it, maybe a bit too roughly. "The couple before you almost called the cops on me when I asked them if they were here for the witching. I just wanted to make sure your report said that was what happened when we first met. Figured we'd give the readers something to really chew on, right?" The deep voice returned. "*You're here for the witching*?" He smiled and nodded, content. "They like that sort of thing, yeah?"

She was sure he had practiced in the mirror a few times before she got here. "They sure do." She kept her smile polite.

A few minutes later, they were sitting in the restaurant discussing witch-hunting tactics over Happy Burgers and Happy Fries. Ted had taken his meal to the car to give the reporter space.

Before Beth could ask him a question, Richard went into his rehearsed spiel. "See, it's my job to restore the balance destroyed by the heinous evil that these things bring upon us. My contacts and I help sniff out these sorts of things and then I *bring the fire for a witch burning*." He spoke as if he was reading from a script, and ended with a stiff smile.

Beth took a sip of her drink and suppressed a sigh. "Is it alright if I record this?" When Richard nodded, she turned on her tape recorder and set it between them. "Who are your contacts exactly?"

Richard rubbed his chin. "Well, I mean, this thing is mostly run by a few of my buddies and me. If we hear something spooky, like, you know, some unnatural change in season or some disappearances, we jump on it, right? We don't want any innocent people getting taken out. This is our vigil to hold, our cross to bear." He waved a hand in front of him and then ate a fry.

"I see, and what do you mean by *bring the fire*?"

"Mostly, I just mean my toolkit really."

Beth smiled politely. "Your toolkit?"

"Yeah! Holy water, grimoire, bell, incense, salt, sanctified jewelry, few vials of this and that." He opened his jacket to show the braided wire and the metal crucifix that hung on a necklace. The crucifix was tiny, but it had what looked like old writing on it and a blue stone inset. "Oh, and a dagger too. You know, the typical stuff."

"Hmm. Can I touch it?" After he nodded, she reached out and grasped the necklace. The metal was rough beneath her touch, but the stone was as smooth as water, and cold. "That looks old."

"Yeah! It's been passed down from student to master for ages. No telling what it's worth. It's supposed to help defend against the psychological attacks of a witch or warlock. I'm probably, like, the hundredth or so guy to wear it, or something."

She rubbed a thumb over the stone before releasing it. "Interesting." She smiled and tried to make the best of things. "So, Richard, what exactly do you expect will happen here? Do you think we'll actually see a witch?"

"Well, you do see a witch." He smirked and waved a hand down presenting himself. "But you mean evil witches, I'm sure. No. They usually turn tail and run. They know they can't go toe to toe with a *Witch Hunter*. Some of the strongest might be able to withstand some things, like the salt or incense, but those guys are few and far between. And frankly," he said, flooding with pride, "my coven has been hunting dark witches for a pretty long time now. We're talking centuries here. So, we know a thing or two about what we're doing." He gave a loud belly laugh that drew irritated glances from customers nearby. "You might just say we've kicked an ass or two, if you get what I mean. No, most likely we'll just deal with their taint. We'll burn that out and move on. The spiritual taint that is, not the... Yeah, the spiritual taint."

Beth's smile flinched, but she held it on. She was professional after all.

Oh God. How can I possibly survive this?

She looked down at her notes, preparing for her next question, when Richard cut in. She spared only a half-second glance at her watch.

He lowered his voice, as if worried about the next table catching on. "So, honestly, how am I doing? Is this interesting for you? I practiced that 'bring the fire' line in the mirror a few times. I just want to make the story interesting for you, you know?"

Richard was certainly kind, but something seemed off. She felt like she could smell the crazy on him.

I really hope this guy isn't a murderer.

"Yeah Richard, it's all good stuff, but just be yourself. Don't worry about trying to impress your audience or anything. I mean, who wouldn't be impressed with a story like this?"

Richard let out a breath. "That's a relief. I mean, this stuff is really exciting for most people, but you get a couple goobers out there that keep screaming 'Photoshop!' or 'Fake!' at everything. I had a picture of a plant with witch's taint, real ugly thing. All wilted and dying—obviously a witch had something to do with it, right? I put it online, and some guy called me a—" Richard glanced around and then whispered to Beth, "he called me a *mouth breathing shithead.*

And said that it looked like I just forgot to water it. It wasn't even my plant!"

"Yeah that's, uh...That's rude." Beth cleared her throat and flipped through her blank notepad. "Well, how do you plan to conduct your investigation?"

"Back to business. Well, first we're going to have to smell out a lead. We'll have to go someplace that has a lot of energy and let the tools point us in the right direction."

"Where exactly is the 'right direction'? It points you toward the witch, or...?"

"No, no, it just points me to the strongest composition of the taint's dark energies."

"I see. And then you'll sanctify the area? Cure it, then it's done?"

"Well," Richard said with a laugh under his breath. "It can be a little more complicated than that. I mean, we're talkin' ghosts, spirits, demons—those sorts of things are attracted to the area. That's their source. It strengthens their anchor to the mortal world. You get a bad enough taint?" He whistled and shook his head. "We're talking a pretty strong ghost there. That type of thing could rip you to shreds! Don't even get me talking about demons either! Don't worry though. I know how to deal with 'em."

"A ghost?" Beth leaned in and feigned interest. "Have you ever seen a ghost?"

He grinned sheepishly. "Well, I've had my fair share." He sank his teeth into the burger and tore off a piece. He hadn't quite finished chewing before he started speaking again. "But, you know, it's usually just light and noises. Haven't found anything too, uh, visual yet." He shoveled a handful of fries into his mouth.

"So I guess you've never encountered a demon either then?"

"Oh yeah, sure, of course. One scratched my arm up pretty good. I mean, some people were just saying it was dark and I bumped against a wall..." He stared off for a moment of reflection. "But my sensei was completely convinced that it was a demon. He knows what he's talking about."

"What *have* you found?" she asked, looking up from her notepad, which was nearly devoid of ink, save for a few scribbled drawings.

"Oh?" he said as though he had misheard her. He glanced up to the ceiling. "I mean, all sorts of things. Like I said, that demon-wall that scratched me once. Saw a few lights too. Hell, even heard something creaking around upstairs while I was clearing the spirits out of an old house once. My buddy said he thought it was a cat, but I've never heard of a cat that can move that fast!" He paused to take a slurp from his straw. "Really though, it's my coven. They're the ones always finding stuff. They always come back with these wicked stories about strange voices chanting the Lord's Prayer, or throwing holy water into a ghost's face! Man, it's righteous stuff. They do some good work, I gotta tell you. I'm more of a lower level cadet or something, but they tell me I have potential."

"Right," she replied and pretended to read something from her notepad.

I'm sure they do. And all for a monthly fee I would bet.

"Well, you said something about locating our next place to go?" Beth was already packing her things away and standing up before Richard could speak.

Richard sucked down the rest of his diet cola and nodded to her. He motioned for her to follow him as he turned to walk out of the restaurant. She gathered her things and moved behind him.

I really hope this night doesn't last long.

Outside, the sun was quickly retreating in the shortening autumn days, allowing darkness to creep back over the streets and houses of Bridgedale. Richard froze for a moment as though he had just remembered something. He stared out the window, looking into the orange sky, then slowly turned to look at Beth over his shoulder, his eyes bright and grin wide.

"*What a lovely night for a witching.*"

2

"DOES ANY OF THAT WORK?" THE LARGER DETECTIVE grimaced, only half seated in his chair as he leaned forward. "I mean with the ladies. Does it ever actually work? God, I hope not."

"Yeah, I mean... I wasn't doing it to try and hook up with Beth! She was following me to go after the witch!" Richard's collar felt tight, choking. He sunk a finger beneath the dirt-stained edge of the collar and stretched it out.

The gray-haired detective breathed out a tired sigh. "So this is the part where you got the knife?" He leaned farther on the wall and rubbed his thick mustache.

"Yeah, I, uh, I needed the knife to find the witch." Richard pulled his sleeve up to wipe the sweat that dripped from his face.

"Pffft." The larger detective shook his head and lowered his voice. He was clearly tired, though he spoke in as soothing a tone as he could muster, as though he were doing Richard some kind of favor. "Enough with the witch. Tell us how you killed her, and tell us the names of your accomplices."

Something hot boiled and gushed in Richard's chest. He slammed his fist down, causing the table to shake. "I didn't kill her! I don't know what happened!" He grimaced, and started rubbing his now aching hand. He glanced up to see the two men staring at him, waiting. "Don't I, um... don't I get a lawyer or something?"

The larger detective leaned in to place his elbow on the table. "Sure, we can get you that lawyer. But I'm thinking a judge would appreciate it more if he could read about how very forthcoming and what a team player you were, how you made all our jobs just that much easier. So how about you keep talking and we can wait it out for the public defense attorney to get on down here? You play ball, and we'll make it easy. Only the guilty have anything to hide after all." Richard could smell the man's stale breath from across the table, could practically taste the shots of liquor the detective had enjoyed earlier to keep the night warm. He was afraid for Beth, and for himself.

Did I really kill her? Could I really have done that?

The room sat in a deathly silence as they waited for Richard to speak. He took a few shallow breaths before he spoke again. "Can I just tell you what happened next?"

The gray-haired detective grinned with coffee-stained teeth. "Sure, Dick, sure. What happened next?"

THE NEWS VAN drove down the old, winding country road. The trees were nearly bare, their dead leaves already fallen to the earth. Raked piles of orange and brown were formed in front of the houses. "Pretty place," the reporter said. "I've always been a sucker for all these autumn colors."

Richard bobbed up and down in his seat, swaying with

the curves in the road and the hills that seemed endless. His initial courage was starting to burn off and the van was closing in on him like a metal coffin. He gulped and wished for a window that he could crack but, much like a coffin, there was none. It was empty, save for a few bits of equipment, and Richard, the lone witch hunter in the back, waiting. "So what's with the camera?"

"Oh, the editor didn't tell you?" Beth turned to see him, and her gorgeous brown, gold-specked eyes seemed to pull him in. "I'll write up a piece for our blog, but we're also shooting something for one of our evening segments." She was beautiful, a slim and stunning woman. Richard's stomach tied knots with itself whenever she looked at him.

It was several moments before Richard realized that he was staring. "So, uh," he sputtered. "I'm going to be on TV?"

"If the editor likes it. But I don't imagine they'd turn anything down."

"Hell, I don't think so," Ted said from the driver's seat, his voice deep and confident. "Not after that garbage Jen had on last week about the neighborhood playground."

"I know, right?" She glanced at Ted and then back to Richard. "Don't be worried though, all right? You'll do fine."

Ted's eyes flashed in the rearview mirror to capture Richard's. And they did. Where Beth's eyes were inviting, Ted's were something else. Ted was the type of man that Richard used to wish he could be back in high school. He was thick-chested, with short, trimmed, red hair, and seemed sure of himself, maybe even with a hint of cruelty. Whatever the case, he didn't seem to have any trouble talking to Beth.

Richard said a silent prayer that he wouldn't embarrass himself. His mouth dried at the idea of Beth or Ted thinking they wasted their time.

I'm going to do it. I'm going to make it worth their time. I'm not going to be like Jen and her playground. Everyone is going to like me.

The van's headlights painted a small, wrought-iron gate just off the road. "Turn here and stop at the graveyard."

"Graveyard, huh?" Ted laughed. "Do witches hang out in graveyards? I always pictured them more as a house-deep-out-in-the-woods type of thing. Little bit of a cliché, huh?"

Richard's stomach hardened.

Beth smirked at Ted and slapped his leg with the back of her hand before glancing into the back. "Why exactly are we headed to a graveyard, Richard?"

Richard cleared his throat. "The, uh, energy, of course. Necro energies. The dead, the afterlife, sadness, and even sometimes relief. These things all hold a lot of energy. On evenings like this, the *dead may dance here*." He couldn't help but smile with that last line.

That definitely won them over.

"That's nice," said Beth.

What? She didn't like 'The dead may dance here'? Man, that's gold!

Suddenly, the van felt a little smaller, his collar a little tighter. That dull and bored look in Beth's eyes sent him scrambling.

Time to spice things up.

He dipped his hand into his rough, old, leather bag and pulled out a dagger. It was a wicked thing, with a curved blade and wooden handle, etched with designs and runes, said to channel ancient energies with arts lost to modern man.

They'll dig this. They have to.

"Check this out." He held the knife up to the front of the van for them to see.

"Whoa, whoa!" Fear spread across Beth's face.

"Oh!" Richard paused when she looked frightened; he slid it back into his worn leather bag. "It's only part of the ritual. It's made of, uh, special materials. And it can point us to where the witch's energy is strongest." He grinned uneasily. "It's easy; we just use my bowl, fill it with local water, drop in some of the graveyard dirt, say a few chants, and bingo! This thing will point us to where we have to go next." He nodded and hoped that was convincing enough.

"But, hey, man, let's not be pointing out any evil spirits while in the van." Ted's green eyes locked him in. "Save it for the camera, yeah?"

"Yeah, yeah, makes sense." Richard put his leather satchel back down as they pulled into the Bridgedale cemetery.

It wasn't a large place, and there were no walls or tall gates, just a simple fence that seemed more decorative than anything. The fading sun cast long shadows that crept out over the gravestones and turned the bare trees into desperate pointed fingers, clawing over the ground as though to wake the dead.

Ted was the first one out, and easily hefted the camera bag with a single arm. "Spooky!" He glanced at his watch. "Hmm. Might have to use the camera light. I hope it doesn't ruin the shot too much."

Beth kept her jacket high up on her neck. "It'll be fine." She laced the microphone through her jacket and then turned to do the same to Richard.

His heart fluttered as she began to pull around his loose jacket, and he immediately regretted not having dressed nicer and a bit warmer. He took a deep breath, and the air chilled his lungs.

"Just a little cool out here, right?" asked Beth.

He puffed out his chest, trying his best to look as tough as Ted.

Beth faced the side mirror of the van to adjust her hair one last time. She then walked over to several large gravestones that were set beneath a crooked tree. With a smile, she motioned for Richard to join her and, together, they waited for Ted.

Ted hefted the heavy camera onto his shoulder. "Ready?" She nodded and Ted counted down.

"This is Beth Sanders with WB19 and I'm here with Richard Fitcher, local witch hunter." While Beth seemed to glow in the camera's light, Richard suddenly felt awkward and unprepared. "He's invited us onto a witch hunt in time for autumn. There have been reports of obscure activities here in Bridgedale, and we're here to get to the bottom of it!" She giggled and turned to Richard. "Richard, earlier today you told me we needed to come to this graveyard because of the dark energy here, and that it will help your investigation. What do you hope to do here?"

Don't screw up, don't screw up, don't screw up.

Now that the camera was actually on him, Richard felt far more aware of his red hat, his faded jacket, the few extra pounds he carried, and a hundred other things that suddenly demanded his full attention.

Don't screw up, don't screw up.

"Richard?" Beth pushed the microphone a little closer to him.

"Yes!" Richard cleared his throat and looked directly into the camera. "There's a witching here in Bridgedale. A blight upon the land, and it's up to those who would stand against the forces of darkness to take up the vigil. We must hold the candle in the dark, lest the darkness cover us all."

"Yeah, fantastic! And we're coming along for the trip!"

Beth smiled, showing her unblemished teeth. "But what is it you plan to do *here,* Richard?"

"Oh yeah, right." Richard composed his voice once again. "With the energies here, we'll locate the source of the blight, of this plague. From there, we'll *bring the fire.*"

"Right." Beth turned back to the camera. "You've heard it here folks, we're out here saving the day so you can sleep well at night!" She smiled wide until Ted turned the camera off.

Ted pulled the camera down and snorted to Beth. "You want to do another shot?"

She shook her head, "I'm freezing. Let's just get what we can and get going." She turned and looked at Richard. "Richard, listen, just be yourself, okay? Don't worry about trying to impress us. Let's be honest here, at best this story's going to be a five-minute clip on the evening news. Just answer my questions and we keep this thing rolling. Let the editors add in the spooky music and what not. That's what they get paid for. You just take it easy."

Richard felt his heart sink deep into his chest. "Oh, okay," he said.

No one told me we were filming any of this.

Beth gave him a soft smile and placed her hand on his. "Don't worry, the editing room will chop this all up and make it interesting, I promise."

"Fine." He slid on the best smile he could and then turned to grab his satchel from the van.

A cold, vaporous trail formed from Richard's mouth as he breathed; the night's chill set in quickly. The moon rose to greet them as clouds rolled over it. He unzipped the satchel and took out a brown-red bowl with carvings on it similar to his knife. He placed it on the ground and knelt to fill it with water from a bottle.

Beth leaned in to watch over his shoulder. "I thought you said it had to be local water?"

"It is. I gathered it from the stream before you arrived."

Richard then walked from grave to grave. He gathered just a bit of dirt from each and collected it in a small paper cup. "Dead man's dirt," he mumbled to no one in particular.

A howling wind came blowing through like a cry of warning, tearing at Richard's hat and nearly taking it from his head. He gasped and held it down. The hair on his neck rose and an eerie feeling crawled beneath the skin of his back. The wind grew weaker, and where it howled before, it only whispered now—whispered tortured moans of warning and threats of pain, in a language Richard couldn't understand. He held for a moment, waiting for it to make sense.

"Maybe that's your witch, huh Richard? Maybe he's getting pissed off!" Ted said with a laugh.

Richard didn't laugh. He turned and looked out across the graveyard and jumped when he saw one of the shadows move out of view, then sighed when he realized it was only a tree swaying beneath the moon. "Yeah..." The whispers stopped, but something was wrong. He felt like something was there, moving in the graveyard. Something they couldn't see. Something behind a gravestone or lurking beneath the ground, watching.

Ted chuckled again, and Richard returned to the bowl. "Are you going to get this part on video?" Richard held the paper cup of graveyard dirt just above it.

"Sure. Why not?" Ted aimed the camera at Beth and turned it on.

She plastered on her practiced grin. "Richard, tell us what it is you're doing here."

"This is a little method I've learned for tracking." His

voice kept steady and without theatrics. "We mix a few things together inside this ceremonial bowl and place this dagger inside." He held the blade up for the camera. It glinted in the light, lethally sharp.

"That's a pretty unique dagger there, Richard." Beth inspected it with some distance between her and him.

"Well, it's a very unique build."

The handle was carved from a tree where a witch was hanged, and the blade was forged by a priest inside a church.

Richard kept that part to himself, though.

"My, uh, organization sent me this one. It's important when tracking a witch."

Beth's smile tightened. She watched as Richard pulled up the bowl and dumped the grave-dirt inside. Above them, lighting cracked as a storm cut through the sky. Richard peeked up at the sky and then looked down at the swirling dirt and water in the bowl. An eerie sense of dread nestled into the back of his mind, just as the wind had. He'd never felt this way before, never had this glut of pained emotions digging its way through him. Ignoring it all, he placed the dagger into the water and held the bowl up just below his chin. It bobbed up and down, the metal blade sinking as the wooden handle kept afloat. Richard began to chant some words, "Carpe et ferrum illud—"

Beth cut in, "So, as you said, you'll chant now and it'll point us in the direction of the witch? Was that Latin I heard?"

Richard cleared his throat and nodded. "Yeah, Latin. After I finish, it should work." Beth smiled at that, the Latin. A renewed sense of energy washed over him.

Richard began chanting again as the knife shifted around in the bowl. "Carpe et ferrum illud. Ostende mihi pythonissam." He slowed the words and finished the chant,

"Ostende mihi pythonissam." The dagger bobbed a little, still angled down over one of the graves. Richard had done this trick before, with the same results.

"I guess we have a winner! I think its rig—HOLY SHIT!" Richard's eyes went wide. The blade snapped up to level with the water, as if a ghostly hand wrenched it into action. It turned halfway around in a quick motion and went dead still. The water seemed undisturbed and was completely motionless despite the movement of the blade. Richard nearly dropped the bowl.

"What was that?" Beth whispered. "What just happened?"

"I've never seen it move like that." The words fumbled in his mouth. "I've never seen it move so fast."

"Did you get that all on camera?" Beth shot a wide-eyed look back to Ted, who gave her a thumbs-up. She motioned for Ted to bring the camera over to her. "You've seen it folks, we're on the trail! We'll be here all night until—" Suddenly rain began to pour down on them. "Ah, this is Beth Sanders of WB19, signing off!" She smiled for the camera before Ted lowered it. Cursing, she ran toward the van. Thunder and lightning clashed overhead as it rained onto them.

Richard held the bowl in two hands and watched as Ted and Beth dashed toward the van. He stood frozen in place, his feet molded to the ground. He pulled his head back to stare into the storm and let the rain beat against his face. He never said it out loud before, never had to, but he didn't actually believe in witches, though he wished at times that they were real. He wished he were a hunter, a man to hunt the wicked in a world of black and white, wished for fantasy that would make sense to him, not the real world that played angles with him and left him confused. He wished they were real, but he'd never seen anything that could get him to believe it. He only joined the group to have something to do on Friday and Saturday nights, some people to hang out with.

He stared into the storm as the wind blew against him and the rain soaked his clothes. As if to answer, a shadow moved behind the clouds and caught beneath the moon's light, he saw a wraith that existed for only a single blink.

Or was it all just the rain in his eyes?

The blade was steady, still pointing in the same direction. "What?" he asked it. Another loud clash of thunder snapped Richard out of his daze.

"Richard!" Beth waved him forward from the van. "Richard! Come on!"

"Yeah, I'm coming!" He snatched his satchel from the ground. He turned and took a few short steps toward the van as he stared down at the blade in the bowl. The rain dripped down from his hat, but he wasn't concerned. Only one thought crept into his mind.

What just happened?

3

"How you doing there, Mr. Fitcher?" A man with deep, aged grooves in his face sat across from Richard. He had a thin, graying beard that covered layers of neck fat and he wore a tan suit that complemented a wide-brimmed cowboy hat. "I'm Jeff Minges, your defense attorney." His words slipped out with a quickness that blended with a southern drawl. He extended an open hand toward Richard with equal speed. "You ain't told them nothing you shouldn't have, right? Sons of bitches will squeeze sap from a twig if they get the time."

Richard had been sitting with his face flat on the table. The night and the weight of the detectives' words had torn from him what little energy he had remaining when the detectives left only a few minutes earlier.

He slowly blinked and looked up to see Jeff's hand still lingering, waiting to be shaken. He leaned up to take it; the other man shook hard. "I've just been telling them what happened, you know? Nothing bad. I didn't do anything." He took a few deep breaths. "They said I killed her though, that I killed Beth. Is that true? Is she really dead?"

"Well, let's be straight on one thing, Mr. Fitcher. They have a video of you doing your best lumberjack impression on that reporter's skull." He was clearly a man who didn't mince words. "I've seen the video. Bloody stuff. How many whacks? Two, three? That was enough to put her down. The other five must have just been for fun."

"Oh my God!" Richard's arms turned to jelly, the strength drained from them, and his head rolled back on his neck. "I didn't do it! It was the witch! Oh God, I didn't believe it before. I didn't know any of it was real. You've got to believe me!" Fat tears oozed from his eyes and dripped down from his chin.

"Calm down, calm down." The lawyer pulled out a tissue and handed it to him. "Listen, I've got it all worked out, yeah? We're gonna get you a deal that smells pretty *damn* sweet, son. I'm thinking we should plead insanity. You go up there, you talk about all that witching and ghouling, and we've got ourselves a case!" He rubbed his thick hands together, the coarse skin scratching together like sandpaper. "Hell, we could *easily* deal for life in prison."

"Life in prison!" Like a rat breaking from a fire, a moan started a hasty climb up his throat. He choked it back. "I don't even remember any of that stuff on the video! I wouldn't do anything like that. I'm not like that." The thought of the axe made his skin crawl and his body shake.

"Easy there, son. Maybe we can play another angle? I got the report on the way in. I have a few contacts here in the PD." His wet tongue clicked between his teeth, and he gave a hard wink that shook his cheek. "You just go on ahead and tell 'em all about this witching stuff. Tell them all about that cult you were in, give 'em the names of all your buddies and they'll cut you a deal, I'm sure. No chair or lethal injection, and that's the Minges guarantee!"

"I can't do it, I just can't! I can't go to prison!" Richard shook his head and clenched his eyes so tight they hurt. "There's a witch out there. You gotta believe me!" His voice broke into sharp jagged edges, cracking like fine glass. "He... he killed my friends."

He must have. I couldn't do that.

Minges sighed and reached up to pull off his hat and rub his pink, balding head. He rested an elbow on the table and fixed Richard with a tired stare through blue-gray eyes. "Now let me be clear here, son. It don't get no prettier for the DA than a video of some slobby city boy smashing some pretty girl's head open with an axe." He puckered his lips to whistle through his two front teeth. "They'd just love to sell you in the media. Bet you didn't even know how much you worship Satan, did you? How you been thinking 'bout killing her for weeks? That's what they gonna say. Some crazy psycho axe-murderer, people love that kind of story. You'll be famous. They'll be lining up to see them stick that needle in your arm."

"But you believe me, don't you?" Richard felt the weakness in his own voice, but could do nothing to stop it. "I didn't kill her."

Minges rolled his eyes. "Sure, 'course I do. I believe everything you say. That's my job, ain't it? But my job's also to play damage control here, son. Know what I mean? This ain't a courtroom. It's an operation table. Sometimes you gotta cut off a hand to save the arm. Just so happens for you, it's a whole leg, and that leg is a life sentence, so we're cutting off the, uh, well hell I'm no good with metaphors. What I mean is, son...," he grinned and raised his eyebrows, "you ain't walking out of here."

Richard shut his eyes tight and pulled his head back. It

was all he could do to not burst into a blubbering mess. "Just kill me now."

"Come on now, son, we're here to beat the system! Course, they're gonna want to get you the death penalty for caving in that pretty girl's head, but we ain't gonna let them, are we? Hell no, I say!" He leaned across the table and stretched his short arm out to pat Richard on the shoulder. "Let me hear something I can work with sweetie, okay? Let me hear the story."

"Okay, okay. I was telling the detective about how I was able to locate the—"

"No, no, no. I got all that! Like I said, got a contact here that likes to sing. I heard all about your goofy ass waddling around in the graveyard. What happened next?"

"HERE?"

The knife had led them to an old dirt road surrounded by trees. Their bare branches reached out in a horrid gesture, inviting the brave and the foolish farther in.

"Guys, this—"

"Holy shit, man!" Ted flipped on the van's high beams and illuminated the old dirt road. "You've got to be kidding me. I feel like some dude in a gas mask is going to jump out with an axe." Ted blurted out a laugh and glanced back at Richard through the rearview mirror. "Richard, did you set this up? Seriously, this is creepy." He whistled an eerie tune.

"Yeah. This isn't so bad, I think." Beth rubbed the fog from the window and stared out. "To be completely honest, I'm not sure if we're allowed to be out here. Is this a private road?"

"Guys...," Richard tried to speak, but it came out more as a squeak.

"Oh hell, Beth!" Ted cut in again. "This story finally starts to pick up and you start asking questions like that? I thought you wanted to be in Syria getting into the shit, and now you're worried about a private road? This will air the week of Halloween, right? People will eat it up."

Richard stared down at the knife and then up at them. "Guys..."

"I'm not saying we drop it, okay? I'm just saying we need to be careful. We need to be—"

"Guys!" Richard took a deep breath, and tried to pour out the words before someone else spoke. "I've *never* seen it do this before. I mean it." His hands trembled beneath the bowl, but the blade stayed steady. Richard shook his head in disbelief. "It usually kinda, you know, just floats there and I play it up and talk about the mystic winds pointing out the land of the damned or something."

Richard heard a snort from the front seat. "Come on man," said Ted. "Save it for the camera, all right? We've done this before. But like you said, this is all about giving a good show, isn't it? That's all we're here for, a good five-minute break in between the riots and depressing key notes on our economy."

Richard tried to protest, tried to say something, anything to get them to understand. This time, he could *feel it*. There was something dark here, something moving just beneath the surface. Something wicked that both scared him and whispered at him to keep going.

"Don't worry, Richard." Beth's voice was calm and soothing. "Ted's right. We'll get our story, and get out. No harm no foul, right?"

Richard tried to latch onto something. "What if there's a

wild animal or something though? Out here in the woods, I remember all kinds of reports..."

"Relax, man." Ted let out a laugh that seemed to be at Richard's expense and sent a nervous shiver down Richard's spine. "I'm armed. Got a Glock. Been carrying for a while now, nothing to be concerned about. I'm licensed."

"Armed?" Richard felt incredibly nervous about the idea of a gun. He reached out for something else. "But you said it was private property, right?"

Ted let out a long, annoyed sigh. "Maybe it is. Our producer would tell us just to go at it. They'll pay the fines if we hit any. You're making too much out of it man, come on. I haven't seen any 'No Trespassing' signs, have you?"

Richard's gaze fell one last time to the bowl and that knife. The edge still pointed cleanly forward, shifting ever so slightly with the turns in the road to keep pointed in one direction. "It's just that—"

"Dammit!" Ted thumped the dashboard. "Listen man, we drove an hour and a half to get *your* story. If you were going to turn into a baby after doing what *you* told us to do, then why the hell are we even here? No one likes a coward, Richard."

Richard fell silent as his back turned into jelly, and suddenly he was that ten-year-old on the playground, the fourteen-year-old at the school dance, and that seventeen-year-old at the butt of the joke. Ted was a fair deal bigger than him, and his anger cowed Richard.

Richard finally nodded and then spoke, though meekly, "Okay. Let's go." He then pretended to turn around and organize the contents of his bag.

What's the worst that could happen?

From the corner of his eye, he could see Beth nudge Ted and whisper: "You didn't have to do that."

Rain peppered the windshield of the van as they followed the dirt road down to an old two-story farmhouse that had not aged well. Old and bleached, blue paint peeled from the sides while large patches were completely devoid of color. Rot was consuming the house; part of the roof had collapsed in on itself while another portion seemed next to give in. Tall, uncut grass sprouted up all around, save for the gravel driveway that held only small patches here and there. A dilapidated shed stood nearby, its door chewed away and swinging loosely in the wind on one hinge, threatening to give even that up at any moment.

Fear washed over Richard, finding root in the part of his brain that told him to be afraid of it, to be afraid of everything—a sensation he was intimately familiar with. He rubbed the sanctified necklace, hoping to find some strength in it, as if the crucifix could swallow his fear. He idly traced the metal cross with his finger; it felt strangely warm. He pulled it up to inspect it closely, but it was just the same small crucifix he'd had for years. He finally looked up to watch through the windshield as they approached the shambles of a once-beautiful home.

Something shifted in the air; Richard could feel it. A strange numbness spread up from his toes and shook him as it stretched through his body. The heat from the cross, still in his grasp, burned for a moment, and the numbness was gone. Richard shivered and looked up to see Ted bring the van to a rough and sudden stop. Both he and Beth silently opened their doors and almost mechanically stepped out into the rain, completely uncaring as it beat down across their faces.

"Guys?" Richard said beneath his breath. There was a twisting in his guts—something he might have called instinct—that told him to be cautious, told him that there was something beyond the sane world nearby. He moved the bowl to his side; the blade kept focusing on the house.

Beth stood unflinching as the rain drenched her neatly prepared hair, slopping it out of place. "Wow, this is just... It's amazing." The words were hollow and devoid of emotion.

Ted stepped several feet away from the van and froze, fixated on the house. "Yeah, some cameramen would give an arm and a leg to film in a place like this. This is the type of story that can make a career."

"Make your career?" Richard mumbled. He stepped out of the van and shuddered in the cold rain.

This is just a crappy old house.

"You guys want to actually go in? What if we fall through the floorboards? Or step on a nail, or..."

"It's beautiful." Beth finally inched forward across the wet gravel and climbed the warped wooden steps. "Wow..." She nearly spun after reaching the porch and looking it over.

Ted broke his fixation to grab his camera from the van and followed behind her, leaving the back van doors open. Hefting the camera onto his shoulder, he moved up to the patio and tested the bronze handle on the front door. It made a painful screech as Ted forced its turn.

Richard could only watch in stunned silence. He thought about just sitting in the van until they finished. He closed the van door but didn't pull his hand from the handle.

No one asked me anything. Maybe they won't care if I just sit in the car.

A flutter above snapped his attention upward. On the second floor, behind a dirty window, he saw the white, fleeting, ghostly image of a woman watching him, her dress fluttering like a torn curtain. He blinked and it was gone.

"Shit!" Richard sprang forward, sloshing rainwater and mud with each step, before he jumped onto the groaning wooden stairs of the porch, racing toward Beth. "Guys, there's someone in there!" He grabbed Ted's arm before he could step inside. "I saw a woman. She was all white and staring down at us. I'm pretty sure she had an eyeball hanging out. She was all like..." He stuck his tongue out and closed half an eye.

Ted ripped his arm from Richard and glared at him with fire in his eyes. Beth stepped behind him. "What is with you guys?"

Richard's mind scrambled for an answer. "What's going on? Why don't you...?" The gears began to turn. The lessons he had learned, the old books he had read. That one book he thought was only good for a distraction.

They're enthralled. This is cursed ground. They don't have the defenses I have. They don't have the necklace.

His hand rose once more, clutching the necklace hard enough that it might pierce his flesh. His heart pumped like a jackhammer, shaking his arm with each pulse of blood.

"Oh my God," Richard said with disbelief. "Listen, Beth, Ted, this place is cursed! You're enthralled. It's drawing you in. These types of places..." He cast his gaze out to the muddy grounds, the gravel road, and the woods that now seemed more threatening than ever. Something was inviting him in.

"The curses, they manipulate your minds! They distracted others, pushed them away from here so they wouldn't come. But we stepped in. The knife, the ritual, it showed us to this place, but I can't... I can't defend you guys!" Beneath his grip, the necklace grew even warmer. "It's real.

It's all real!" He begged them to listen, but his words found no ground, nothing to connect to, scrabbling against Ted and Beth's dull fixation. There were no words that the enthralled could hear, none that would draw them from the curse's snare.

"Amazing..." Beth strode past Richard and brushed her finger against the wall, leaving a neat trail through the thick dust and exposing the yellowing grime beneath.

"Listen to me, dammit!" Richard seized Ted's sleeve with both hands, pulling it tight. "We'll get stuck in here, it won't let us leave. It'll never let us go!"

With frightening speed, Ted shifted toward Richard, and slammed an open palm against Richard's chest. Richard lost his breath and stumbled back.

"Richard Fitcher," Ted said. "Witch hunter. Why are you such a coward? Isn't this your job?"

Richard sucked in a breath. A hundred words came to mind, but he couldn't find the breath to speak.

What's he saying?

"Ted Court," Beth said with toneless words. "Cameraman. Angry sports fan. Asshole."

Then Richard felt it; an itch inside his brain. It scurried beneath his skull and tried to hide. He didn't know how he knew that it was there or that it was trying to deceive him, hide from him, but he knew just the same. It was there, clawing its way through the grooves of his brain. Prickly spines sunk through his mind and pulled forward, slithering around through the recesses of his consciousness. He went weak in the knees and collapsed onto the dusty floorboards. Ted and Beth remained undisturbed as Richard writhed in pain. They simply wandered around the house, their minds lost in the fog.

Richard's shaky hands went up to the sides of his head

and snagged on a root of hair. It felt like it would rip from his skull, but somehow that pain was more bearable. He raged, silently, in his own mind, clenched his eyes shut as the throbbing pain sharpened and cut pieces away.

Get out of my head!

The itch dug though his thoughts and sent bits of information away. To where, Richard did not know. The itch fit its claws beneath a layer of thought and pried pieces of him loose.

Richard's thoughts were dragged back to other times, times in the basement of his club meeting, just after their Dungeons and Dragons games, when their training would begin. His sensei told him of the things from the dark that could pierce the folds of your brain and take what they needed. It needed your name. It needed to know your sins, needed them to play wicked games with you. And now, it knew all their names and their weaknesses. It knew Richard, knew who and what he was: a coward and a charlatan.

Ted's voice broke Richard out of his internal struggle. "Beth Sanders. Desperate reporter." Then his voice shifted to something darker. "What the hell are you doing? You ready for the shot?"

She had found a dusty, cracked mirror. Enamored with her broken reflection, she picked small strands of wet hair and smoothed them into uneven fashion, a mockery of the skill she had before. She swayed and lazily turned her head toward Ted. "Oh, yeah, right." Her dull grin slipped across her face, but she ran one more dusty hand through her hair, leaving a filthy black streak in its trail. "Richard?"

Richard let his hands loosen on his head. The itch, the pain, it had gone as quickly as it had come. He rubbed his necklace and staggered to his feet. "Guys, we have to get the hell out of here. This place is haunted. I'm not dicking around! It's going to play on our emotions and tear us apart and—"

"Whoa, whoa, whoa." Flat words as Ted brought the camera to his shoulder. "Hold on a second there, buddy. I don't have the camera on just yet."

"Dammit! No, I'm not saying it for the camera! You don't get it. *It's in here with us.* It's playing with our emotions. You're going to get angry, depressed, scared, more than you've ever been in your entire life."

The camera came to life, illuminating the dusty old house, pushing the shadows back and blinding Richard, who put a hand up to shield his eyes and turned his gaze down. On the floor, he saw their footprints in the dust, only their footprints.

No one has been here in a long time.

The floorboards creaked with each step Beth took toward Richard. Something about her was terrifying, her toy-like grin and makeup running down her face, streaks of grime in wet hair slithering around her head. She looked unnatural.

She came close enough that Richard could feel her breath across his face. "Richard, you said there was something in here with us. What is it?" Richard's heart thumped in his chest, sending hot blood through his veins as Ted's camera painted him in light.

They're not going to listen. They're enthralled.

Richard took a breath and finally spoke. "There's a spirit, or a ghost, or something that's here with us. It's angry."

"And why do you say that, Richard? Why do you say it's angry?" The words dripped out of her mouth, lacking any real taste or emotion. She was a slave to a dark embrace, a puppet moving on strings in a grisly theater.

"Because I feel it clawing into my brain." He ground his teeth together, less in frustration and more in fear of what might come next.

A forceful gust of wind blew through the house, blowing Beth's hair farther out of place and slapping the wet strands against her coat and face. She laughed for the camera as she tried to fix it quickly, but succeeded only in smearing more black grime across her face.

Richard's lungs filled with heavy mouthfuls of the stale, dusty air; his eyes scanned the rooms off to their left and right—nothing but old rotting furniture and moldy rugs. He tried to calm himself, control his breathing, but the scent of the house, damp and musky, sent him into a fit of coughing. He forced himself to take in more of the environment.

The wooden floor was cracked and peeling, along with some of the wallpaper that had been torn down or stripped away crudely. Behind Ted stood the warped wooden steps that led up to the second floor. The steps went up halfway before they turned suddenly to the right and finished in a hallway. It was impossible to see where that hallway might lead from this angle, or what things prowled the shadows of the second floor.

"So what will you do, Richard?" She forced herself closer to him again, trying to get him to refocus. "Are you going to perform a ritual or something?"

A ritual!

Richard had been too afraid; he hadn't even considered a ritual. "Of course!" His eyes searched across the ground and came to his satchel by the door; he must have dropped it while he was struggling. He snatched it from the floor, his flesh prickled the second his hand touched the leather bag. He felt eyes piercing him from the dark.

He turned toward the stairs, but caught only a fleeting

glimpse of the pale woman. Her dress was full of holes and her skin was a translucent blue, but it was her that burned into his mind—pained but curious, confused maybe. "She's here with us now! Did you see her?"

"Yes." Joy dripped off Beth's smile as she addressed the camera. "Our expert is reporting clear signs here of spiritual activity. Richard, what do you expect this ritual will do for this spirit? What do you think will happen?"

"I, uh..." Richard's thoughts were bare, his mind blank in a scattered state of confusion and panic. Ted's camera light was blinding.

A chill rolled through the room like a flood of oil and cut to Richard's bones. It dug its fingers into his leg and climbed.

A pained, hollow gasp came from the room next to them as the apparition took form and floated effortlessly inches above the floor. Her gaunt eyes sank deep in her head and pain, fear, and desperation dripped from her taut flesh. Her long hair, unhindered by gravity, floated at all angles, stretching out in web-like patterns. The faded woman howled a low, tortured moan and gestured to them with thin bony fingers, pleading for them to close the distance and join her in the dark.

Throughout his life, there had been occasions when Richard would freeze in fear, or blabber away endlessly. There was a time during his training when his friends had played a joke on him; they convinced him that a ghost was just outside the room. He fell into a chattering mess and pressed himself against the wall, only stopping when they started laughing. Another time, when a man pulled a knife on him, he went stiff, unable to even retrieve his wallet before someone else showed up to chase the man away. He didn't know when his body would freeze or when it would send him into a blabbering mess. He wasn't sure he even had a pattern or rationale for how he did things.

Now he was a blabbering mess. "We're uh, just hanging out here. Thinking about leaving," he said to the floating specter. "You look busy though, and tired and... How are you?"

She moaned tearfully, silencing him. Something cracked inside Richard's heart. He felt her sorrow; he felt her tortured existence and the clear hell she lived in, a spirit forced into the world and unable to leave it.

But then he saw the other hand, the one that held the rusted scissors that were slowly opening and closing with only a faint squeak. *Chip-chip-chip.*

"The hell?" Ted asked from behind the camera.

"Are you getting this?" The reporter couldn't draw her focus away from the ghost. Richard fell to a knee and dug through his satchel.

The ghost started to glide forward, the ends of her frayed dress licking the floor. She reached out her fingers, cruel things that had rotted to sharp bones, a sharp contrast to her face, which seemed to smooth into an unblemished surface as she flowed toward Beth. Her hand was held out in front of her in a plea for mercy, for compassion, for love, all while her other hand opened and closed the rusted scissors in rapid succession: *Chip-chip-chip-chip-chip.*

The tortured spirit moaned once more while Beth stood still beside Richard, who focused solely on the pained eyes and miserable face of the woman. A tear dripped down Beth's cheek. The ghost glided forward and slid her hand over Beth's face. The reporter shuddered, but did not pull away. The aberration's head tilted slightly with curiosity. Her lips cracked as she made a tight insidious mockery of a smile and the hand with the scissors rose up quickly.

Richard stepped forward and dashed the spirit with water. It screeched loudly and dissipated, burning away like tissue paper.

"Holy water." His voice cracked as he spoke to no one in particular. "It won't hold it for long." He fell to his knees again and rummaged through the small leather pouches and pockets of his satchel, working open their fasteners as quickly as he could.

"Can those things—that ghost—hurt us?" Beth asked with some focus, as though some part of her was starting to return. She motioned for Ted to focus the camera on Richard.

"Yes!" Richard's head shot up and he quickly got to his feet. He reached for Beth's hands and squeezed them tightly. "Oh God, you're listening now! We need to get out. Something in here has control of you two. Something is not letting you think clearly."

She blinked and held the same unconcerned expression. "What do you mean, Richard?" She pulled free and fluttered her hand toward Ted. "Make sure you're getting this!"

She's desperate. She can't do anything but think about how she can use this for her career. She's lost, and so is Ted.

Even then he could see her focus fading, going back into the mists. "Just be ready. That won't hold it for long." Richard retrieved a crucifix from his bag. It had a long metal wire loop coming from it—a thing he often used for show but now prayed had some real use. He hung it on the doorknob and then reached into the bag to pull out a few flat-bottom candles. He placed one near where the ghost had been, another by the stairs, and then ran past Beth and Ted to place one on the other side of the door, creating a triangle around them.

"Richard?" said Beth.

He struck a match and began lighting each candle, one by one, as he chanted in Latin, a language he knew very little of, but had memorized a few short chants.

"Da ex manes praesidium! Da ex manes praesidium!"

"Richard, what are you doing?" Her voice had sweetened, as if she enjoyed what was happening.

He didn't know how to force Beth to understand, to explain to her the danger they were in. So he didn't. He went back to work while Ted followed him with the light of the camera, painting his shadow against the old walls of the house.

Richard ignored them until the last candle was lit. He then slid down the front of the door and lay back against it, huffing. "I hope that works..." His pulse thumped in his ear, the pounding of it drowned out his thoughts of Beth and Ted. Richard didn't meet their gaze, but instead searched the shadows behind them. The candlelight flickered, and the shadows crept and danced.

God, I hope this works.

Beth leaned down to him, close enough that he couldn't ignore her. "Richard? What did you just do? What's happening now?" A curious smile stretched across her face.

He swallowed and took a deep breath. "It's a shield. It will keep the ghost out of here until I can think of what to do next." He rubbed his tired eyes. "I have to, uh..." The words slipped away, his thoughts lost to the exhaustion of the moment. Beth leaned farther down, prompting him to speak. His head felt as if it was filled with lead and he could raise it only slowly. "I'm going to..." The words wouldn't come.

This isn't supposed to be real.

"Exorcise the ghost?" Her head shifted to give the same plastic grin to the camera.

Richard licked his lips and slowly nodded his head. "Just stay inside the triangle." He waved his hands toward the candles, their only source of protection from the horrors of the house. He slumped down farther, pulled an old, leather-bound book out of his bag, and laid it out in front of him. With careful fingers, he passed through the crisp, aged pages, reading each section carefully but as quickly as he could.

Beth bent down alongside him, pausing for a moment to smooth the wrinkles on her pants. "What are you looking for?"

"It's not..." He shook his head. "It's not so easy as just saying a few words. I have to identify what type of ghost it is and find the right passage. We should have thirty or so minutes before it's back again. So we just have to stay calm and focused, and we should be okay." A gust of cold air blew through the house again, as if to prove him wrong. He saw the candle flicker. "Or maybe it was thirty seconds?" He considered for a moment before throwing caution to the wind. He began to tear through the book faster.

"How do you think she died?" he asked Beth and Ted, hoping that they could provide some insight, however small. "We need to know how she died to exorcise her if we don't know her name."

"I don't know." Beth looked over his shoulder at the book with a joyful and curious smile.

"There were scissors, right? A torn dress?" Richard wiped away the sweat that had formed on his forehead, even as the chill of the room grew stronger.

Oh God, what should we do? She's reforming...

"What about her hair?" Beth asked absent-mindedly, warm vapors coming from her mouth as the room grew colder.

Richard shivered and pulled the collar of his jacket tighter. The temperature was plunging by the second; the ghost would be here soon. “What about it?”

“Didn’t you see how it waved? How she was blue? She floated?” The excitement grew in Beth’s voice.

“Yeah?” Richard was dumbfounded.

“Does that mean she drowned?”

Adrenaline surged through him. “Yeah! Maybe.” Richard pieced through the book’s yellowed pages to rest on a section that read ‘Drowning,’ written at the top in decorative black ink. A picture fell below the words: it was a large rippling lake. There were words written in Old English and others in Latin, still more in languages long dead and lost on Richard. He placed a finger beneath one section and began to recite the words in their ancient tongue Another shriek echoed through the house.

Ignore it, keep reading. Keep reading.

His guts twisted into knots and the strength in his knees began to melt. He bit his lower lip and forced himself to focus on the pages, on the ink, on the paper, anything to stop from thinking of the shrieking terror that would have him.

He recited more of the Latin incantations, his large finger trailing beneath them in an effort to aid his focus. “Da ex manes praesidium! Disperge manes!”

A gust blew in and flowed upstairs, where it took form as an aberration: the shrieking woman. The moment she finished her manifestation, she began to glide down toward them with a hideous moan and the accompanying sounds of her rusted scissors, *chip-chip-chip-chip-chip.*

Richard’s concentration broke; his gaze was drawn toward her hollow stare. Ted finally spoke from behind the camera. “Sounds like you’re pissing her off, Richard.”

Richard shook his head hard to refocus and returned to the book. He began his recitations again, louder this time, in an effort to drown out her cries.

"Da ex manes praesidium! Disperge manes! Da ex manes praesidium!"

The ghost's feet did not so much as touch the stairs; only the frayed ends of her dress slid across the steps as she descended. She moaned quietly and slowly raised the rusted scissors, *chip-chip-chip-chip.*

Richard raised his voice and blurted the words with what little strength he could wrench free from the knots of fear in his stomach. He turned his mind blank, a canvas for only the words to be painted on.

"Defendat nos a malo! Removere mortuus!"

The recitations found ground, visible in the pain that cracked across the wretch's face. The ghost whiplashed from side to side, thrashed by some unseen force. Its face twisted, swirled, and contorted in inhuman movements. Whatever youthful beauty she had once had now melted from her face to a worn and taut-skinned horror. The lips shrunk away, exposing crooked teeth; eyelids melted into hollow, solid-white orbs. An unseen force gripped her and pulled her to the floor, her limbs thrashing like an animal as it did. Struggling against the force, she hissed in anger and whipped her hands out to the stairs, using her nails to drag herself down the steps, finally stopping at the base of the stairs in front of the candles.

It's working! She can't get through!

Ted swung the camera to film her, bathing her in its bright light. Despite the chaos erupting across her face, she stared at Ted with a zombie-like fixation. "The hell?" Ted gazed back through the camera with only a few feet and the candlelight between them.

What is she doing?

Richard allowed himself only that one thought before he returned to the recitations, his finger still tracing beneath the words. Somehow, reading made the shaking stop, and he was afraid what might happen if he stopped reading.

"Removere mortuus!"

The aberration shifted from side to side. Her expression melted from anger to one of sorrow and pain with the movement of the muscles beneath her slim face. Her hand rose in front of her and extended toward Ted, but when her fingers came above the candle line, white, scentless smoke sizzled from her index finger like charring meat. She hesitated, then brought her hand up to her eyes to look more closely at it, though she didn't seem hurt, only confused and curious.

No, something's happening.

The ghost's eyes shifted away from her hand to fix again on the cameraman. Richard bit back the fear that leaked in even now and stopped reading, his eyes once more drawn to Ted and the ghost, how they simply stood and scrutinized one another. Richard could see her thin stub of lips begin to move as she tried to speak, but she could only emit a faint whisper, ghostly words without a language. Ted's head twitched and jerked. He pulled the camera from his shoulder and set it down on the floorboards.

"Ted? What are you doing?" Richard watched as Ted slowly bent down toward the candle to inspect it closely. "Don't listen to her, Ted." His words were meek and maybe only a whisper.

"Why did you stop filming?" Beth's lip curled, showing her teeth. "Pick that camera back up again, dammit!" Ted paid her no mind; he reached out toward the small flickering flame.

"Ted. Ted, don't." Richard's voice quivered. A braver man

might have grabbed Ted, but Richard felt unable to move, incapable of doing anything but sit, watch, and beg as the fingers of fear gripped him. "Don't touch the candle." Ted reached out, slowly and unsurely cupping a hand around it.

Ted put his fingers into the flame, letting it burn him. The ghost watched him as he pinched the wick, unflinching. Her eyes then slowly shifted toward Richard in anticipation, in wanting. Richard saw something behind her eyes; gone was the confusion or pain, replaced with something that craved and desired, something that hungered. He curled in on himself, watching his fate unfold in front of him, unable to stop it.

He swallowed, took a deep breath, and tried to curse. "Oh geez," was the best he could muster.

"Pick that fucking camera up!" Beth stomped a foot. Her outburst ripped Richard from his fear-stricken paralysis. He suddenly became aware of himself again, of the flask of holy water in his pocket. He stood up and hurled the holy water at the ghost again, but the ghost shifted. The water splattered against the dusty stairs behind her as the candle went out between Ted's fingers.

The ghost glided past Ted and toward Beth. Without thought, Richard pulled the crucifix from the door, holding it high between Beth and the ghost. He tried to hurl the holy water at it, but again it shifted out of the way. It turned from them and shot to Ted, moving not past but through him. The crucifix clattered to the floor; Richard was unaware that he had lost his grip on it until he heard the crash.

Richard watched as the ghost's hand pierced through Ted's chest, gripping onto something inside him, and pulled deeper in. Ted shuddered and convulsed before falling to his knees. With a moan, the woman sunk her face into Ted's. The cameraman's eyes rolled back into his skull and his teeth chittered. His gasp was loud and low, sending a haunting cry through the house.

Run. Run!

No longer paralyzed, every instinct filled Richard with fear and adrenaline and roared to take flight. Fear told him to run to the van, and leave Beth and Ted to their own fates. But something stronger than that weakness took control, something against his instincts.

I can't leave her.

Another sense whispered to him, an idea, a last-ditch effort. Richard pulled open his jacket and stripped his sanctified necklace from his neck, wrapped the braided leather around his hand, and pressed the metal cross into his own palm.

Beth gasped as Ted fell, but she was more stunned than afraid. "What's happening?"

Ted rolled around in quick, painful jerks, hooting and gasping for breath as he did. His back contorted into a wide horseshoe shape and his arms cracked down by some invisible vice-grip.

With the necklace now wrapped tightly around his palm, Richard reached over and grabbed Beth's hand, the same one that had sent his heart fluttering hours ago. She shrieked the moment the necklace touched her skin. "Oh my God!" The chains of the spell now broken, she stared down at Ted with horror on her face.

With no more time to waste, Richard pulled her toward the door. "Let's go!" With his free hand, he tried the doorknob.

Ted came to his feet with startling speed and shot over to the door. He slammed against it, cracking the wood and making Richard stumble back.

"Richard? I want to talk with you." He spoke between

grinding teeth, his veins popping from his neck. Richard looked down to see Ted's arm shake with frustration, as if he was only barely holding himself back. "You can't leave. No one leaves."

Richard still hadn't found his footing, and he stumbled back. Beth's tight grip kept him on his feet.

"Ted..." It was all Richard could say. He had no other words. Men like Ted had bullied him his entire life. He could only stare at Ted and slowly inch away.

Beth had regained her composure. "Ted, we need to go now. It's time for us to go," she said, slowly and deliberately.

"No." Ted wouldn't look Richard in the eyes; he only stared at the floor. "Everyone is always jerking me around. No one ever takes me seriously." His hand slid beneath his coat and to his holster, freeing the pistol. "Everyone treats me like *shit*." He grinned as he lifted his head, and the pistol followed.

"Ready for your final shot, Beth?"

Without thinking, Richard kicked forward with all his weight, landing a solid blow to Ted's midsection and sending him tumbling over.

Oh, God. I hope that was a good idea.

Richard spun on his heels and yanked Beth's hand, dragging her with him. Unable to leave, they instead went deeper into the house. Their feet beat loudly against the loose wooden floorboards as they stormed up the stairs. Richard spared only a moment to glance back and see Ted lazily pulling himself to his feet. Beth kept a close pace behind, moving more smoothly than Richard.

They entered the hallway at the top of the stairs; it stretched out in two directions, neither of which was inviting. Beth took charge and pulled Richard down one of the dark hallways, guided only by what little moonlight shone through the cracked windows. She then pushed into one of the aged doors. The door was stuck, forcing her to throw her shoulder into it. They slammed the door closed behind them, the rusted bolt of the metal lock groaning as she slid it into place.

"What can we do now?" Beth's voice was afraid but steady.

"Ow, ow!" Richard whimpered and tapped his foot.

"What?"

Beth's hand was grinding the bones in Richard's hand against one another. "You're squeezing my hand." Richard said through gritted teeth; he never did have strong hands.

"Oh. Okay." Beth eased up on her grip, her face calming.

"Don't let go, though!" Richard said, grabbing her at the elbow. She nodded, her face determined. He could see she was brave and in control.

Stronger than me...

A loud thump silenced Richard. Beth leaned in, her warm breath spreading across Richard's ear. More thumps followed.

"He's coming up the stairs."

Richard's gut twisted again, turning inside out. His body shivered—he needed Beth. Needed her strength. He had none of his own, only impulses or flashes of self-preservation.

Ted's voice came from the hallway. "Beth, Richard." It was hard to hear from behind the door, and his words seemed slurred, like a drunkard's. "Where are you guys? Come on, guys you don't have to be afraid of me. We're friends, remember?"

"Can't you do anything?" Beth pleaded to Richard, her hand tensing on his again. "You're an expert, right? Is he possessed?"

Yeah, I'm supposed to be the expert. She needs me. Think!

He swallowed his fear, and whispered, "Yeah, he's possessed." Richard's mind ticked away for a few quiet seconds, until the gears began to turn and pistons came to life.

"My book!" He whispered back as loud as he dared, "I don't... It must be downstairs. I left it by the door." A sudden numbness overcame him; he felt as if he might pass out, and his knees started to shake. He squeezed his eyes shut before he could speak again, getting a grip on himself. "We can just..." He found no more words.

Beth pressed closer to him; her lips came to his ear again. Her heat gave him goose bumps. "Can we go out this window? Jump to the ground and get to the van?" She pulled away with a realization. "Ted has the keys."

A loud knock at the door made Richard jump. He stumbled back from it, and locked his hand on Beth's as tightly as he could. His heart thumped in his chest, loud enough that he was sure Ted could hear, one heavy beat after the next as the doorknob slowly turned. The door pushed inward but caught on the bolt—the rusted metal was all that shielded Richard from Ted simply walking in. "Beth? Richard?" Ted's voice was sweet, calm. "Let me in? Please?" The door rattled calmly against its frame.

A moment of silence passed, but Richard couldn't calm his own breathing. He loudly sucked in breath.

"Open it!" Ted banged against the door. "Open it! Open it! OPEN IT!" He shouted over and over again, yanking the door and banging it against the frame.

Silence returned. Ice water poured through Richard's veins, freezing him stiff. He felt a tug on his hand; Beth reached over to grab a curtain rod off the dusty floor. It was a flimsy thing that Richard was sure would make a poor weapon, but he didn't have a better idea.

We're going to die.

Bam! A blast from the pistol burst a hole through the door. "Dammit!" Ted screamed and roared like a beast in anger. "What did you make me do? I got wood in my eyes, you pieces of shit!"

Fear gripped Richard as he saw visions of his coming death; his jaw hung loose and tears streamed down his cheeks. Beth's curtain rod fell to the floor. "Richard, help me!" She pulled him toward the window and put the palm of one hand at the top of the window frame. Richard followed her lead mindlessly and pressed his hands onto the window and waited.

"We can't wait here, he'll be in soon!" Beth said while pushing as hard as she could against the window, trying to slide it up.

The window was tight; it had likely been locked in place for years or decades. It groaned but refused to move. A light rain began to drizzle and pattered the window as they strained against the glass. Another day and another place, Richard might have found the rain soothing.

But today wasn't that day. Richard watched as Beth shot a look of panic back at the door. He had seen that miserable look before. He remembered it in his dog's eyes when they found it on the side of the road after it had been hit. A look that said death was soon to come. He was powerless then as his best friend died in front of him. He was just a boy then, frozen in fear.

He wasn't a boy anymore.

He pushed the fear away and found strength and purpose through Beth's need of him. He clenched his jaw and shoved up as hard as he could, letting adrenaline give him strength. With a loud crack and a groan, the window finally gave way, pulling a string of dried paint that had been sealed within the crack behind it.

"Let's go!" Beth went first, sliding her thin legs through the old windowsill and ducking her head as she stepped onto the overhang. Richard planted one hand against the cracked frame and followed hastily behind. The overhang creaked as it threatened to collapse beneath their weight.

Richard felt as if Beth's thin, soft hand could slip from his at any moment, leaving him no choice but to trail quickly behind her. The shingled overhang became slick as the rain grew heavier. Richard stepped with careful feet, as quickly as he could, for fear of slipping, but Ted bashing against the door behind him prompted him to move ever faster.

Beth moved to the edge to see the ground beneath. She turned to him, preparing to say something, but never got the chance. The roof finally collapsed to the soft wet grass with a loud wooden crack. Richard's elbow slammed a rock. A shot of pain surged from his elbow to his fingers, forcing him to cry out. Several painful seconds ticked by as he gripped his elbow before he realized he had lost his hold on Beth. He struggled to his feet in the slop as the rain peppered his face.

Richard took two steps forward, sloshing through a small puddle before he spun around and began searching for Beth. He caught sight of her, his red hat gripped tightly in her hand. He had to rub the rain from his eyes to be sure, but she was sitting, playfully, in a rain puddle.

"Richard Fitcher." She spat his name out and twirled the hat on one finger, her tone much darker than before when she was enthralled, her warped voice now drawing nails across his ears. There was something behind her eyes, something that wasn't Beth. She stretched her neck at him, twisting it inhumanely. "He's going to find you, Richard." She gave a sweet chuckle with the promise. "You better run fast, little witch. Faster than those fat legs have ever carried you."

Terror clutched his chest and squeezed the blood from it. He wanted to scream, to run, to do anything except move forward—anything except be here right now. Instead, he reached down and snatched Beth by the hand as quickly as he could for fear that she might bite him or, worse, keep talking.

She gasped when he connected and the fog lifted once more. "Richard?"

"Let's run, he's coming!" The words spurted out as he grabbed her wrist and pulled her to her feet. Her jeans were caked with dirt and soaked from the rain.

"What about Ted? We can't leave him," she said, despite her fear. It was surprising how quickly she could pull herself together.

Richard found courage in that—in her—once more. Terrified and fighting for her life, she refused to leave Ted. Something about her gave him strength; she helped him overcome his own fear.

I can help him. I know how. I know how. I know how.

He told himself over and over again as if that made it true. The gears began to turn in his mind, the trials of the witch he'd gone through before exorcism. He knew how, but he needed something.

My crucifix. My book.

"We'll need to get my book. Ted's probably on his way out now, but he can't come out the front door. I dropped my crucifix there and he can't cross it while possessed. That should stop him, I think. I hope."

Oh God, I hope that's true.

Beth brushed a strand of wet hair away from her eyes and nodded, and together they dashed toward the front of the house. They could hear Ted curse and fire off another round. The blast made Richard stop dead, but Beth pulled him forward—her steps became his. They crept slowly through the wet grass and up the groaning porch to the front door. Richard had been content to let Beth lead the way, but now he stepped forward. He let out a choked breath as he reached for the doorknob and slowly turned it. It croaked open, and Richard could still see two of his flickering candles. He peeked in through the crack of the doorway, between the peeling paint and wood. He slowly pulled the door open and reached for the book.

"Richard!" Beth tugged him back, pulling him away just as a shot blasted into the floor near him, sending chips of wood into the air.

Richard slipped back, but still on his feet, lurched forward again and grabbed the book from the ground, yanking Beth with him. Another blast went wide from the top of the stairs, slamming into the porch near Richard. Richard jolted up and turned to run with Beth. His legs felt uneasy, about to collapse with each step, but he managed to stay up.

Mud from the dirt and gravel road slung up and splattered both Richard and Beth as they slopped their way through it. Richard saw the trees there, still holding their inviting gesture, still calling for him to go deeper into the woods, farther into the dark. They had no other choice.

4

"WELL HOT DAMN, SON," MINGES SAID THROUGH A YELLOW-toothed smirk. He leaned back in his metal chair, looking like he'd be more comfortable with his feet up on the table. "That story sure as shit makes you sound like a lunatic." He pulled his hat from his balding head and fanned himself with it. "Lay it on a bit thicker. Let's hear about that cult back home a little more. Problem is that them sumbitches had you all confused and murderous, right?" After a wink, his entire face shook as he chuckled.

"What? No! I was never in a cult. We mostly played Dungeons and Dragons. My sensei... eh, my Dungeon Master also taught us about real-life occult magicks."

"Mmhmm, mmhmm." The lawyer bobbed his head. "How to be summoning all them demons and talking to ghosts, yeah? Them dungeon masters, they kinda like a BDSM thing, that right? I think I can work a tortured soul angle on that. Your pappy never touched you funny, did he?" He strummed his thick whiskers as he played with the thought.

"No, nothing like that! Our sensei just told us how to

find them, how to use the texts to fight them, how to defend ourselves. God, I never believed any of it."

"Sounds to me like you wasn't doing too well though, am I right? From what you told me, you and that girl were just running to the woods with that other fella chasing you. What happened to that old boy anyways?" Planting a heavy arm against the table, Minges leaned forward. Richard finally looked up to stare into the lawyer's strange blue-gray eyes.

"It wasn't like that. We didn't know what to do. I didn't *really* believe this, any of this. I thought it was a game we were all playing, that we were all just fooling each other. But it's all real..." Somehow he couldn't break his gaze from Minges's. "Ted is a big guy, scary even when he isn't waving a pistol around. And he had the car keys. What were we going to do?"

"So this is the part where you get the axe, right?" He cleared his throat and considered. "No wait, I saw the video. You were by some gas station, yeah? How'd you finish the old boy then? We gonna find another body out there somewhere?"

Did I kill Ted too? Is he still out there? No. No! I didn't kill anyone. It was the witch!

Richard clenched his teeth and shoved the thoughts back before he could speak again. "Well, like I said, we couldn't get in the car. Ted had the keys. We couldn't just *leave* him there. Who knows what would happen after that? We just needed to get some space so we could think."

"IT'S FRIED." Beth held her phone, which was refusing to turn on. "What the hell happened? It got too wet?"

"Maybe. Mine won't work either." Richard dropped his phone back into his satchel. "But it might be this place. These perverse energies, they can mess with electronics." His whisper barely carried a few feet.

"Ted's camera was working though..." Beth said.

"I... I don't know. God, I don't know anything." Richard rubbed his head, trying to think. "We need to get somewhere safe so that I can look at the book."

They had run off the dirt road and into the dark woods, leaving Ted in the house. How they had outpaced Ted, Richard had no idea.

Thankfully, the rain had lightened from its moment of downpour, but it was still hard to move quickly through the untamed woods where roots twisted up from the ground and sharp branches pointed from eye level. Richard had heard plenty of stories of people breaking a leg by tripping on a root or rock at night—as if a ghost, a mad man, and the terror of the woods weren't enough.

The trees seemed to hold hollow faces full of pain—each seemed a cover for the wicked to hide inside. Richard took a deep breath and considered whether talking would help him to remain calm.

"There's so many stories about the woods at night and the strange things that live in them." He was wrong, the talking wasn't helping, but he kept on anyway. "Everything's twisted here, demonic. Evil has corrupted everything."

Or is that just my imagination?

"I can't see anything." Beth said and sprung a small keychain light from her pocket and used it to light their way. "We have to be careful, Ted could see the light."

"Let's just..." Richard looked across the dead trees and foliage. "Let's just get behind a tree somewhere. Can you give me enough light to read?"

They could hear the sounds of the night responding to their intrusion: bugs and birds chirped and screeched. A crow flew overhead and landed in a tree near them. It gave a haunting squawk and watched them closely with its orange-ringed eyes.

Richard shuddered in fear of the crow. But in truth, he was sure that if a squirrel was to drop from a tree next to him, he could just as easily lose the strength in his knees. He was scared of everything, scared even to meet Beth that morning. He had thought that she might not take him seriously, that maybe he wouldn't be interesting enough. He had a whole routine in mind that all went down the drain the second that knife came to life.

He was trying not to think of that now though; those were all years in the past for all he was concerned. He knew now he had to focus, but the fear kept coming back. Thoughts of Ted and his gun plagued his mind. Strangely, though, he found focus through Beth's hand. He knew that if he had been alone, he'd certainly be dead by now. He'd never been particularly religious before, but he reached up to the crucifix and prayed to whoever might be listening.

He felt Beth tug his hand. "How did you know this would work?" She held up the hand wrapped in the necklace.

"I didn't."

"You just thought it might work and took a shot? That was brilliant, Richard. Good instincts." She rested her other hand on his shoulder. "Thank you."

He felt warmth fill his cheeks and only smiled in reply.

"What makes it warm?"

"It's never been that way before." He shook his head. "But it's working."

"I know what happened, Richard. I know you begged us

to go. I can't explain it; I knew it was happening but I didn't care. I didn't care about anything. Not until you touched me —then I got it all. But something else came over me when you let go of me the second time. Something else clawed its way inside of me."

Richard only listened and trembled. He remembered that look in her eye when she twirled his cap in the rain.

"What was it?" she whispered, her eyes soft and unsure.

A demon.

He refused to say it out loud. He only shook his head, feigning ignorance. How or why it was here, he had no idea. Beth gave a shallow nod and looked as if there was something else she wanted to say.

"None of this is your fault, Beth. There's something at work here. It got into your mind." He held a breath to say more, but couldn't, and he hoped she wouldn't ask him again. Instead, he turned away and started to go through his satchel with his free hand. He pulled his tome out and opened it, doing his best to shield it from the pattering rain.

"Do you need the light?" She leaned over his shoulder and looked down.

He nodded as his thoughts refocused. He parted the leather covers and ran his finger down a page. A single drip of water splashed against it, despite the cover of a tree. He sighed and stretched out farther, pulling his streaked jacket across it and continued. It did well enough to cover the book.

The crow squawked again, not wanting to be forgotten. It jumped and fluttered its wings before landing on another branch not far away. Its orange-ringed eyes turned to them again, watching them closely.

"Shoo! Go away!" Beth reached down for a stone to hurl

at the crow. The stone bounced not far from the creature. It blinked and twisted its neck, completely unbothered.

There was a scream somewhere far off. Or was it a roar? Richard couldn't tell. He only took in a deep breath of the cool night and hoped whatever it was doing, it was doing it somewhere else.

"It's Ted. Just try and go fast," Beth said, dashing his hopes. She turned the light back to the pages.

Richard leafed through, but found it difficult with just his one hand. "Here. Possession."

The crow squawked, drawing an angry look from Beth, who didn't bother with another rock. "The stupid crow is going to give us away." It hissed at her before its head twisted away to find something else of interest.

Ignoring it all, Richard tapped a neatly inked paragraph. "The ghost is anchored to the house, I think. If we get it out of Ted, I think it'll be forced back into the house. We can chant and force it out, but we'd have to hold Ted down before it starts and I'd need my candles. We could try and drive it out if we knew its name, but we don't..." He sighed in desperation. "The only other option is to find her body and where she drowned, it might even be a bathtub for all we know. I just... I don't think we can do it, Beth. I think we have to leave him."

Beth turned her gaze in the direction of the house and bit her lip. "What would happen to him if we left him? If we got help and came back?"

He might kill himself.

Richard knew that much. Being possessed wasn't the same as wearing a coat or pulling on a shirt. There was a relationship there, between the possessed and possessor. "A symphony of insanity," one passage had called it. He had read the sections on it, never thinking that they could be true and one day useful. It was a strain, though, to have something else in your head, and ghosts and spirits were not such easy things to understand. They were the restless dead. Perhaps without even knowing it they could drive their hosts insane or suicidal. More than a few testimonies had come to that end: suicide. But not all.

"He could be okay if we got help and came back." Richard's words might have been true, but they may as well have been a lie. He certainly didn't believe them.

Beth had clearly smelled his doubt. "I can't. I really can't. But you go, Richard. Go and get help. Leave me the book and the necklace, I'll go and see what I can do for Ted." Her eyes were honest. She really would face it by herself.

His mouth dropped; he hadn't expected that. "What... what are you going to do?" He struggled to keep his voice from quivering. He wasn't sure if it did or not.

"I'm going to find the body." Her voice was still, resolute. "You said the house seems like an anchor. Does that mean the body is there?"

Richard lifted a shoulder and turned to read some more. "It might be. Maybe she always lived there and can't stand the idea of leaving, or maybe she did leave once and that's when she was killed. There's really no way to tell."

"Let me see the book." Beth leaned in and looked over the pages. She traced over the passages that had been translated into English. "It says that she likely died unnaturally? Richard, do you think there might be something else in these woods?"

Richard felt the fear creep back in, and the hairs stood up on the back of his neck.

The knife, it pointed toward a witch, but they found a ghost.

"The knife. It told us where the witch was. That's why we're here. Not for a ghost."

"We can't just leave Ted, Richard." She shook her head. "What would happen to him? Think, Richard, think. You're a *witch hunter.* You've been right on *everything* so far. What can we do, how can we save him?" She squeezed his hand tighter.

A witch hunter. A game, yesterday.

"You're right." He straightened his back. He clenched his hand, hoping that this would somehow give him the courage he needed. "We're going to go back in, get my candles, and find the source. And then we're going to rip it out of Ted. After that, we're getting the *hell* out of Dodge."

5

"Getting the hell out of Dodge?" The lawyer was clearly skeptical. "You really say that? Sounds like something you were practicing in the mirror again."

"Dude. No, it just totally came to me." Everything was starting to come back and Richard was feeling better. "Though I'm pretty sure I stuttered that last part. I was just trying to play the part, be confident for Beth, you know? She was knee-deep in all of this and holding it all together. I had to try and do the same."

Minges grunted. "Why didn't ya'll just leave and let the chips fall where they may? You just told me you hardly knew what the hell was going on anyway."

"Like I said, we didn't know what could happen He could kill himself, or maybe anyone else that showed up would be just as controlled as Beth and Ted were. I just didn't know what would happen. Besides, we needed to find the body of the ghost somewhere in that house, if that really was her anchor to the world. Imagine trying to find the body and use it for a ritual with police help."

"Mmhmm. S'pose I can see how that line of insanity

could pose a problem for ya'll." Minges laced his fingers together on the table. "So you can't or won't leave, and your phones are dead. Mighty convenient."

"Convenient?" Richard spat back at him. "It's the freaking opposite of convenient! I couldn't call anyone, even my group back home! They might have been able to tell me something, give me some help."

Minges flicked his tongue against his teeth and presented a sharp smile. "I'll be needing the phone numbers of your cult buddies too."

"I don't have them right now. Who remembers phone numbers these days? They're all programmed into my phone, and that got fried. I got them in my book somewhere, wherever that is. Everything is still blurry." He rubbed his temple with his palms. "God, it's so hard to remember what exactly happened."

"Could be the drugs, or something wacky up in your dome." Minges pointed a finger at his own balding head. "Memory can be funny like that, change things around with the right prompting. Get you thinking all kinds of things that didn't actually happen."

Richard squeezed his eyes shut. It was true, it was hard to remember anything, but talking made it all come back, like waking from a bad dream. "I know it's hard to remember, but I know I didn't kill Beth. That's a lie. The witch..." Richard struggled to remember, but it came only in pieces. "He could do things."

"Yeah, I got that part." The lawyer said, donning his white hat once more. "All kinds of things, I'm sure. And that's the story we're going to go with, right?" His smile opened wide. "We're going to say those voices were talking to you, made you do all that evil shit you did."

Richard clenched his teeth hard enough that they might

chip. "I didn't do it! I didn't do any of it! You have to believe me!"

"Well, son, we got a body. But let's keep playing with the idea that it wasn't *really* you."

God, I wish it was Beth. I wish she was the hunter and I could just follow her. I wish she could be here right now. I wish she was alive and I was dead.

He squeezed his eyes tight, trying to stop the tears from coming. "Beth was so brave, so ready to just get into it all. She would have been a great reporter. She could have done some good work."

"Sure." Minges's words were bland. "So ya'll were walking up to that spooky old house that ya'll shouldn't have been at in the first place. What happened next?"

"We went in." Richard said simply. "What else was there to do? We had to go in and find the anchor."

RICHARD SLOPPED through the mud as they closed in on the house, and he wiped rain from his eyes. He wasn't a hunter or tracker, but he could clearly see distinct boot prints in the mud that must have been Ted's. A single trail made its way out onto the road and curved off onto the grass. Richard couldn't tell where it went from there, but he hoped Ted was now deep in the woods and nowhere near the house. He ran a hand across the van as they passed it, wishing he could jump into it, search it top to bottom for a spare key, and drive away, but Beth's hand still pulled him forward.

Swaying in the cold wind, the front door creaked open and closed, the flickering candlelight illuminating the house from within.

What if Ted is there, waiting for us?

Richard didn't have long to dwell on the idea. Beth easily led him onto the creaky wooden stairs, and he was unwilling to refuse her. She reached for the worn door and pushed it the rest of the way open, and the quiet groan of the metal hinges welcomed them once more. Holding his breath, Richard crept inside, picked each candle from the floor, and blew them out.

He tilted his head and focused on the dark of the hallways and crevices of the gloomy house, praying that nothing was watching them. "Where should we go? The body could be anywhere."

Beth shined her light across the floorboards and exposed their disturbance in the dust. "The basement, maybe. Where else would you put a body?"

Richard couldn't argue with that logic. "Great. Well, how do we get into the basement?"

"Not through the living room." She shined her light across the room and settled on the entrance to the kitchen. "Maybe here? That's where the basement door was in my parent's house—the kitchen."

The tip of Richard's nose itched. He rubbed it, but the feeling didn't go away. More than an itch; he knew Beth was right. He felt drawn to it, as if hands pressed his shoulders forward. Was it instinct, or intuition, or something else?

A breeze passed through the house and whispered in the wind. The quiet sound crawled up Richard's back and slithered onto his neck as if it had a thousand legs.

It was hard to see in the kitchen; guided only by Beth's small light and the moonlight piercing the window. Richard grunted as he cracked his shin against a stool, which clattered against the floor a few feet away. He frowned, then gave a sheepish smile of apology to Beth.

They both stood still and waited to see if anything had heard them. "I think we're okay," Beth said.

A strange yellow and orange rot grew in the corners of the kitchen's floor and climbed up the sides of the peeling wallpaper. A pile of dishes sat in the sink with a layer of gray dust that coated everything. A door in the rear of the kitchen was busted in and had collapsed to the ground some time ago. Dirt was everywhere, as if some animal had broken in and dragged the wild in with it. Richard took a deep breath and watched the door as they moved past it.

"Something broke in here," he said as his focus stayed on the door, waiting for something to lurch in, though nothing did.

"I don't think so—look at the dust. We're the only ones leaving tracks." Beth shined her light across the floor. "If something broke in, it was a long time ago."

What could it mean?

He'd heard countless tales of other things beyond witches or ghosts that ran through the dark and preyed on men, any of which might have been able to break a door but not leave tracks. He would have laughed at the idea just yesterday, but now he didn't know what to believe.

He shook the thoughts away and brought his attention back to the kitchen. The basement door was there, just as Beth had guessed. Beth tried the old, stiff door latch. "I can't get it open. Can you try?"

Richard nodded and wiped his hand on his pants, more for fear of opening the door than anything else. Reluctantly, he grabbed onto the handle with one hand while he gripped Beth's hand with the other. "I might have to put my shoulder into it." She nodded for him to go ahead.

He pressed down on the latch as hard as he could and threw his shoulder into it. It popped open, and a shower of dead bugs and dust spilled down over them, causing the two to squeal and pull back.

After brushing off the filth, Richard turned to look down the stairs. He gave a stiff, unsure look to Beth as he took a step closer to the basement, but all he could see were steps that descended into a black pit.

"Just... just give me a second." With an uneasy hand, Richard fished a candle and lighter out of his bag. He had Beth hold the candle while he made several attempts to ignite it. Beth finally asked to try. She lit the candle after a few attempts.

"I'll go first, Richard," she whispered, even as she moved to get ahead of him.

"No, no, it's okay. I'll do it." Richard didn't even know he could say those words, let alone take the first step into the dark. He took several steps down before his mind caught up to the idea. Beth kept pace with him as they slowly descended. His candle's flickering flame and Beth's light pushed the darkness back and brought the ground into view.

So far, so good.

The last step creaked, and the dark took notice, seeming to shift and move farther away. "Did you see that?" Richard nearly shouted.

"Richard!" she hissed, and glanced to see if anything was approaching. "Stay quiet."

He gulped and braved another step forward. "We'll have to find her bones," he whispered in an effort to distract himself and force another step forward.

The basement floor was packed dirt, and the walls were stone. Water trickled down the sides and into the dirt, creating slop. Large pieces of trash were stacked, one upon another, so rusted that it was impossible to distinguish what it might have once been. The mounds of decayed metal created a maze of rusting filth. The thick musky smell of the basement was hard to ignore, but it wasn't just that.

Something is rotting here.

Richard held the candle high and saw the string of a hanging light. He reached and pulled it a few times, but it gave only a quieted *click-click.*

"No bulb," he said between nervous laughter.

"We're going to have a hard time finding anything down here," Beth said.

But somehow, he knew Beth was wrong. "Something's down here." He took two steps forward. "I can feel it." Something pulled at his soul, something that was trying to warn him, to speak with him, but he didn't know what it was.

It's watching you.

"Richard?" He heard her but could no more slow his feet than he could stop the call to move forward. He dragged Beth a few steps before she caught up.

"Can't you smell it? Feel it?" He took in a breath of musky air and held the candle up as they moved past another heap of rusted trash. He turned back to look at Beth and sank into her eyes, unsure of what he was feeling.

Is this a curse? Did it get me too? Is it compelling me?

Something clattered at the other end of the basement, causing Richard to nearly yank Beth off her feet when he jumped.

I'm the witch hunter. I can't jump at noises. I need to be strong, for Beth.

They wove through the strewn-about trash maze, avoiding the sharp edges that stretched to greet them as their candlelight illuminated the back stone wall of the basement. Richard leaned down and placed his candle on the floor. "Beth, can you shine the light here?" He didn't know how or why, but as sure as a hook and line in his lip, he was drawn there.

Beth turned the light up onto the wall and Richard raised his hand to touch the stone; it was smooth and cold. He rubbed his fingers together, feeling a layer of grime that had come from the wall.

"What are you looking for?"

"I don't know." Richard moved farther down and stopped.

Erlend Boberg.

Richard found the name carved into the stone, inked in red that leaked from the edges and down the stone. It swallowed him as he stared at it. A simple thing that he knew meant more than it appeared.

"What is it, Richard?"

He hesitated. "I think it's the witch's name." He drew in a deep breath. He couldn't find it in himself to say it aloud.

This is power. This is its strength.

Beth didn't have such troubles. "Erlend Boberg?"

Something in the darkness replied. Rusted metal dragged against rusted metal, screeching a hail of terror. Richard felt Beth spin around and aim her light into the dark. Two small green orbs shone and floated in the abyss of the basement. The orbs became eyes as a creature moaned and whimpered, stepping out from darkness, between them and the stairs.

Its skin was a putrid white. It wore tattered rags and was covered with boils and patches of coarse, black hair. When it spoke, Richard could hear the menace in its voice. "Long has the age been since I've last feasted on the living." Its lips curled up, showing splintered teeth. Its back arched as it pounded forward, with the knuckles of one long hand beneath it like a third leg, and the other three-fingered hand reached toward them. "Your flesh will relieve me from the torment of my hunger."

Richard stumbled back, his shoes sliding in the slop of the dirt. They couldn't fight it; he didn't even know *how* to fight it. His brain raced, trying to find something, anything, he could do. He didn't want Beth to die here in this cold basement. He refused to freeze again. He refused to fail Beth. He refused to die.

Do something! Do something!

He fumbled for words, and they spilled out. "I uh, I have a Snickers in the car."

The creature halted. Beth's light shone up to find its face, but it didn't seem to mind. Its features twisted even more horribly as it spoke. "You would snigger at me? The memories of your death throes shall fill the enjoyment of my slumber!"

"What...? No!" Richard pulled Beth back against the stone wall. "No, no! It's a candy bar! A Snickers is a candy bar! It's chocolate with nougat and peanuts and caramel and I think there's usually like some cream mixed in..."

Run! Run!

Its soulless eyes fixed on his. "Caramel?"

"Yeah." Beth took up Richard's pitch. "I have some other things too, in my purse outside."

The flesh pulled tightly on its face, making it difficult for Richard to see if it was angry or curious. It twisted its head up to an odd angle. "In what measure could this *Snickers* be compared? What manner of beast surrenders its flesh toward this *Snickers* that it may be more delicious than that of the meat of man? I know not of any creature of *nougat*."

Work the sale, work the sale.

Richard took a breath and breathed fire into his nerves. His hands didn't twitch; he wouldn't let them. His feet stayed strong on the ground; he refused to let them do otherwise. Something was different in him, something he had never known before but had come just at this moment.

"Have you ever had chocolate before? It's not made of flesh. It's made of some kind of bean thing I guess? I don't really know. It's a bean thing, right? With milk?"

"Yeah." Beth agreed, but stayed a foot back. "It's really sweet and I think I have a can of chips in the van too..."

Richard didn't know what the thing was, or why it was there in that basement, but he did know one thing about it.

"Chips?"

It's an adventurous eater.

6

"Listen here now, boy. You mean to tell me you got yourself face to face with a wight and you talked your way outta having your ass on the dinner menu by giving it a Snickers and some 'tater chips?"

"Yeah." Richard squinted. "Wait, how'd you know it was a wight?"

"I got HBO, son. Bit of a *Thrones* fan myself." He laughed. "So you mean to tell me that if we go back there we'll find ourselves an old gangly creepy sumbitch hiding out there in that basement, munching down some junk food?"

"No, no you wouldn't."

Minges simply stared at Richard, waiting for him to elaborate.

"Well, we talked with him." Richard sheepishly looked away. "I had a snack pack in my bag in the van. Witch hunts are usually a lot more 'low key' than this one. I mean, usually we just walk around in the woods or an abandoned house while I say a few words in Latin and flash my light around asking people 'Did you hear that?' or 'Did you see that!' But now I've got a knife that's pointing me through haunted woods, a ghost possessing our cameraman, and a wight that wants to eat my face but likes the taste of honey butter more!"

"Listen, son!" Minges brought him back. "Calm yourself and let's get back on track now, you hear? So, where we at? You persuaded this wight not to start chomping down on some man-meat in exchange for... snacks. So you went to the car, grabbed that snack-pack you were hoarding, snuck past some angry cameraman that's God-knows-where at this point to go back into the basement and have a discussion with a creature that clawed its way out of hell. Am I right so far?"

Richard shrugged and looked down at the table. He couldn't quite believe it himself. "Well it sounds stupid when you say it all like that."

"Yeah, well. Whatever. We need to make sure that we have all this craziness at least in an organized fashion to present our case of you as a brainwashed lunatic deserving of some special care, not a lethal injection in that fat arm of yours."

Richard stared at the cracks on the wall of the cell. "What a nightmare."

"Just you leave that nightmare talk to me son. I'mma paint this whole picture as one big nightmare for you. Juries love this kinda shit. *But*. Let's continue to elaborate. Tell me now, son, what'd that rottin' wight fella talk to you about?"

"*HUNNY BUDDA*? Such a treat must have led to many great wars to secure it amongst the most powerful empires of man. You have done well, male, to bestow such a gift upon me." The wight plunged his hand into the bag and pulled out a handful of honeycomb-shaped snacks and shoveled them into his mouth. A bounty of snacks was placed before the wight, all that Richard had plus a pack of crackers that was in Beth's purse.

"Oh yeah, *Honey Butter* is a big thing coming on right now." He gave a proud grin and shrugged his shoulders. "I get those chips from an import store. They're from Korea. You have to pay a little extra, but you can spend half as much for something that tastes half as good. But are you looking for a meal, or are you looking to enjoy yourself? That's my thoughts on it." Richard knew this was all insane, but he couldn't explain it, couldn't even understand it himself. Their mutual love for exquisite snacks was uncanny.

The wight bobbed its head. It plunged a crumb-covered hand into the bag again and pulled it back empty. It started to lick its fingers with a tongue the color of spoiled meat. "A king's fortune!" it said between licks. "A king's fortune for such a bountiful treasure."

Richard watched the wight proudly before Beth pulled his hand. She motioned to him that it was time to go. She'd sat there, silent and patient, while Richard and the wight had quietly discussed the finer points of the flavor of BBQ chips versus sea-salt bitterness.

He's not so bad, when you get to know him.

Richard cleared his throat. "So, a wight, huh? What's a wight doing here? I mean, why are you in this basement? Why aren't you out raiding villages and plundering homes like the old stories? Why are you trying to eat anyone that comes here?"

The wight glared for a moment before turning again to rip at the next bag. He seemed uncaring if the chips fell to the floor; he simply reached his inhumanly long arm to grab them without so much as bending over. "The last of your line of questioning should be clear. I hunger, so I eat what I may." It grabbed a few chips from the ground and dropped them into its maw. "As for the others..." It turned and then stretched its arm, several feet in length, before it pointed a finger toward the name, *Erlend Boberg*, on the wall.

"He put you here?" Beth cut in. "Why'd he do that?"

"Warden of the Calling. His name." The wight nodded. "It is not a rarity for warlocks of sufficient power to imprison the likes of myself as a keeper." He presented his teeth in a fanged and disgusted snarl. "I was enslaved, dragged in from the pit to the realm of man and chained to this hellish prison." He bit through and noisily chewed a candy bar without unwrapping it.

"So you're just left here to guard his name?" Ever the reporter, Beth persisted. "That's what Warden of the Calling is?"

"Such revelations surprise you female? A name holds power. It connects and gives form to a thing. With a name, a thing can be called upon. It can be controlled. This much I know of the rules of witchcraft."

"But why would he write it on a wall if it's so powerful? Why leave something like that out to be found?" Beth's gaze darted between Richard and the wight.

The wight simply stared at Beth before turning its head to Richard.

"Ah, she's new to this sort of thing." Richard said calmly. He cleared his throat as the wight resumed eating. "There's certain, uh, rules—restrictions, maybe—that the *Other World* must adhere to. The warlock's name is here for him to garner power. How, or why exactly here, I don't know. But there's nothing in the lore of them doing something like writing it on a piece of paper and throwing it into the ocean or putting it into a safe deposit box."

The wight burped and continued eating. Beth shook her head in disgust. "So what do we do next, Richard? We have his name, but Ted's still running around out there, God knows where, and now... *this*." She tipped her head at the wight.

"Oh yeah," Richard chirped. "We were looking for some bones from the ghost upstairs. Any idea where they might be?"

"Bones of the fallen? I know nothing of a spectre among these grounds. Nor of bones laid here amongst my humble domain. Likely a spook drawn or forced here by the warlock."

"Damn." Richard stomped a foot. "I don't know what to do then, Beth." He considered for a moment. "What can we call you, by the way?"

The wight had bent to the floor and was now clawing beneath a piece of furniture for a chip that had fallen there. It looked up toward Richard and spoke in a monstrous, gargling noise. "To properly say my name, you must separate your tongue into three sections of equal length and master the language of Abyssal, with its various overlaying and under-lapping mouthing postures."

His throat went dry; the look of the wight grew suddenly uncomfortable. He shelved the fear. "Oh, I see." Richard smiled politely. "Mr. Wight then. How's that? Would you happen to know what we could do for our friend? He's possessed and moving about somewhere around here with a weapon. How can we exorcise the ghost?"

"Simplicity would demand you dash his skull with a blunt object. Typically, at the base of the skull. I've found men to detach from their head with ease when proper strength is applied to the base of the skull. Spirits find the dead difficult to inhabit. Perhaps with a large bludgeoning weapon? Or something with a proper, narrow focal point would be best in exorcising this spectre from your friend."

"Oh yeah? Hadn't thought of that one." Richard gave a scratchy laugh. "But we were thinking of more of a way where he'd still live and we could leave with him. So we'd rather not have to crack his skull or anything, you know?"

"Are you angel-touched, or dragon-tongued? Hmm? Have you any tears of saints? Perhaps powdered devil's bone, or lycanthrope blood? No? Water blessed of a holy man?"

"That one!" Richard nodded his head. "We have holy water!" He was still gripping Beth's hand as he reached down into his bag and pulled it out.

"Under the proper use of incantations, a spirit will find itself unable to retain the bounds of the host should the host first ingest this holiest of waters." It stretched out one of its long, pointed fingers at the small bottle. "Drain this within the host's mouth-hole. Do not be confused or attempt to insert through any other flesh-hole, you will not receive the desired results."

"Yeah. Mouth. Makes sense."

Beth spoke again. "So we get Ted to drink this holy water and then you say your words, Richard?" She considered this. "Would you help us hold him?"

"I? I am bound to this horrid prison, which you refer to as '*dank basement.*'" The wight sneered, showing its dozens of small, pointed, yellow teeth. "I am a slave until the time in which he releases me, or upon my destruction."

Richard cleared his throat. "What if I were your master?"

"What witchcraft do you declare, mortal?" The wight looked up baffled. "Be you a warlock of old with genuine power to challenge the master that has enslaved me? Or hath you devil's blood in your veins? Perhaps a lick of faery magicks?"

Richard's heart picked up and his pulse throbbed in his ear. He shook his head to all of those. "No." He licked his lips, not quite sure of himself. "But I know his name. And I think I can undo his control of you and take it myself."

The wight threw its head back and spat out a hearty laugh. Richard was sure Ted would hear that.

"Perhaps our union here has run its course?" It drew a lip up into a fanged sneer. "Would I trade one master for another? What depravities would I be commanded to perform under your name? Would you have me toil in your *hunny budda* mines? Better now to feast upon you than subjugate myself to new humilities."

Richard squeezed Beth's hand tightly; he needed every little comfort he could get. Whatever he had fooled himself into thinking before, the monster was exposing itself for what it truly was.

"No." Richard was trying hard to make sure his voice didn't break. "Help us rescue our friend, and we'll get you even more food. But just, no eating people, alright? *No people.*"

The wight pondered Richard's words, "And what do I have to ensure such a promise?"

"Nothing." Beth cut in and took a step closer to the wight, as if to show it she wasn't afraid. "But your alternative is to sit here in this basement from now until the end of time. What could be worse than *that*?"

Its head jolted from side to side as it mumbled to itself. It bent down and repeated Richard's words, rehashing them for its own purposes. It shot a glare at them and then back to the ground. Richard was sure that it was done, that it would turn on them.

It's going to kill us.

But it stopped. And then, standing up and straightening its back and lowering its tone: "The proposal is accepted."

It wasn't long then for Richard to light a few candles and go through his book. He rested on the page: *Binds of Servitude and Commandment of the Infernal.* He spoke in Latin, chanting incantations that the world very likely hadn't heard in some time, from a book writ of heroes long-dead, in form long-forgotten.

"...conteram domo servitutis, *Erlend Boberg...*"

Using the strength that was the warlock's name, he broke the ethereal chains that hung around the creature. A sizzle of smoke arose from the wight's face, curling up and twisting in the air, forming symbols and strange patterns. It hissed, clearly in agony, as Richard continued. But as he set about placing his own incorporeal locks across the creature, his own mind betrayed him.

"...ligabis ad me—"

What am I doing? This was fake for me just this morning and now I'm binding something dragged out of The Other World *to my will. I can't control this, I can't survive this. I'm going to die. I'm going to get everyone killed.*

He must have frozen, the doubt holding him still, because Beth whispered in his ear, "Keep going, Richard. We have to save Ted." It was enough.

"Ligabis ad me. Magister *Richard Fitcher.*"

A surge of new energy filled him and he finished the last of the words. The basement grew quiet as the wight slumped to the floor, looking drained. Everything was quiet, and still, except the light of the candle that continued to flicker.

Slowly, the pale white creature raised its head. "Your bidding, master?"

Richard stiffened his back and smoothed his jacket out. A powerful new confidence spun through his bones. "We've got a spirit that needs a little ass kicking. And a friend that needs saving." Richard spat the words out. Beth laughed and her eyes softened.

She believes in me.

The thought was comforting for Richard. If he couldn't be brave for himself, then he was going to be brave for her.

"We need to find Ted, and you'll have to hold him down while Richard and I feed him the holy water," Beth said to the wight.

"A trivial task." Then the wight tilted its head. "After, surely, we will feast? Preferably on the flesh of some mammal. You still have some enslaved, yes? Or have they finally risen up to throw off the yolk of their masters?"

"Uh, yeah. I guess we still have cows and pigs enslaved." Richard furrowed his brow.

"Excellent. I will gorge myself at the earliest of opportunities. And what of these 'junked food'—will they be plentiful as well?" The wight's three-forked tongue licked the air and twisted as it spoke.

"All the fried and dipped chips you can eat Mr. Wight, and maybe even a burger or two," Richard assured him.

"Then let us hastily commence our kicking of the spirit's ass." The wight planted its foot on the first wooden step leading out of the basement. "My hunger for the budda of hunny grows more terrible by the moment."

7

MINGES STARTED FANNING HIMSELF WITH HIS WIDE-BRIMMED hat the moment he sat down. He had just been outside for the last fifteen minutes on a bathroom break, and came back with a bottle of water and a paper cup. He gasped deeply a few times, but his cheeks were flushed and he looked as if he might vomit.

"You okay there, sir?" Richard was keenly aware that the man looked as if he might spill his dinner then and there across the table while Richard was stuck in the chair.

And if he throws up, I'm going to throw up. I always throw up when someone else throws up.

"Need some water?"

Minges wheezed and coughed. "You get up there in years and sometimes you get some of those, what I like to call 'em, *how-do-ya-do* illnesses. Like a sudden kick in the nuts that twists your guts an—" He was interrupted by a dry gag.

"I think you might need to get that checked out? You want me to call the officers in?"

Oh man, is he drunk?

Minges shook his head and waved him off as he continued to fan himself. He poured water into a paper cup and gulped it down. "I got them all, son. Bad heart, bad lungs, bad stomach. That last one there's why I carry a little air cleaner around with me. No trouble with a little gas between boys, right? But we don't want them ladies getting a whiff, do we?" He laughed loudly but it turned back into a fit of coughing.

"Uh, yeah, sure?" Richard was also keenly aware of the smell; it had been there for about the last twenty minutes. "Maybe we could crack a window though..."

"Window? What window?"

"The slider right behind you."

Minges turned around to glance at it. "Right, right. Must have missed that on the way in. I think the law would prefer if that window kept itself the way it is there son. We can't do nothing 'bout it."

Richard gave a weak nod. "Yeah."

"You're locked up in here tight, boy, gotta get that into your head. You ain't going nowhere. Best you can do is make it easier on yourself and give me something to bite onto, yeah?" Minges seemed to wait for that to sink in. "So how about you go on ahead and tell me what happened after you got that old boy out of that cellar and up the stairs? Let's not spare them details, yeah?"

"You believe me? About the wight?"

He leaned forward on his elbows to stare, his blue-gray eyes piercing Richard's. "I tend to believe you ain't no liar, son. But I wouldn't go so far as to say you ain't losing your mind. S'okay though, son. I've met more than a few crazies in my time. Ain't such bad fellas. Maybe we'll get you locked up in one of them hospitals—more of a resort really. Get you all them funny pages and dragon-dungeoning as you'd want, you'd love it. But let's stay on track here and get this business done. How'd you keep it all together in all this? You said that you came face to face with a thing dragged from the pit, and you were discussing *corn chips*. That sound right to you, son? Can a man that's afraid to talk to girls really do some business with something like that? Clearly you got a wire loose."

"I don't know." It hurt Richard to admit it. "You're right. I mean, I kept thinking it myself, how I'm just simply not afraid. What does that mean? I just felt like this is what I'm supposed to do. This is my meaning in life. Am I losing my mind? I've heard before that it proves you're sane if you have to wonder if you're insane."

Minges bellowed a laugh. "Pretty sure that last part ain't true, son. But enough with the musings." He thumped a heavy hand down onto the table in front of him, making Richard jump. He then leaned close enough for Richard to see the pits on his cheeks and the tiny flecks of black in his blue-gray eyes. "Let's hear what happened next."

"SURELY THE FLESH of the tribes of the Mediterranean—their skin, mixed with their particular taste of sweat, offers the most delicious of the flavors of man." The wight reflected on that thought, as if to reassure itself. "If questioned for the best flavor of meat, I would surely say that of the Greeks."

"But we didn't ask. No one asked," Beth shot back at him. "Aren't you supposed to be tracking the ghost for us anyway?"

Richard wondered if the wight noticed her disgust and just chose to ignore it; perhaps he even enjoyed it. Either way, it didn't seem to affect the wight as they moved through the old house and into the foyer.

Despite its size, the wight crept with a grace that didn't cause any of the boards to groan, nor did it seem that Beth's light was needed for him to move quickly and quietly through the nearly pitch-black kitchen.

This is one of the things that eat men. It sees in the dark and moves in complete silence. This is why the old kingdoms feared the dark.

Richard wasn't quite sure what he thought about that. The wight took a whiff of the air and slunk quietly forward. Richard noted that it walked on the tips of its arched toes and sometimes used its fingers to go on all fours, leaving only faint tracks in the dust.

"Beth," Richard said in a whisper and pulled her back a few feet. "He's just really lonely. You don't have to be so mean." In truth, he was trying to convince himself as much as her.

"Lonely? Richard, he was going to eat us! And now you want to chat with it?"

"Well, yeah. But do you hate a bear if it attacks someone, or do we just say it's just their nature? Let's just... let's just be a little nicer to him, maybe just keep him going in more of a corn-chip direction?"

"You're taking this whole situation very calmly, and that in itself is unsettling. Here we are, holding hands to make sure we don't get wracked with an evil spell, all while following a monster that likes to eat people and looking for my possessed cameraman. And you're worried about me being mean to the man-eater?"

"Yeah..." He faked a happy expression. Maybe Beth understood, as she let her own annoyance drip away and just gave Richard a reassuring smile.

"Male, female. The spectre is nearby." The wight pressed the front door open and stepped out onto the porch. It stretched out on its legs, standing at least a foot taller than Richard. It stuck its nose up and sniffed the air. "I smell something... hot?"

"Maybe it's Ted's gun? He was firing it," Beth whispered back.

The wight twisted its head toward Beth "What's a guhn?"

There wasn't a chance to reply.

Bam!

A loud blast exploded in the air and something struck the wight on the side of the head, knocking it against the outside wall of the house. Black, tar-looking blood sprayed out from it, painting the side of the house with its small flecks.

"Balls!" Richard lost his footing and tripped on the ledge of the front door and slipped back into the foyer, nearly yanking Beth off her feet with him. A fit of dust came up when Richard landed, causing him to cough.

"Get up, Richard! Ted's coming!" Beth grabbed Richard's other hand and helped to pull him up.

Richard looked out to see Ted emerging from around the van; his gun was still pointed at them. He fired off another round that hit the door, showering them with shards of wood.

"Run!" Beth's screams rang in Richard's ear as he got to his feet. Richard started to move, but spared a glance back at Ted. The wight laid on the porch, with a dark sludge leaking from its wound. It didn't so much as move. Its only use was as a small obstacle for Ted to step over.

Ted's head reared back, showing the whites of his eyes as he sprinted forward, roaring.

Richard froze as the fear crept back in, making him shudder. He couldn't fight Ted, couldn't outrun him. Beth screamed in Richard's ear, but he couldn't move. As Ted charged him, his mind went blank, like a deer in headlights.

Beth reached into Richard's bag and pulled free of his grip. She threw Richard's heavy book at Ted. A metal clasp on the edge of the book caught Ted in the face, cutting him just above his eye. Ted stumbled forward as blood poured from the wound. He held a hand up to his face and collapsed to one knee in the mud.

"Kill you!" He bellowed and raised his still-smoking pistol.

Beth fell to her knees and screeched only a few inches from Richard. It was enough to force him to regain control. His mind snapped back into place.

"Beth, no!" He grabbed her hand and pulled her as another blast came from Ted's gun. Richard turned his back to him, expecting the hot lead to pierce his body, but each shot fired at him narrowly missed.

Richard saw the focus return to Beth's eyes the moment he grabbed her hand. She leapt to her feet and the two of them dashed through the living room; Beth ripped chairs down behind them. Only small rays of moonlight through the window and the flashes from Ted's gun seemed to provide any light to guide them. They had no time to be careful, and they slammed into furniture on their way through.

Ted stumbled after them. "Beth!" his voice was weak and sickly sounding. "Beth, you bitch, you cut my face." He fired off another wild shot.

"Dammit, dammit." Richard's eyes were wide with fear. "I kinda thought the wight would be able to take a little more punishment than that."

Beth pulled him into the shadow of a side room and held up a finger. "Shh!"

Richard closed his eyes tight and hugged the wall, trying his hardest not to breathe.

"Richard," she whispered. "We're going to have to wait for him to pass and hit him from behind. We have to hit him together."

"Yeah..." He wanted to protest, but couldn't.

"Richard, you fat son of a bitch, where are you?" Ted called again. Richard could hear his voice closing in. "Richard. I just... Just come out here."

Beth stared at the ground. A tear rolled down her face. "Richard, I'm sorry we made you come here when you didn't want to. But we're all getting out of here, okay?" Despite the tear, her voice didn't crack.

More than ever before, Richard wanted to be brave. He wanted to prove to someone that he wasn't worthless. He wanted to stop being afraid of everything, and he wanted to believe her that everyone was getting out.

I'm going to save them.

Ted's steps thumped louder as they drew nearer. "Hey guys, everything is starting to get a lot clearer, and I'm starting to feel a lot better. But what the hell was that I shot in the head?" His words came with a drunk's slur, filled with anger. "You're not going to answer me? Are you hiding from me? Are you hiding from me? Do you know what I'm going to do to you when I find you, Beth? I'm going to rip that hair out of your scalp and then beat your pretty face against the corner of one of these walls until... Well, I haven't thought much past that part." Something crashed in the other room.

Bam!

The blast resounded, and the flash of the shot lit up the room next to them.

"Am I getting close yet? Got another clip in the car just in case I run out."

Each blast in the confined area of the house shook Richard to the bone. His ears rang deafeningly as another blast ripped through the walls.

"How about there? These rotted walls are weak, yeah? Maybe a round will make it through and shake things up. Kinda hard to see in here, you know? Figured I'll find you both soon, but it makes it more fun if you're running, right?"

His steps crept closer still, and Richard had to bite his own lip hard enough to draw blood as he struggled not to move or even breathe.

"Richard. Richard! Do you know what I'm going to do to you?" Richard could hear furniture clatter to the floor as Ted threw it aside.

Please, please, please let him walk past us. Please let him walk past us.

"I'm going to rip that fat head of yours straight off, Richard. But I'm going to cut you with a piece of glass first. Cut you until it's not fun anymore." Ted burst out laughing and stepped past their room with his back to them. Beth ripped forward, Richard in tow, despite how much smaller she was.

The two slammed into Ted, knocking into him. Something broke beneath them as the man collided with the floor. His gun fired, filling the room with a moment's flash of light.

Richard hit the ground too, his head had been too close to the gun. The intense buzzing now made him sure he was deaf. His head seemed to whirl uncontrollably, the buzzing drowning out everything else as he brought his hands to the throbbing pain in his head.

It was several long moments before he began to feel

lucid again. His legs felt weak, making it impossible to stand, even as the ringing somehow grew louder. He blinked several times. The flash from the gun and the force of hitting his head on the ground made it hard for him to think.

When he could move again, he forced his eyes open. He could see Beth screaming, though he heard nothing beyond a dull ringing. To Richard, she only sat there screaming to a silent world. Then Ted was on top of her, grabbing her by the hair, jerking her from side to side like a dog with a dead rabbit.

Richard tried to scream, roar at Ted to let go, but he couldn't hear anything come out. Ted turned to him, his hand still laced with Beth's hair, as she dug her nails into his arm. He raised his pistol to Richard's eye level.

Richard could smell the gun, could see the smoke slither out from the barrel, but he couldn't do anything. He was frozen in place; he simply waited for Ted to pull the trigger. The shock of everything was too much for him to command his body to do anything else.

This is how it ends. I'm so sorry, Beth.

Ted pulled the trigger once, twice. It clicked. Beth shrieked again—her mind lost to the witching effect—and her screams finally cut through the ringing in Richard's ears. Her cries of pain compelled him to act. Now, with the gun empty, Richard lurched onto his feet and bowled into Ted. He hit the thicker man on the chest, knocking him back against the wall.

Ted's hand was pulled from Beth's hair, ripping strands with it, as he stumbled back. Drawing a breath, Ted growled as he whipped the pistol forward and caught Richard in the lip with the grip.

The blow connected with Richard's teeth and knocked

him flat. Richard spat blood, and a white shard of tooth with it. He tried to call for Ted to stop, to remember who he was, but the blood kept flowing down his throat. Each time he tried to speak, he coughed up more. He could only hold up a single pleading hand.

Ted reached out and grabbed Richard's hands and then twisted the fingers. Richard felt them all pop and feared they might break; the muscles in them tightened and the bones felt crushed together beneath Ted's grip.

"Stop, dammit! Stop!" Richard's blood spattered out with each word. There was nothing Richard could do to save Beth, or to even save himself. Ted's cruel strength overwhelmed him.

Ted dragged him up by the hand with apparent ease and kicked him hard in the stomach. Richard collapsed against the wall and gasped for air as he spat out more blood. The red dribbled down his lips and sprayed across Ted when he coughed; Ted remained unflinching. Richard tried to cry out again but couldn't find the air to even attempt. Ted slammed the grip of the pistol down on Richard's skull, splitting open the skin. A wet sensation leaked down Richard's face and over his ears.

Richard squeezed his eyes shut and waited for the next blow. He suspected that it would be the last, but the thought of Ted finishing him and moving on to Beth gave him the strength to lash out one last time. He turned and swung a wild fist up at the bigger man. It connected with Ted's arm to little effect.

"I'll rip you apart, Richard! You fat-ass son of a bitch!" Ted slammed a fist into Richard's head, catching him on the ear and knocking him loose.

I can't fight him. We're dead.

"I'm going to cave your brains in, Richard. Isn't that

wonderful?" Ted stepped to the side to grab a piece of furniture that had broken in their struggle. He yanked up the broken wood and gripped it tightly. The makeshift club was splintered in sections, leaving cruel-looking shards across it. He swung it hard and caught Richard's arm. Its large splinters of wood shoved deep into the meat of Richard's arm; he wasn't sure if the blow had broken his arm or not.

Ted stepped over Richard's legs and raised the chair leg up into the air. His expression mocked lurid happiness, his eyes stretched wide open. Despite the blood that slowly ran down his face from the head wound, he seemed to be enjoying himself.

In that last moment before death may have taken Richard, a long white arm stretched out from the dark and grabbed Ted. Three long white fingers clamped down over the top of Ted's head before pulling him off his feet and into the air.

Richard blinked, then tried to wipe away the blood that was dripping into his eyes, layering his darkened world with shades of red. He watched as the wight took a bite from Ted's arm and heard Ted's blood-curdling scream. Like a wounded animal snagged, Ted struggled and raged to fight the creature, but it was of no use. As weak as Richard had been against Ted, Ted was weaker still against the wight. Its strength overwhelmed him, and with only an empty gun, the wight met little resistance. The creature held Ted off his feet by his head. It shook him from side to side, hitting him against the walls as it tried to beat the fight out of him. Ted's club clattered to the floor as his neck twisted and turned.

It would have been the easiest thing in the world then to stay quiet and watch the wight finish Ted off. Men like Ted had stepped on Richard his entire life.

The spell's effects drew out the worst parts of you. Beth

was afraid—of what, Richard didn't know. But Ted was clearly just an insane asshole when his inhibitions were stripped away. Richard's face was slick with blood to prove it.

No, that's not true. He's possessed. It wasn't Ted. He doesn't deserve this. It's the ghost.

The wight thrashed Ted into a wall and pinned him against it. Its head reeled back and the sharp, inch-long, yellow teeth extended from brown gums. It wrenched Ted's head to the side to expose his neck.

"Hey." It was a struggle for Richard to get the words out, to even find the air to fill his lungs. "Hey! Let him go. Don't kill him!"

The wight bellowed in anger and then looked back at Richard. "This male would seal your fate. Cast death upon you! I shall fill the void within my stomach with his flesh!"

Richard couldn't find the strength to get any more words out. With cold and pained eyes, he stared at the wight and shook his head. His neck ached and his eyes were heavy; he thought of closing them and letting what happened next come without his interference. But his eyes were drawn to the sharp movements Beth was making—she sucked in air loudly and convulsed like she was stuck in seizure.

He rolled onto his hands and crawled to her. His limbs were unsteady beneath him and threatened to fail him at any moment. The way the room seemed to swirl around him made him think he might also have a concussion. He reached up to touch the top of his head and came away with wet, bloody fingers. His eyes stayed locked on the redness as it rolled down his fingers. He wasn't sure if he'd ever bled like that before.

Beth was no longer screaming, only gasping. She looked up at Richard, scared. He reached a hand out to her and held it still. Beth's eyes didn't hold thought or reason, but there was a flash there. Richard knew she was strong though; her resolve pushed her even in the throes of hysteria. Her lips trembled as she strained to reach out and take his hand. Richard could see the witching effect visibly drain from her, and the first breath she took after their hands met told Richard she was going to be fine.

"Oh my God, Richard." Together they came to their feet and embraced. Richard began to cry as he hugged her tightly. He felt her also give way, and the two held each other, sobbing.

"Delightful." The wight cut in. "You both live. Mayhap now we revisit my request to consume him?"

8

"Quite the story we've got here, son. Got yourself some witches, got yourself a ghost possessin', got yourself a wight that's apparently one of the hungriest sonsabitches out there. Then we got you, the reporter-brain-smasher." Minges's smile oozed with as much arrogance as it did sweat. He fanned himself, apparently tormented by a heat that Richard couldn't feel.

I bet he was drinking right before he got here.

"Why do you even care then, if you don't believe?" Richard fought back the sneer his lips threatened. "Why do you even want to hear it if you don't think it's real?"

"Real? What is 'real,' son? Real is a perception. What's 'real' to you is bullshit to me. But I can tell you, I can spin shit like it's silk and get you what you need from the jury. So I like to hear everything I can from what my client has to say 'bout what happened. Makes sense, yeah?"

"I guess." Slumped in exhaustion, Richard reached up to feel where his head had been struck. He rubbed the spot and pulled his fingers back to find flakes of dried blood. It was sore, but he felt mostly fine now.

"Got a booboo there on your head, eh? Good, we'll use that. We'll say them boys in blue were beating your ass real good when they were bringing you in, eh? Yeah, yeah, I can work with that." Minges rubbed his thick beard. "So. Where were we? You got the bigger boy beaten near death and ya'll did what with him?"

"The wight held him as I went through the ritual. We exorcised the ghost."

"Exorcised a ghost? You make it sound like it ain't no thang, just another day at the office."

"Well, it certainly wasn't the strangest thing that happened today."

"Sure enough." Minges continued to fan himself before falling into another fit of coughing. He hacked up something into his hand, and inspected it before wiping it beneath the table. "Seems like I'm coming down with something. You ain't got them AIDS or nothing, right?" He looked Richard over with eyes full of suspicion.

With a tired sigh, Richard shook his head and continued with his story. "But, uh, when we were exorcising the ghost? We had a bit of a mishap. Kinda, uh, burned the whole house down."

"What?" Minges seemed almost angry as he pulled out a handkerchief and coughed into it. "You burned the house down? How in the hell did that happen?"

"I've never done an exorcism before! It was my first time!" Richard shot back. "We had everything set up. The candles, the incense; I got my book back. It wasn't too bad, just had a little blood and rain on it. Everything was how it was supposed to be. But, you know, things got a little out of hand..." He barked out an uncomfortable laugh. "We all got out in time."

"*We all got out in time.*" Minges puckered his lips and

mocked Richard with a whiny voice. “You know what this’ll do son? It’s gonna look like you were destroying evidence!”

“I don’t even know what to say.” Richard grabbed his hair and started to pull, nearly tearing it out from the stress. “You have to believe me, Mr. Minges. There is a witch out there and he’s manipulating people. I’m not crazy. Maybe I just...” Something caught in Richard’s mind. He pulled his hands back down and stared at them. “My necklace. My sanctified necklace—that must have been when...” The necklace was absent from his neck.

“Ain’t no jewelry making you more hardy, son. It’s all in your head. Don’t need no fancy charm bracelet to keep your shit together. Just take a deep breath. Tell me what happened next, yeah?”

Richard nodded. Talking about what happened helped bring him out of the painful memories, and he desperately wanted to be anywhere else but here. “All right. Well, the wight held him down while we fed him holy water and I began the chant. It all went ass-up after that.”

TED HOVERED NEARLY a foot from the ground, held by phantom forces, as he thrashed in the air. Flickering candles surrounded him, providing the energy needed to expel the spirit. Ted took in long, desperate breaths before words spilled out of his mouth, all backward and chaotic. Richard tried to chant loud enough to drown him out, loud enough to ignore those ghastly deaths promised to him in reverse through Ted’s mouth.

Did it just promise to eat my spleen?

Ted kicked and whipped his limbs around violently, trying to find something to hold. Richard was thankful to have enough distance to not catch a foot in the mouth. One of Ted's boots dipped a little too low, though, and kicked a candle into a wall and beneath a curtain; an old, moldy, decrepit thing that burned quickly.

Oh. Yeah, I guess I should have put those candles a little farther out.

Richard did not stop chanting. Beth's hand pulled tight against his; he spared her only a half-second glance. Clearly, she wanted to get away and put the fire out, but couldn't without letting go of him. And he couldn't move closer without breaking the chant.

Richard sat on the ground, the book laid out in front of him and trying hard to focus. "Idcirco præcipio exeatis hinc!"

Ted began to whirl in the air, turning over on himself. His eyes rolled around while he gave a low hiss. His mouth stretched wide enough that Richard thought his jaw might break. Two white, ghastly fingers slowly stretched out of Ted's mouth and started to pull their way free. Richard spoke louder and faster still, using the ancient words to force the spirit from Ted's chest.

The ghostly arm stretched farther out from its captive. The head finally emerged, dragged out by the mystic strength of the chant. It turned to look at Richard with hollow eyes before shrieking. The wight, hunching down like a panther ready to pounce, watched from a few feet away.

"Richard, hurry! It's lighting up!" Beth's screams broke his concentration; he turned to look at the fire. The ghost started to flow back into Ted the moment Richard stopped.

"No, keep going!" Beth screamed again. Richard resumed the chant, and the ghost shifted direction again.

Slowly, inch by painful inch, the creature was ripping

free. Ted's jaw was stretched to the limit; his eyes turned red and looked ready to burst from his skull. With half its body loose, the ghost shrieked from behind the candles and sunk its fingers into the floorboards.

Hmm. I didn't know it could do that.

When its foot came loose, it jolted up and shot to the edge of the candlelight. Richard cut the chanting, and Ted fell flat to the ground and groaned.

"Now! While it's weak!"

Beth hurled a cup of holy water at the ghost. It splashed across its face, leaving dark crevices where the water burned. The ghost melted in agony down to a puddle, crying out in tortured moans as it sizzled away, until there was nothing left to scream.

"That won't stop it." Richard couldn't stop the anxiety in his voice. "It'll be back when it regains itself."

"Grab Ted," Beth yelled at the wight. "And don't eat him!" The creature reluctantly obeyed, grabbing the unconscious man and following them toward the door. The fire crept up the walls and to the ceiling, too far gone for any hope of stopping it. The old, dry house, with its peeling wallpaper and brittle walls, seemed to be too well-suited as tinder for fire to do anything to stop it.

Richard grabbed Ted's camera from the ground. The weight of it strained his forearms. Groaning, he pulled it up and was led out by Beth.

Richard planted his foot in the mud and turned around to see that the flame had gotten to the second floor in dizzying speed, as if the sins and dread of the house ached to be burned.

Beth pulled at his hand, but he couldn't help but watch quietly and think of the irony that the rain had stopped now that the fire was catching. He was starting to turn away, to join the others in the van when he heard the sobbing. His gaze was drawn to the second-floor window where he first saw the ghost. She cried out for her home and the harm Richard had done to her. Despite all that had happened, Richard felt a tinge of sadness and sorrow for her. The woman who had lived in this home for countless years, now forced to remain as it burned.

Rest, now...

Whatever the reason for her tortured existence, her cage was alight, and if that would free her or push her into the afterlife, Richard didn't know. He turned and ran toward the van, without any real desire to find out.

Calmness washed over Richard. How exactly he couldn't say, but he knew they were going to be all right. "I think you can let go now, Beth. I think it's done." She released his grip and rubbed the palm of her own hand for a minute before refocusing.

The wight set Ted's unconscious body in the back of the van next to his camera. It then crouched over him with a blank look of bewilderment. Beth fished the keys out of his pocket and started the van. Before Richard had quite closed the door, the van was already turning around. Beth slammed the gas, spitting pieces of gravel into the air as they raced down the road.

Those dark trees, the ones that had been so threatening before, now raced by his window and into the rearview mirror. "H-how do you feel?"

"I'm okay." Beth's grip tightened on the steering wheel hard enough to turn her knuckles white.

Richard let out a deep breath and looked into the back of the van. The wight was still hunched over Ted, staring, mere inches away from his face.

"Hey," Richard laughed uncomfortably. "Let me see how

he's doing." He climbed into the back and sprinkled a little of the water from his flask onto Ted's face. Ted stirred. "Hey buddy, how you doing?"

Ted blinked several times and was greeted with Richard's battered, bruised, and bleeding face. He wiped a hand through his red hair and took in a breath as the wight leaned in and showed a monstrous, toothy smile.

Ted screamed. "What the hell is that?"

Richard held his hands up to try and calm Ted. "It's a wight. Don't worry, he's cool. He nipped at you before, but when I told him not to eat you anymore he quit, so nothing to be too concerned about. Everything is *under control.*" The wight nodded in agreement with Richard.

"He what? He fucking bit me?" Ted crawled back and pressed against the side of the van, his eyes fixed on the wight. He spared only a slight glance down to his still-bleeding arm.

"Yeah." Richard nodded. "Maybe you should hold something against that? It doesn't look too deep, though. More like a pretty good scratch, right?"

"Why the hell are we riding with it?" Ted shot back.

"Human! It was I who stopped—"

"Wait, wait, let me take care of this," interrupted Richard. "We humans are a little sensitive about things trying to eat us and all." Richard said with sincerity as he turned back to Ted. "In all fairness, you were being kind of a dick when you were possessed. You *did* shoot him in the head first."

"Yes! Be glad I took so little of your flesh, male!" the wight piped in again. It pointed a hooked finger at a single leaking black hole where its brain should be, thick tar dribbling down.

Richard motioned for the wight to calm down. "So yeah,

you shot him in the head, but apparently that's not such a big deal for him, I guess?" Richard shrugged and gave a confused smile. "Anyway, yeah, you shot him and were chasing us. Mr. Wight here was pretty instrumental in exorcising that ghost. So you kinda owe him, man." Richard grimaced. "He's due a solid."

"He did kind of save you, Ted," Beth said from the front seat. The wight looked deeply irritated and started aggressively nodding with everything that was said.

"A solid is due!" the wight spat.

"This is insane!" Ted snatched up an old jacket that was lying in the back of the van and pressed it to his wound.

"Well, you were possessed, man. You were running around shooting people and trying to rip our heads off. We had to exorcise the ghost from you."

Ted's eyes faltered. "I can remember pieces of it. God, I'm so sorry. I'm sorry Beth." He held a hand up to his head and squinted his eyes in pain. "I remember going in… the rest of it I just get in pieces."

"Yeah, well, the wight helped," Richard said as he let his head fall flat against the headrest.

Whatever forgiveness Ted had, it dripped away almost as fast as it came. "We got away from the ghost and now we're riding around with this scaly ugly son of a bitch that crawled out of hell and eats people?"

"Ugly?" The wight shook in frustration. "Such a hideous man would call me ugly? You have the hair of fire! The abyss is rife with the likes of your kind, the red-headed devils! Such soulless men fill the halls of hell!"

"Ted," Richard cut in again, trying to calm the situation. "I'm just going to put it out there, but you're being *kind of* a dick right now. You were trying to kill us, and he helped us. Frankly, I think without his help, you would have killed us and still be stuck in that house for who knows how long."

"This is insane," Ted repeated, shaking his head in disbelief.

The wight looked like it might cut in again before Richard waved it off. He whispered to it, "Just give him some space. We *really* don't like it when things try to eat us."

The van went quiet as Ted held his head in his hands, trying to come to grips with what was happening. The wight stared out the window with what looked like a grin, happy to be out of the basement.

Richard crawled back into the front seat. "So now what? You guys heading back into the city?"

"I'm just going to need a minute, Richard." Beth shook her head and focused on the road.

"Okay." Richard glanced around, at a loss for what to do next. He pulled up his bag to check and make sure everything was still there. He pulled out his cell phone; it had eaten up a good chunk of his monthly bill for the last few months. Now it just seemed like a brick.

Man, I'm hungry. Maybe I can talk them into pulling over somewhere?

The thought hadn't struck him as strange until he looked back at Beth, who stared out the window while Ted quietly rocked himself. He looked to the wight, who returned the glance with a wide grin. Something else crossed his mind then, and not for the first time—why was he so calm? Why was he so able to put this all aside?

Why am I always so damn strange?

Richard stared out the window and considered the night, the knife that pointed him to the house, the name, the ghost, and the wight.

What am I going to do now?

Richard wasn't sure how long he was lost in his own thoughts, but he was pulled from them when Beth parked on the side of the road.

"Guys." Beth shifted to look into the back of the van to include everyone. "I'm going to keep going."

Ted raised his head to look at her. "What do you mean, 'keep going'? Keep going with what?"

"*This,* Ted." She hit the steering wheel. "This story. This is our story. This is what I'm supposed to do! Witches are real and they're *hurting* people. I can't stop. I have to keep going." She brushed the hair from her eyes and turned to Richard. "But I can't ask any of you to come with me."

"Beth..." It was all Richard could murmur before going silent again.

"Richard." She reached out and grabbed his hands. "I was so scared there. Scared that I got you killed, that I dragged you into something." She bit her thin lip and pulled her hair back to tie it into a ponytail. "I don't want you to come or put yourself in danger for me. I don't want you to get hurt because of me."

"This is ridiculous!" Ted blurted. "We barely survived *that,* Beth! I even had this freaking thing try to eat me!" He thumbed to the wight. The wight immediately sneered in offense.

"But a nibble! You moan like a cow for only a nibble! Among a brood, we regularly take bites of each other. It is a sign of bonding!" the wight shouted.

"Oh, is that so? Then we must be *really* good buddies for you to try and take a bite out of me! Oh yeah, we're like the damn odd couple, right?"

The wight skewed its eyes suspiciously. "What is this 'odd couple' you speak of?"

"Beth." Richard squeezed her hand. "Let's... let's be smart

about this, okay? Let's leave now and come back later. We'll restock, we'll get help. We'll hunt the witch."

"Such prattling," the wight scoffed.

"What the hell is prattling?" Ted shot an angry look at the wight.

"You talk as if you have the jaws of rabbits. Nattering? Inevitable failure," the wight responded. "The warlock knows that his name and domain have been disturbed. He's felt such. He's weakened until he can locate another suitable location and perform the proper ritual to transcribe his name again. The warlock will have fled this location, abandoning all that he has to regain his safety. There is no tomorrow in this war."

"Then it has to be tonight." Beth's voice was resolute. Richard knew there wasn't a way to change her mind.

"Tonight?" Ted shouted. "Who gives a flying shit if there's a warlock running around out there, Beth! We didn't even know they existed until tonight! What harm could they do?"

"Such occurrences are formidable to detect. He draws his essence from the life of the town around him, causing torment, sorrow, suicide, terror." The wight spoke nonchalantly. "It empowers him and gives him life. From time to time, further sacrifice is needed from the blood of—"

"Shut up! Just shut up!" Ted yelled over him. "You don't get a say! You eat people, probably people he gave you! No one is going to listen to you!"

"He's helping, Ted! No one says you have to go. We'll drop you off in town. You go right on your way. But for me, it's now or never." She turned away from them to look back at the road.

"I'm going," Richard said.

Ted ignored him, "You're acting like a lunatic, Beth.

You're not equipped to fight a damn witch! Hell, your only real qualification for reporting is your bra size."

"Dammit, Ted! Get out!" Beth yelled back.

"Watch your damn mouth!" Richard finally shot at Ted. He was filled with anger, and his outburst brought everyone to silence. "I'm tired of you!" Richard turned around and pointed a finger at Ted. "You're the type always telling everyone what they can and can't do, you're always talking trash to everyone! Always telling us we're fat, stupid, or weak just because you hit the gym and have more girls' phone numbers than just your mom's, that you're somehow better than us! I'm the only one that has *any* kind of training. And you know what? If it weren't for me, you'd be dead! In fact, you almost were dead and it was only because you *didn't* listen to me!"

Ted shook his head. "So, what then? We form a war party to hunt a warlock that knows we're coming to help people who don't know we're helping them, all the while taping it for people who won't believe it when they see it anyway?"

Richard tapped his finger against his chin, considering. "Yeah, yeah, I think that's what we're going to do."

"Fine, fine." Ted gestured toward Richard. "I'll come along. Can't sit out if he's going."

Beth shook her head. "No one is asking you to, Ted."

"Who's going to hold the camera? This thing back here?" Ted tipped his head toward the wight. "I don't think the creature with the strangely extensive vocabulary will know how to run a camera if it doesn't even know the etiquette about not eating people."

"No. I do not attend myself to such modern magicks," the wight responded.

"Exactly. He doesn't play with magical camera gear. I'm

in. In until it becomes suicidal—then I'm out," Ted promised. "But I'm going to need that extra magazine from the dash."

Richard hesitated, letting a second tick by before popping open the glove compartment and finding the clip there. He handed the extra bullets back to Ted. He decided this time he would feel more secure with Ted's insistence on the pistol; they might just need it.

"Then it's settled." Richard turned to look up at the full moon in the sky and let his voice drop low. "*Such a lovely night for a witching.*" He let a few moments pass before he turned back to Ted. "Can we try that again but you get it on film this time?"

9

Strings of mucus shot from Minges's mouth as he coughed; Richard had to cover his face and turn his head as the snot and spittle hit the table.

"Sorry 'bout that, son." Minges slurped down a paper cup of water. "Getting steamy in here, eh? Aww dammit, supposed to be cooling down here. It's autumn ain't it?" He stretched his collar.

"You don't look good at all. I think you need some medicine or something, like seriously." Minges's health concerned Richard; the air wasn't particularly hot. He looked as if he had eaten something bad, drank too much, or had the plague.

"Don't rightly believe in them medicines, son. That's how they get you. You ever know someone that went to the doctors and didn't have to go back in again in a few years or what-not?" He smirked, assured that he had made his point. "Me, naw, I don't go to them. My pappy and grand-pappy never went to no doctor, and they lived well into their sixties."

"Oh yeah, that makes sense." Richard tried hard to be

polite. "Well anyway, that's what we did. We all decided we weren't going to give up, just going to keep pushing on. Go kick the big guy while he's down. Make the world a little safer for everyone." He felt a warm sense of pride with that.

Minges coughed. "Yeah, that was the plan, but instead you ended up just smashing the reporter's head in, right?"

Richard's smile slowly left his face. "I'm still just..." He couldn't find the words to finish.

"Why not just go home then, son? You said it yourself, you folk didn't even believe in all that until the house. What do you owe the world that you'd go and tango with something you don't understand? Makes no rightful sense."

"Ted didn't want to go, that was very clear, but I think he just didn't like the idea of being left behind, feeling like he was the weakest. And me? Well, this was something I could do that no one else could do. I mean, how many other people have that much importance placed on them? This could be the most important thing I do in my entire life. And, well, Beth wanted a story, and she was getting one. Maybe that's just her blood, right? Maybe finding the truth is just what she's about."

"*Was* about." Minges reiterated.

"Yeah..."

Minges nodded slowly. "So how does an amateur witch hunt begin? You gather yourself a posse with some ropes and pitchforks then set out to beat a lil ass? Or is this the part where you and that blood orgy come in?"

"Blood orgy?" Richard's eyes went wide. "Whoever said there was a blood orgy?"

"Son, I've heard enough of these stories to know that there's *always* a blood orgy. Weirdoes are always working toward a blood orgy." He laughed and slapped his leg. "Trust me. I've seen my fair share of the weirdoes that hit up them blood orgies, and you fit the bill, son. No fooling me."

Richard shook the thought from his head. "No, no, no! I just called my sensei and told him about what had happened."

"Your sensei." Minges snapped back into attention. "What'd you say that old boy's name is?"

"He's *intense*. We just call him The Kord."

"Cord? Like what you plug in a vacuum with?"

"No, The Kord. Kord, with a K. He's a... he's a god in one of the RPG games we play. The *name* The Kord though, not my friend. No, my friend isn't actually a god or anything." Richard laughed shyly under his breath.

"And you guys worship Kord?"

"No, no! He's not the *real* god, it's just for a game!"

"Mmhmm." Minges looked skeptical. He said nothing else, only stared at Richard.

When the silence became too much to bear, Richard finally murmured. "Uh?" "So, got a phone number where I could contact this *Kord*?"

Richard nodded. "Got it logged in my phone, but it got fried. I guess the police have it? I also had it jotted down on a note in my book, but I don't know where that is. Oh, and it's not under '*Kord*,' but '*The Kord*.'"

"You don't know the damn number? Kids these days. Hell, I used to have just scores of ladies' numbers burned in my mind, down to the last digit! Now you're all '*I don't have my phone*,' " he mocked.

"I have his email. It's *The Kord six nine six nine at*—"

"Eh," Minges waved him off. "I don't do none of that computer crap. We like to keep it basic around here."

Richard shrugged. "That's all I've got."

"Mmhmm." He trailed off into silence for another few long seconds. "So you called your buddy. Then what?"

Ring Ring.

The telephone continued unanswered. Richard turned in the booth and smiled at the camera; Ted was just a short distance away, filming everything, which, at the moment, was nothing at all.

Richard took a breath; the phone booth smelled like cheese. He hadn't been in an actual phone booth in years, but he was happy to have found one of the only working ones in the state, though he was also careful not to touch anything. He moved his feet around from the discomfort; the bottom of his shoes peeled from the sticky floor with each step.

Oh man, this phone booth is so dirty. I'm pretty sure someone peed in here.

They were parked at a gas station, and the lights were still on, despite how late it was. An old, tired-looking attendant flipped lazily through a magazine, paying them little attention as they went about their business.

The night had grown so cold that Richard had to keep his jacket zipped all the way up, and it was starting to drizzle again. The moon was at its apex, and seemed to be shining an abnormal amount of light down on them.

"Still ringing," Richard said with a shy smirk to the camera.

"Procure more of the rings of onion!" The wight cried from the driver's side window in the van, its body stretched from the back and its green, beady eyes piercing the darkness. "My hunger grows more desperate with each moment's passing!"

Beth held up a finger and shushed him.

Richard sighed. Finally, the phone clicked over and a tired voice came on. "Yeah?" It was The Kord.

Richard gave a bright smile and thumbs up to the camera. "Kord? *The* Kord? Is that you?"

The voice on the other side yawned. "Who is this and why are you calling me so damn late, or is it early? I have to work at The Comic Bin in the morning."

"It's me, Richard. Kord—The Kord, it's real. All of it, it's real." Richard saw the lenses on Ted's camera shift and move as it followed him. He gave the camera a thumbs-up.

"What's real, Richard? Wait, the casting rumors are true?" His voice grew desperate. "Are they really casting Mark Wahlberg as The Weasel?"

"No, no, nothing that bad. Witches, I mean. Warlocks. Man, they're *all real*." Richard's voice grew in excitement; he had to keep himself from spewing all the words out at once. "We're hunting one right now. We went to—"

The Kord cut him off. "Richard, I know it's real. I've been training you for years."

"What?" Richard's voice fell flat.

"Are you joking? We're a cabal of witch hunters. Our hunting ground covers the tri-state area."

"It's... I thought we were joking?" Richard couldn't hide his confusion. He slid his hand over the receiver before looking up to speak to the camera. "He says he knew that already. He says that he was training me for it."

Beth and Ted exchanged an awkward glance.

"*Richard*," The Kord yelled back. "Richard, what have you been doing when we sent you out on missions?"

"I don't know? I was just looking around, playing along! I thought we were all just really into roleplaying."

"Oh my God, Richard. You always came back and told us of your struggles with demons and ghosts! Shit, wait. Is that your real name? Richard?"

Richard stopped to consider if he was joking. "Uh... Doesn't Harry use his real name too?"

"You think his real name is Harry Deezenutz?"

"I thought it was Polish!"

"So when you told everyone your name was Richard Fitcher and we all laughed at how terrible that was, you were actually telling us your real name?"

"I thought you guys were just being dicks!"

The Kord groaned. "Richard, we made you take a ceremony, we told you it was real, over and over again. We made you study it and told you to prepare for what you might come across. You told us you've done it before. You've been practicing Latin for years!"

"I thought it was *very* serious role-play! Like LARP or something. Why do we always play Dungeons and Dragons at the end?"

"Because we *like* Dungeons and Dragons. What the hell else is a group of witch-hunting nerds going to do?" The Kord sighed and took a breath. "Okay Richard, okay. What are you hunting right now?"

"A warlock, here in Bridgedale."

"Mmhmm, mmhmm. I guess Deezenutz put you on that?" The Kord listened carefully. "Have you come into contact with the witch yet?"

"No, not yet..."

The Kord cut him off. "Richard, listen to me very carefully. You should know all this already, but I'm going to tell you anyway and I'm going to speak slowly so that I make sure you understand. If you've been using your real name, *you're in serious danger*. Names have power. They can touch you by knowing your name, and I don't mean that in the physical sense, though they can certainly do that too. No, I mean in the spiritual sense, *they can reach out and touch you.* They can enter your mind and wreak havoc with your brain. You're not strong enough to resist. You need to leave the area immediately. Like, *now*. If you haven't confronted him yet, then you probably still have a chance."

"Uh, it's not that simple." Richard laughed under his breath and smiled to the camera again.

"Why not? *What did you do*?"

"We found a wight that was guarding for the warlock."

"*You found a freaking wight?*" The Kord screamed into the phone. "How in the *hell* did you kill it?"

"See? That's the funny thing. We didn't actually kill it. We more or less got past him, though."

"*More or less*?"

"It's uh, it's pretty cool actually. Basically, we freed it and it's traveling with us now. It's eating chips in our van right now." Richard spoke quickly then. "I know what you're going to say, I *know* what you're going to say, but hear me out. He's not really so bad when he's not eating people. And I've kinda bound him into my service."

"Not, eating... It's traveling with you, and you bound it to your service? Holy shit, Richard! I'm impressed, that's not easy." The Kord cut out for a few seconds. "*Wait.* What was it guarding?"

The rain broke in the sky, pouring buckets. "Aww, dammit..." Ted cursed as he moved to get under an overhang.

Richard licked his lips and then spoke. "The warlock's name. *Erlend Boberg*."

Something shifted then in The Kord's mood, Richard could tell. He could sense it. "Richard, I can feel that name. You're onto something ancient, something old. Can you feel it? When you read the name, when you said it, can you feel how powerful it is?"

It was true. He felt it. He felt the power climb up his neck. Instinct, the world, maybe God... something told him what a wicked name it was. Something told him he should fear it. Richard shifted his weight and looked at Beth and Ted.

How can I explain this to them? How can they understand the itch on my neck or the whispers in my ear? The things that tell me what to do? My instincts...

He had known from the moment he saw the name that they were onto something powerful, something old and evil. He couldn't explain how—he was sure that no words existed that could fully describe it—but he had a sixth sense that told him of the power, of what he would soon face. "Yeah, yeah I feel it too."

"Did you destroy the placement of his name? Like we've trained you?"

"Yeah, but not on purpose. It burned down with the house. It was on stone, but that should have been enough to burn the name off."

"Listen to me Richard, listen carefully. That name, I don't know whose it is, or what they can do, but I can *feel it*. He's a cancer on the world, and he's killing that city, and he's probably done it many times before. He's draining them. And I don't even mean that in a figurative sense. I'm sure, if we looked at medical records, that they are going to have an abnormal number of diseased deaths, suicides, and deformed births. Richard, we have to take care of it." The Kord was speaking slowly and carefully. "But don't say that name again. Don't you dare say it until you're ready to hurt it. It might be listening. It's not human anymore; something that powerful, that old, can't be described as human, as a mortal, anymore."

"Okay, okay. What should I do then? We're committed to going after the warlock..."

"You and that news crew? Do they know what they're getting into? You know what, it doesn't matter. You need all the help you can get until we get there, but they're *your* responsibility, Richard." There was silence on the other end as The Kord let that sink in. "If it's really as powerful as I think it is, we need to hit it quickly. I'm going to go wake up Harry, Katrina, and Severin. We're going to come down there and kick some ass. But every second counts, Richard. We're going to need you to gather research."

"I can do the knife trick again, see if I can track him down that way. Get a lock on him?"

"No, I think it's best if you get into the library and check the local papers for odd occurrences and whatnot. Get that news crew to help you. I want to have a general idea of how long the bastard's been there and what kind of things it's been doing. Can you get your team looking for anything out of the ordinary?"

"Yeah, but the library is closed, right? It'll be closed tomorrow too I think, since it's Sunday."

"Richard, we're hunting a warlock that may possibly be hundreds of years old. It could be a necromancer bringing the dead back to life, or it could be a vampire that's left a trail of half-drained bodies around, or it could be any number of other horrible things that hide out in the dark, waiting to snatch our last breath. We have its name, and now we need to know what it is. You'll manage with a locked library, won't you?"

"Yeah, of course. Of course." A nervous laughed gurgled out of Richard's throat. "I just meant, *in theory* we'd be locked out of the library. Not that it'd give us much trouble to break in and check the records for local deformed babies or anything."

"It's important, Richard. If we don't know what we're dealing with, we won't know how to fight it. Find us something. This is who you are, Richard. You're a slayer. You're a witch hunter, you're a killer, you're the light in a world of dark. Be brave. We don't fear the dark, the dark fears us. Bring the fire. It's time to show the world you're worth a damn. I'm out now." He hung up. Richard nodded, despite the fact that The Kord certainly couldn't know if Richard was nodding or not.

Damn, that guy is intense. That was a whole string of badass one-liners.

He glanced at Ted and Beth, who were still filming. Richard cleared his throat. "I guess I'll have to employ my skills in *murder* and *hunting*."

I'm overdoing it, aren't I? I think I'm overdoing it.

"We'll draw the fiend in and cut that bastard to the *bone*."

That last line was definitely overdoing it.

He hung up the phone and turned to the others. He marched through the rain to the overhang with Beth and Ted; he stood just outside, still in the rain. "The Kord said we need to get more information on our warlock, the type of witch he is, and then we'll hunt him. We need to know what weaknesses and strengths he has. The only way to do that is to try and find out how he's been affecting this town." He stopped to wipe the rain from his face with the tail of his shirt. "We're going to break into the library, check the local papers, and hope that the law doesn't show up."

Beth stepped out, holding a hand over her eyes to block the rain. "Richard, we're with you. We're going to do this together," she promised, and Richard believed her.

She means it. She's here to bring this thing down.

"Yeah, we'll do it together." He scowled and turned back to the van. "Let's roll."

"The chips!" The wight yelled from the car. "You have forgotten your promise of a bounty of chips!"

10

"So we wrung the wight for all he was worth, which was little, honestly. He said he was more a servant and 'did not hold confidences with the warlock.' Seriously, the guy knew way less about his master than what you'd think. The wight said that he usually just 'slumbers in eternal ennui,'" Richard scoffed. "Where the hell does this guy even hear words like that?"

"Yeah, sure. Sounds like you boys were having a helluva time. But the library?" Minges said, clearly trying to refocus Richard. "The hell's in the library that'd help ya'll out?"

"Dude, tons of stuff, lots of historical newspapers and whatnot. This is a pretty old town, few hundred years old. Who knows what clues a warlock might leave behind?"

"What clues indeed. So we're going to have to see to those charges of breaking and entering too, then." He wheezed and coughed up a chunky piece of brown phlegm into his palm. He inspected it before again wiping it under the table. "Damn son, why's it boys like you always waking me up in the middle of the night? Can't you all go and get caught at a decent hour? These midnight runs, they run a mess on an aging man's stomach." He rubbed his belly before reaching into his jacket. "Better take a shot of some of the medicine I do approve of." With a wink, he took out a metal flask, unscrewed the top, and took a swig.

"Maybe you shouldn't be doing that right now." Richard clenched his lips.

"Nonsense! Shot of the good stuff'll keep you going, so long as you pace yourself." Minges nodded. "Now you called this man, what's his name? Kord? The Kord? We going to find that old boy out there smashing heads too?" He offered Richard a shot.

Richard winced and waved it off. "I don't know. I don't know where The Kord is. We're a few hours out; maybe he's still on his way?"

Minges nodded. "Look son, I think our best game here is to roll one over on ol' Kord. He's the one filling that head of yours with all that demon-worship and those blood orgies, right? Sounds like a ripe sumbitch."

"That's, uh—"

Minges picked up again. "What we're going to do is give everything to the police, son. Let's not dig this hole any deeper; let's start clawing our way outta this pit. How's that sound, old boy?" Richard was about to speak but Minges cut in. " 'Course, if you choose to ignore what I say and your blood orgy buddies skip town, Sheriff's gonna be looking at your lumpy ass twice as sideways if he don't have no one else to pin this nice little case all up on. Why you being so damn quiet all of a sudden, anyways?"

Richard took a moment to see whether he was finally allowed to speak. "I wasn't! You won't let me say anything!"

"*Exactly*." Minges gave a hardy laugh and another wink to Richard. "You got yourself into this mess, but it's up to ole

Jeff Minges to get your ass outta it, right? What we need here is a one-way street on the understanding. Get me, son?"

Richard shook his head, "It's not that easy! It's real, it's all real! I can't just... I can't just let it all go..."

" 'Course, son, 'course it's all real. You're going to keep spewing that all the way up until that judge's hammer hits the block. Let's show 'em how much of a crazy sumbitch you are."

Richard let his head rest in his hands. "Gavel."

"What's that there boy?" Minges raised an eyebrow.

"It's a gavel, not a hammer."

Minges laughed. "Boy, are we gonna start arguing semantics? We gonna build this case by making sure we got all our commas in the right place?" He rolled his eyes. "When the hell did a comma ever do anyone any good?" Richard hung his head and exhaled loudly. Minges tilted his head back and prompted Richard to speak again. "Well, what'd ya'll do in the library? Find anything interesting? Break anything expensive?"

"Just did some research. I've used the newspaper scrollers before. Microfilm readers."

"And where'd it lead you, son? Might as well keep this downward spiral goin'!" He slapped the table and guffawed. "All this talk of wights and ghosts is pretty interesting anyways. I'm a bit of a *Potter* fan myself."

"Yeah, it's still a little rough in my head. I think getting inside the library was the easiest part, though. The wight said he could just rip the front doors off and kill any 'constables' that showed up or something. Took us a bit to explain to him that not eating people also meant he couldn't kill any humans, even the ones that annoyed him. I think we got to him, I *really* think we got to him, though. Dude isn't such a bad guy, really, just confused. I mean you wouldn't get mad at a lion that ate someone right? You might shoot it, but that's just its nature, right? So long as we gave him chips, he was cool. He explained to us that he's basically just starving all the time."

Minges tapped his watch and motioned for Richard to hurry up. "Yeah, I got it. You've got a pet poodle, he's gnarly as hell, and he's traveling with you. Back to how you got in."

"Well, like I said, that was the easy part. Beth said she was a realtor before and knew how to pick a lock." Richard squinted his eyes. "Not really sure how that relates. Seemed to make sense at the time though."

Minges nodded and drew a circle in the air with his finger, motioning for Richard to hurry up and start again.

"Yeah, yeah. Anyway, we found a side door that was locked. Beth got through it pretty easily."

"So why *people*?" Ted asked, shining the light of his camera on the wight. The wight was standing, stretched fully out, in front of the library's brick wall.

"Man?" the wight responded. Its tattered clothes were barely hanging on, and it brought a finger up to its chin as if considering. "Have you ever consumed the succulent flesh of man?" it responded earnestly.

Ted's impromptu interview continued as Beth knelt to work on the lock. She pulled the picks out of a small case and leaned forward, Richard could tell she knew what she was doing.

"No, I haven't." Ted kept the camera light on the creature. "But *why*? What is it about being a wight that makes you want to eat people and not animals?"

The wight's glassy black eyes, with their strange, green

shine reflected some of the camera's light. "My being lives in eternal damnation, a struggle against hunger for the flesh and the taste of fear and woe. We are by nature the enemy of man. There is no greater thing in life than to see your enemies crushed and driven before you, and to hear the lamentations of their—"

Richard burst into laughter. "The lamentations of their women? Dude, you're totally ripping *Conan* off." Richard continued to laugh as the camera light moved to illuminate him.

"*Conan*?" the wight said curiously. Ted panned between Richard and the wight.

"Pfft, don't act like you don't know *Conan*. You're totally ripping it off." The wight gave him a blank stare. "Ripping off? Copying? No?" The wight still didn't seem to understand. "You're imitating *Conan*."

"I imitate no man," the wight said angrily. "Clearly this man of *Conan* has dealt with wights before, and now..." The wight hesitated as Richard stifled a laugh. "Where is this man of *Conan* located? I will feast upon the flesh of him and his children for such an insult!"

"No way man, no way." Richard shook his head. "No one can take *Conan*, *no one*. He was always cutting the heads off snakemen."

"What would I have to be impressed by such a feat of beheading the impuissant snakemen? I've rent the flesh of their warriors, sucked the marrow from their bones. Such feats do not astound me!"

"Snakemen are real? Seriously?" Richard wasn't sure if he had heard the creature correctly.

"Got it." Beth came up from her knees and turned the doorknob. The sound of the door opening snapped Richard's attention away.

Mental note: find out more about these real snakemen.

"Realtors are awesome." Richard's smirk stretched from ear to ear. The library doors swung open, revealing a dark hallway.

As Beth stepped in, she smiled and flipped on a flashlight she had taken from the van. "Let's make this trip as fast as possible." She shined her light against the walls, revealing aging posters and reminders of monthly events.

They crept down the dark hallway with their lights to guide the way. "We're going to have to turn the power on if we're going to check for the newspapers," said Beth.

Ted stepped in behind them, filming them as they spoke. The wight followed shortly, mumbling to itself and closely inspecting everything with fascination.

"I used to work at a gas station. We had the electrical box in the front but you needed keys to turn it off and on." Richard turned back to look at the camera. He raised his hand over his eyes to shield them from the light. "Are we sure that we really want to tape ourselves committing a breaking and entering?"

"Fair enough." Ted peeked from behind the camera.

"I would feast upon his eyeballs!" The wight shouted from behind.

"Are you still going on about *Conan*? He's a fictional character."

"Ah, the fictitious," The wight sneered, showing its rows of yellowed teeth. "The fictitious and the dead are all who would be saved from punishment for such an insult."

"Anyway," Beth cut in from the front of the group. "We're taping this for our own purposes, Richard. We're going to document *everything*."

The group made their way through. Ted still seemed uncomfortable letting the wight stay behind him, but the worst they got from the creature was the occasional cry for food.

It didn't take them long to make their way to the front desk and then to the main doors. As they had suspected, there was no sophisticated security system in the library of the sleepy town of Bridgedale. Ted shined his light across Beth's back and the security box.

Richard and the wight were cast in darkness as Beth worked her picks. Despite how oddly comfortable he'd grown with the wight in such a short time, Richard couldn't help but feel his mind run wild with thoughts of blood and pain when he saw the creature hunched in the dark. Each breath it took made its thin chest expand farther than Richard imagined it should be able to. It returned a stare at Richard, more dull than malicious.

"So uh..." Richard scratched his chin. "Where did you study English?"

"Hmm?" The wight reflected. "What is *English*?"

"Oh come on! You know the word 'impuissant' but don't know the word English?" Ted spat from behind the camera.

"Got it!" Beth said as she opened the lid on the power box. She held her cellphone's light to it. "I don't think we want the whole place lit up, right? Let's go for this." She flipped a switch and lights came on in the back.

Richard could see through the entire library. It was two stories, but the center was open enough that he could see up to the second floor. Stacks of books were carefully organized and placed on nearby wooden racks and huge metal shelves —an impressive collection for the town.

The building itself was humble, but did house a few computers in the back. It took a few minutes, but Richard was able to find the newspaper scrollers. The model was different than what he was used to working with, but he figured it out quickly.

The two peeled through countless local newspapers and articles but came across little of value. Ted had set the camera down and started a computer, doing what research he could too.

"Any luck?" Richard sighed. "I haven't found anything."

"I might have something here," Beth said, staring intently at the screen.

"Finally." Ted let out an exhausted breath and then walked over to grab his camera.

"Apparently there were several animal deformities born around the same time here in the sixties." Beth scrolled through an article, quickly scanning it. "It talks about one farmer delivering a two-headed cow, another complaining about all their chickens going sterile, another about a horse with a third eye..." She grimaced. "What do you think it means, Richard?"

"Animal deformities," Richard said aloud as he dug out his heavy tome and let it drop onto the table with a loud thump. He undid a clasp on the aged leather cover and began to leaf through it. "Maybe he was born here? The witch? Or maybe there was a ritual performed here. I think it's a fairly widespread sign. It's hard to pinpoint with just that."

There has to be more.

"What can we do with this, Richard?" Beth looked up from the screen.

"I, uh, I don't know." He looked from page to page, the book groaning crisply with each turn. "If he was born in the sixties, then maybe he's in his fifties? Certainly not ancient. But that's just a guess. Maybe he's much older?"

"Can someone just be *born* a witch?" Ted asked from behind the camera.

Richard looked up to the camera, not sure how to answer the question. "No, not exactly. But it's possible that a pact with a demon was made, or that there is some inherent strength in his bloodline. No one is born a witch, but some can be born 'better' at it than others."

Beth's brown eyes focused on Richard as she spoke. "How does that work?"

Oh man. I'm supposed to be the expert here.

Her sweet eyes made it hard for him to think; he wasn't sure if he had ever seen that exact shade of brown before. He blinked several times to focus himself. "Well, you might hear about a family of mechanics, right? We say it's 'in their blood.' Witches can be the same. Maybe someone in their bloodline sacrificed something for a ritual before they were born? Witches or warlocks aren't necessarily evil, either. Though this Ere—uh." He reconsidered repeating the name. "This E.B. we're dealing with, he certainly seems to be a dick."

"Yeah," Ted cut in, "this one has a monster hiding in a basement of a haunted house ready to eat anyone. I'm pretty sure we're safe to assume he's evil."

"Yep, there's that," Richard agreed.

"Richard," Beth said. "You're the only one here with any knowledge of what's going on. Give us your best assessment. What is he?"

"Well, with what we have in front of us." Richard glanced back at the screens and then to them again. "I think we're dealing with a witch in his late-fifties or -sixties. I'm guessing this because this town isn't in complete ruins. He's probably something of a corrupting force, based on these mutations and birth deformities. There's probably something about people being born deformed. I imagine there was an unnatural spike in them, small town like this might be less willing to put something like that in the papers."

"There seemed to be something in the season too, right? And the woods? Nothing here seems natural," Beth interjected.

Richard nodded. "Yeah, but we're going to need to look for more. This... this just isn't enough to make a good call." Richard puffed up his cheeks as he blew out a mouthful of air. "We need to look specifically for any types of strange deaths. Mass suicides or ritual murders could maybe give us a better understanding of how he's getting his power or how he's using it. I get a feeling there's more to him than what we're seeing here."

"How long were you there?" Ted flashed the light of the camera onto the wight. "In the basement, I mean. How long?"

It scoffed, and spoke with a voice like broken glass scratching together. "I saw no moon nor rising sun. I slumbered for weeks or years at a time until meat was brought to me. By what count could a being judge? By what measure could—"

"Yeah, so you don't know." Ted stopped him short. "Pretty long time though." Ted shifted the light from it back to the others.

"What could you tell us about him, though?" Richard said. "What did he look like? How did he act?"

The wight spoke from the dark. "He consumes the eyes."

"Shit," Ted shuddered.

"He eats people's eyes?" Beth stood up from the desk. "How do you know?"

"The master would occasionally feed me from the remains of his sacrifices. Their eyes were always missing."

There was a moment of silence in the room; only the buzz from the microfilm reader continued. Beth looked at Richard, as if to ask what it meant.

Richard gulped and took a deep breath; he knew the words but found them difficult to speak as his throat dried up. He turned to look at his book, though he knew he didn't need to. After taking a moment to center himself he finally spoke. "Were they men or women? Adults or children?" Richard felt the room grow tense.

The wight considered. "Children?" It stepped farther into the light and bent down on its haunches. "Small humans? On an occasion, those born with death have some value to one like him. Others were men. Man-meat."

"Stillborn." Richard shuddered. It felt as if the tips of claws were raking his back. He took another deep breath and pondered. "The year of animal corruption, the eyes of adult men. Stillborn children." He licked his lips and nodded. "I think we're dealing with a blight warlock, a plague witch. Bringer of disease and corruption."

"A blight warlock?" Beth stood up and moved to Richard, her eyes filled with horrid wonder.

He nodded, still unsure. "I can't say much for certain, but it looks like his presence is a corrupting force for sure."

"So what? Cancer rates are twice the nation's average?" Ted asked from behind the camera.

"Likely. The blight warlock spreads disease, sickness, and madness." Richard licked his lips and glanced down. "I would bet that there is a significantly higher rate of Alzheimer's here too. Suicide, wild animal attacks." He bit his lip. "People in the city look at places like this and think the people here are just insane, but the truth is more sinister than that. He feeds off of their pain and energies. Depravity and sin fuel his magicks." He drew in a deep breath. "He'll swallow them all up, and when the well runs dry, move on down to the next town."

This is big. Very big.

"Then there's just one more question." Beth stepped in and grabbed Richard by the arm. "What do we do about it?"

Richard nodded his head—his soul filled with resolve. He turned back to his book and flipped through the pages. He mouthed the words as he read through them, and then looked up. "We need something pure—pure soil, herbs. Something uncorrupted, untouched by his plague."

"So, what, a handful of mountain soil? Some holy water?" Ted kept the light focused on Richard.

Richard bit his lip and shook his head. "No, it's never as easy as that." He looked down at his book and mouthed some words again. "I see some names here of flowers. I think? And some herbs?" His voice was clearly unsure. "Does anyone know what Mintunsun or Korvison is? Anybody?" He looked between them before glancing back to the book. "How about root of Newyen?"

"No idea, let's search the Internet?" Beth stepped alongside him to read.

Richard was about to respond when they heard glass breaking. Ted spun around, flashing the camera light into the dark. "The hell was that?"

The wight's tongue licked the air as it spoke. "I smell something wicked. Can't you taste it in the air?"

"What is it?" Ted asked while using the camera's light to probe the darkness.

The wight squinted, its thick white eyelids creating a narrow slit for its eyes to shine through. It took a three-toed step forward and used the knuckles on one of its arms like a third leg. "The air—I taste the abyssal form upon it. But I know not what it is." The wight's tongue flicked out again before it corrected itself: "What *they are*."

Skittering came from the east wing of the library. Something else jumped up to the second floor, just far enough into the shadows to be hidden.

"Everyone, get close," Beth said, moving in. She flashed her light behind them.

"They're surrounding us." Ted set the camera down and pulled out his Glock.

Richard pulled his book up tight and turned his back to his friends, suddenly much more reassured by Ted's pistol.

Something clattered to the ground behind them. "*Will you help me?*" The soft girlish voice carried out from the dark. The few lights from the main library suddenly cut out, dropping a cloak of darkness onto them.

"What do we do?" Ted asked Richard. "What the hell is it?"

"It's uh..." Richard started to tear through his book. "I need light!" Beth held up her cell phone to the pages.

"*I'm hurt*," The pitiful, childlike voice whimpered from the shadows. "*Help me, it's hurting me.*"

Beth took a step forward before Richard grabbed her hand. "Wait, just... just wait."

Fear the dark.

"*Please! It's trying to find me!*" A childlike shape formed near the main hall of the library. The light didn't stretch that far, but the moon's light cast her shadow down. "*Help me!*" It dashed away on its small legs to hide behind something.

"*Help us*!" Another voice said from the above them.

A third voice cut in. "*I'm hurt, my leg is stuck!*"

The voices cried out and sobbed in the dark. Moving and darting about unseen, each pleaded, asking them to come farther out of the light to help them.

The wight growled, but otherwise didn't move.

"Go out there! Get it! See what they are!" Ted yelled at the wight, waving his hand forward.

"You hold no bond over me, male," it snarled back at him.

Beth let out a breath and took a step forward. "Let's all just go together?"

"No!" Richard shouted at her as he scanned the dark. "Just give me a minute to think. I need a minute to think." He licked his lips again and his breathing grew rapid. He mumbled words to himself as he kept scanning through the pages.

"*Help us!*" A girl's voice shouted again. A young boy's voice joined in, "*I'm hurt, I'm hurt!*" Another girl's voice cut in from behind them. "*My leg is stuck!*" More voices joined in from other places.

How many of these damn things are there?

"No!" Ted stepped forward and yelled. "Shut up! Shut your damn mouths! Be quiet!" He raised his pistol up and aimed into the shadows; Richard could see nothing.

The voices went silent for a few moments. Eventually one started to giggle and the rest joined in, their laughter rapid and unnatural. The voices changed from children to something deeper and more vicious. It echoed through the halls of the library.

Richard's finger landed on a line, scribed in faded ink. *Infernal illusions,* it read.

"I cast you out!" Richard roared and stepped forward. He held the book up while reading from it. "In the name of Christ! In His name I cast out thy tormentors and demonic illusions! Into the pits of darkness, through the gates of hell! I rip away your façade and cast you down!" Richard's voice shook as he spoke. "Latitudo autem ante faciem perdere!

Revelare verum!" More strings of Latin followed, practiced from his times in trial. He held his voice as resolutely as he could.

As the last of his words echoed among the dark, a shape took form in the front of the lobby. Its feet patted the ground as it moved forward. Though it moved feverishly, its childish legs could not carry it quickly.

How? How did they know we were here?

Ted grabbed his camera and focused on the creature. It stepped into the light, holding the shape of a young girl. In the shadows, its face might have resembled something human, but now its facial features were burning away into something horrid and maligned. It had the snout of a pig and the yellow, slitted eyes of a cat. Smoke poured off it, burning away the last of its human features to reveal the monster beneath.

All I could do was burn away its illusion.

The smell of something terrible cooked in the air. The small creature's maw dragged up and spittle slid out from the ragged edges of its mouth, reflecting what Richard could only assume was excitement.

"*We're going to have so much fun together!*"

11

"Hot shit, son. Thems sounding nasty." Minges shook his head, and the rolls of his chin rippled. "Now you sure you boys weren't doin' nothing too hard before this, right? Not a thing that'd be givin' you delusions, yeah? Ain't no reason in keeping it secret, son. They're gonna test you, that's for damn sure. Sure as you're handcuffed to that chair, son, they'll get you."

"What?" Richard raised his hands. "I'm not handcuffed."

A flicker of doubt crossed Minges's eyes. "Hmmm." He looked at Richard and shrugged a heavy shoulder. "Guessing you got a bit of luck, son." He laughed. "Now here I could'a sworn..."

He's so freaking out of it.

Richard exhaled loudly. "We didn't do any drugs, nothing. They were little monsters—Sankai, I think."

Minges raised an eyebrow. "Sankai?"

"A creature from Japanese lore. It's when a mother gives birth to something that's not human. These things had faces like pigs or raccoons or raccoon-pigs." He emphasized each word. "They were terrifying!"

"Now son, why would a Chinese pig baby be running around over here? You see how I have to be a little skeptical 'bout the intoxicants, right? Hell, a ghost would at least make sense."

"Well, I mean they're not Japanese, of course. But I think the Japanese are the only ones who have a name for it. Maybe he was using the stillborns to do it or something, I don't know."

"Yeah, I guess he just ran down to the ol' doctor-dumpster to grab himself a few, eh?" Minges rolled his eyes. "Just ain't no logical sense to it, son. Sometimes, when people do horrible shit like you do, hack a poor girl to death, it'll make you play these jokes on yourself."

"I'm not making a damn thing up. I *know* what I saw and none of it was a joke! And I know every minute I'm sitting trapped in here is another minute he's out there tearing this town apart. You don't get it. We kicked a hornet's nest. He's got to heal, got to defend, got to run, but he's pissed! *He's going to be ripping this place to shreds.*"

Minges laughed under his breath. "Now calm down, son. You been nice and calm this entire time, don't go—"

Something about the dismissive tone opened a vein of emotion in Richard. "Do you know what a human *pig-baby's* brain looks like splattered across the ground? I do. It's purple and bloody." Fire burned in his chest. "How do you think I got out of there!" he yelled. "There's no lore for fighting something like that! No magic words to send it back to hell! Only lore I could find would strip the guise off and let us see what piece of hell was crawling its way into that library!"

Minges inched backed in his chair just as Richard was standing up.

"I grabbed a chair, smashed it against the first little son

of a bitch that charged me!" He clenched his fists into rocks as the heat burned hotter in his chest and bellowed out from his lungs to spit fire at Minges. "When it broke, I grabbed the largest piece and turned to the ones that were still laughing."

Minges clumsily stood up and started moving toward the door.

"Get back here! Don't you tell me I killed Beth! Don't you tell me she's dead and there's nothing I can do about it! Don't you tell me this is how it ends! *Don't you tell me this is how it ends*!"

"Sit'cher ass down, boy!" Minges finally snarled as he retreated. "You sit your ass down right there and cool off! I'mma get you a damn cola, and you just take yourself a breather." He turned and pounded on the door. "Get me outta here! I need some damn air!"

Richard was huffing air in a labored attempt to cool the hot coals in his chest. Finally, something snapped in the anger. He wasn't the type to yell at anyone, and just as quickly as it came, it started to fade.

What am I doing? He's my lawyer. Am I really losing my mind?

"Hell, Richard." Minges shot a look back at him. "I hate to think what it actually was that you were beating the brains out of."

A uniformed officer with a scowl drooped across his face showed up and opened the door to let Minges out. Richard went back to his seat and slumped into it, letting his head fall into his hands again. He started to cry. He wasn't sure if it was the rage he was coming down from, or the situation he was in.

What it actually was...

Minges's words ran through his head as he questioned his own memory.

No. No, I'm not insane. I'm not insane. It all happened. I'm not crazy.

He told himself that over and over again. It was several long minutes before he started believing it. After some time, Minges returned with a can of off-brand cola in one hand and what looked like coffee in the other. He approached Richard more cautiously than he had before. He took his seat and slid the cola over to Richard. "Cheer up, son. We're gonna get you the help you need, yeah?" Minges took a sip of his coffee.

Richard glanced up and sighed. He popped the tab on the soda. "So, you want to hear the rest?"

He took a drag of his coffee. "Yeah, you all right telling it?" Minges had cleaned up his attitude; he was less demeaning now.

God, maybe I am just tired. Maybe I am just imagining things. Did I really do it? I couldn't have. I wouldn't have.

Richard gulped and took a breath, filling his lungs, and stared into the lawyer's eyes. "I'm not insane. I want you to know that. And, if I die, I want you to tell someone else. I want *someone* to know what happened here. I don't want it to die with me."

Minges nodded. "All right then, son. Let's hear the part about smashing pig-babies and whatnot."

Richard gave him a long hard stare before he started to speak again.

RICHARD LET the broken wooden leg fall onto the creature again and again. He didn't know what the creature was—he could only guess—but he knew the sound it made when it died; it was a terrible squealing noise that Richard was sure would haunt his nightmares for the rest of his days.

Something had happened when the laughter stopped and the echoing giggles faded, a rush of bodies—thin and small, but full of teeth—descended onto them. Something had changed between this place and the last. The war in Richard's mind that he had been fighting all night had been won.

This time, when death came, he stood to meet it.

The flashes from Ted's gun almost blinded Richard. The light allowed him to catch enough of a glimpse of one creature leaping quickly from side to side as it rushed toward Ted. It jolted from one leg to the other, dodging each shot of Ted's gun. The creature lunged at him, nearly raking his face, as more monsters joined the fray.

The wight let out a horrible, curdling roar as it snatched the creature lunging for Ted in midair, and dug into it with clawed fingers. Richard watched in horrid fixation as the wight tore the smaller creature apart. It split down the middle, dumping purple entrails out like slop from a fisherman's bucket. The smell of rancid meat hit them at once.

Oh, God! Run!

Richard's brain screamed as he watched in horror. But he couldn't watch long; more of them were coming out of the dark. They ran up to him on all fours like rabid animals.

He clubbed the nearest on the back of the head, slinging what blood had already been there. It cried out but pushed forward and grabbed onto his leg. It bit into his shin, pushing its needle-point teeth clean though his jeans. Richard grunted in pain and kicked it against a table. It wrapped its fingers around his leg and sunk its teeth in farther, doing what it could to hold on while it growled like a mad dog and dug at his flesh.

Beth rushed in from the side and kicked it. It barked before it let go. "Oh God, Beth!" It was all Richard could say. He limped forward as more rushed toward him.

The wight jolted in, swinging its long arms out and grabbing several of the monstrous horde in its claws. The jaw of the wight unhinged and stretched down like a snake's. It was hard for Richard to see exactly what was happening in the dark—he saw only light and shadows—but he heard one of the small creatures wail in terror as the wight shoved it into its gaping maw; a dance of shadow horrors presented the show. Richard was thankful for the dark.

Richard turned to flee with Beth but bashed against a table and shoved it aside. Ted's camera had been sitting on the table; it spun off and clattered to the ground, resting its light on the wight. Beth and Richard turned to see the wight pull several of the creatures apart before falling on them to feast on the pieces. It started with the ones that were still alive. Richard turned away; the creatures' screams were enough to make it clear what happened next.

"We need to get out of here!" Beth screamed.

Ted was still firing into the dark when Beth grabbed him by the arm. He turned, with panic in his eyes, and nearly shot her. "Let's go, Ted!" she yelled at him.

Ted took two steps forward with her before he looked back. "I need my camera!" He turned around and went to pick it up. As he spun it around, the light shined across a creature in a little girl's dress with saggy eyes and ears far too long, already nearly upon him. Her jaw, long and drooping, hung open as closed in on Ted. He tried to pull the pistol up, but Richard was faster.

Richard had closed the distance between them and

slammed the chair leg across the creature's head; the force of it jolted his hands painfully. "Let's go!" Ted plucked the camera from the ground as the two moved off with Beth.

Beth spun around as they were running and called out: "Wight! Come on, go!"

Richard caught a glimpse over his shoulder of the wight thrashing its long arms in wide, sweeping patterns as it continued its war with the monsters that swarmed it.

How could there possibly be so many of them? How in the hell did they get in? How did they know where we were?

He was at a loss.

They closed in on the front doors, but Richard felt something lurking just beyond the glass. His instincts told him of the things sitting still beyond the doors, eagerly awaiting them. "Wait, wait!" Richard cried out as Ted rushed to the door. "Just... There are more of them. They're waiting until we come out."

Ted turned and looked out over the quiet entrance, then shined the light from the camera out. As the light touched the hedges along the paved entrance, creatures shifted and moved, and one gave a childlike giggle when the light caught its face. The giggling face looked like a piece of rotting fruit, caved in the center, with the same animal snout and large, exposed teeth. It stepped forward on its thin, short legs and brought its arm up to point a stubbed finger at Richard. It burst into hideous laughter, with more soon joining in. Richard stared back, transfixed by the horrid deformities.

"Come on, we can't stop! Let's go!" Beth's words went unheard at first—Richard was mesmerized, unable to turn away from this thing crawling loose from a nightmare. "Richard!" She shoved his shoulder, bringing his attention back. "Let's go!"

The three hurried up the stairs to the second floor. Little hands reached out between the steps and grabbed at their feet as they ascended. Ted stomped on the hand of one, making it scream as it pulled back its mangled fingers. "How many are there?" Ted screamed.

"I... I don't know." Richard responded, as the fear threatened to cut away the strength he had mustered. "I don't know how there can possibly be so many..."

Beth rushed up the stairs in the front, "Richard, what can we do? How can we stop them?"

"I don't know!" Richard yelled back in desperation, tears dripping from his eyes.

When they reached the top, things became a blur. One of the creatures jumped out and slammed into Ted, knocking the camera from his arms. It fell down the steps, crashing loudly with each hit. The light from it flashed around and came to a rest on the base of the stairs. It illuminated the fixed grin of one of the terrors.

The top floor was pitch-black. Richard tripped and his head collided with the hard tile floor. The air was knocked out of his lungs, and his club slipped from his fingers and went skating across the floor. Looking up, he couldn't find Beth or Ted; in the confusion, they had scattered.

"Beth?" He came up to his knees. "Ted? Beth?" Richard blinked and tried to clear his head. Something screamed, a bloodcurdling shriek that reached inside of him and scratched his bones.

Oh, God, that was Beth!

Richard climbed to his feet to see two blurs fighting in the shadows. He heard Ted curse. Something slammed into a bookshelf and knocked it over.

One shelf hit another, sending books clattering to the ground and spilling down to the first floor. "Beth!" Richard bellowed, drawing the attention of one of the creatures running up the stairs. It snarled and barked as it galloped on feet and knuckles at Richard. It lurched into the air; Richard swung his heavy bag and caught it in motion, knocking it over the railing and down to the first floor.

Richard sucked in labored breaths and pulled his bag up from his side. He fumbled around in it and came out with a lighter and a candle. He flicked the lighter three times until it finally caught, then touched the flame to the wick and held it in front of him.

A few feet away from Richard, Ted screamed "I'll kill you!" and brought the heel of his boot down onto the chest of one of the snouted creatures, forcing it to purge the contents of its stomach through its nose and mouth.

Another creature crawled on all fours, right to the edge of the candlelight. It snarled. Richard stumbled and turned to rush away, but it pounced on his back. He fell on his chest again and dropped the candle. The creature skittered up his back and tried to sink its teeth into the soft flesh on the nape of Richard's neck. Richard threw an elbow back and knocked it loose, then rolled over, scuffling with it until he came out on top, his full weight pressed against it.

Richard's fear and anger found an outlet through violence. His hands were on the creature's small throat, choking away its life, before he knew what he was doing. Its throat was thin and he crushed it quickly. It suddenly reminded him of wrestling with his younger sister.

Oh my God, what did I do?

The creature's head rocked back. Its thick brow over-shadowed its eyes, making it hard for Richard to see them clearly in the dark. The eyes looked like solid white gel with something yellow shifting beneath the surface. A long dark tongue hung between its thick teeth. The monster's stink rolled off in waves. It wore a little girl's pink dress with smiling elephants.

I'm going to puke.

Richard's stomach lurched and he emptied bile onto the floor next to the creature's head. He heaved three times before he could take a breath.

He quickly spotted the candle, still burning despite having been dropped. It had rolled into a stack of fallen books, and the aged paper was aflame. "Oh shit!" Richard's eyes went wide as the flame started to spread into the second fire of that night.

Richard pivoted to Ted and heard him cry out as a dark-skinned creature bit into his flesh. He pulled it free and threw it over the railing. Its screams echoed through the library, followed by a thud.

The flames were spreading near the edge of the stairs. The creatures hissed, unable to move past the flame.

The fire—they're scared of it.

Richard turned again to Ted, who was still battling one creature latched onto his arm. "Ted! Ted, throw it into the fire!" Richard grabbed it by the waist and tried to pull it loose. Ted shook and thumped his fist into its head until it came loose. Richard saw the soft head cave in from the punches.

Richard held the flailing creature as he took two steps toward the fire. It panicked, screeched, and clawed at his face. Braving the scratches, Richard threw it into the flame. The creatures behind the flame cried out as their brother melted like wax.

"Go! Get out of here! We'll kill you!" Richard threw his unconvincing threats across the flame. Some of them scurried off, while others turned to crawl over the railing and come over the side to face them, relentless in their attack.

Richard didn't wait; he turned and fled, stopping only long enough to grab Ted by the arm. "Where's Beth?"

"My camera—"

"Beth!" Richard shouted. "Where the hell is Beth?"

"I don't know," Ted responded with wild eyes. "I don't know where she is!"

The fire continued to grow behind them as Richard entered the dark. He searched desperately between the stacks of books for any sign of Beth.

He came around a bookshelf to the corner of the second floor. Shelves had clattered to the floor here, scattering their books across the ground. One of the creatures hunched over a pile of books laughed inhumanly with its back to them, so filled with maniacal glee that it didn't take notice of anyone else.

"Get away!" Richard screamed as he barreled forward. The twisted thing turned to see him, but not quickly enough. It had been dragging its broken fingernails across Beth's face, enjoying her pain. Richard brought his fist down on its head hard enough to feel the slop beneath its skull push out its ears. It slammed into a fallen shelf near them and fell into a fit of spasms in the throes of death.

"Beth, Beth, are you okay?" Richard could see her arm pinned beneath a fallen shelf, along with piles of books on her.

She drew in a raspy breath. "Yeah, yeah I'm fine. Just get me out of here." Her voice was weak, and blood dribbled down from the uneven claw marks etched across her face.

Ted had come up behind Richard. "This place is going up like a Roman candle, and they have the first floor blocked! The little bastards are spreading the fire!"

Richard yelled, "Just help me get her out of here!"

Richard got beneath a shelf, sliding his hands across the

metal edges, as Ted did the same. Richard groaned and felt the corner edges of the shelf cut into the flesh of his hands. Ted grunted next to him as he powered through it, the workhorse of the two. Adrenaline flooded Richard's body, causing his strength to surge as the two pushed it off. Richard doubled over as Ted took a knee to help Beth to her feet.

Two sets of bare feet padded against the ground at the edge of one of the rows. Their snouted, drooping faces snorted laughter, as if finding the desperation of Richard and the others intoxicating. They galloped in, wailing and screaming with outstretched arms. Richard kicked at the leader's chin, and connected. The solid blow threw him off balance and back into another bookshelf, overturning it. The flame behind them grew greater, as did the putrid smell of the burning creatures.

From the corner of his eye, Richard saw dancing flames. The creatures had ruthlessly ripped arms and legs from their fallen to use as torches. Scaling the walls, they set flame to the curtains and books.

They want to trap us on this floor and burn us out, even if they burn like oil themselves.

Richard hadn't long to dwell on the thought of the mindless sacrifices the creatures seemed to be capable of. Two more creatures—the ones from before, or new ones altogether, he didn't know—jumped onto him and latched their pointed teeth into his arm. The pain curled up from his arm and surged up his throat into a scream; this seemed to drive the creature to sink its teeth deeper. He swung his arm down to hit one, but it moved up and pinned his arm behind him.

Ted came forward and ripped one of the beasts from Richard's arm and hurled it into the fire. Richard brought his hand up and was able to get it into the creature's face. He shoved, trying to pry it loose, but it bit into his hand.

Richard's own blood splattered back into his face as he pushed through, finding strength in the pain.

It snapped two, three times on his hand, each time digging deeper and trying to tear off a larger piece of flesh. Ted returned and pulled it back, but by then it had already locked hard on Richard's hand. When Ted yanked, it pulled Richard too, dragging his arm with it. "Ah shit!" Richard screamed.

Ted either didn't know what was happening or didn't know what else to do. He yanked on it again. Richard bellowed again in pain as its teeth opened the wound farther. Richard reached in with his other hand and stuck fingers in its eye and nose, prying its mouth open and pulling his hand free. Ted dragged it loose, but Richard saw the creature cursing at him and reaching for him even as Ted lifted it and threw it down into the flame.

Beth seemed unsteady on her feet. "We need to get out of here," she said under her breath; her face was tired, dazed.

"We'll have to look and see if there's another way." Richard cranked his neck from side to side, searching fruitlessly for an exit, for any hope of escape. "At least most of them are down on the first floor. The fire is keeping them back."

As if to spite Richard, the aging sprinkler system finally caught the smoke and came on, killing the fire and beginning to return the library to darkness.

A large, white, clawed hand stretched over the railings of the second floor. The wight pulled itself up; it was clearly hurt, with numerous bite marks all over it. Dark blood oozed from its wounds, with lighter shades of blood dripping from its arms and face.

"I have feasted my fill," it said in a daze as it came over the railings, clearly war-torn. "I do not enjoy their taste."

"Yes!" Ted shouted in joy. "You big, beautiful, ugly bastard! Let's get out of here!"

The wight swayed to face a large window and began striding to it. Its large outstretched legs crossed the distance easily. The three rushed behind the wight and to the window.

The wight looked out and saw the van. "Our horseless carriage rests here." Without another word, it burst through the window and landed on the van, denting its roof.

"Well shit!" Ted roared frantically. "What good does that do us? How do we get down?"

Beth shook her head. "We're going to have to find another way."

With the fire on the stairs dying, more of the creatures were coming up now, and they caught sight of the three by the window.

"Where in the hell are these things coming from?" Richard asked with bewilderment.

"Then it's out the window." Ted shook his head. He looked down at the wight who was now standing up. "Hey, catch us!"

"With certainty." It uncoiled its legs to step from the van and to the ground.

Ted spared one look back at the two and then jumped. The wight moved and Ted collided with the hood of the van. He rolled back and cried out. "Dammit! I think I broke my ankle! You were supposed to catch me, you piece of shit!"

"I was not entirely familiar with the concept." The wight looked confused.

Ted screamed, "You said... Never mind, just catch them!"

The wight turned its attention up to Beth. Richard grabbed Beth's hand and said, "Okay, you go first."

Her eyes met his, a moment's pause before she turned and jumped out. The wight caught her and set her down.

Richard shot one last glance back, just in time to see one of the creatures lunge at him. He tripped as it latched onto him and sent them both out the window, a piece of glass from the window cutting into Richard's leg as he fell. He landed short of the van and smashed into the ground. The creature had gotten beneath him and had taken the force of the fall when they landed. Most of what was left beneath Richard was a wet puddle of chunks. "Uh, sorry?" Richard apologized on instinct. He pulled himself up, and the gooey mess stretched thin between Richard and the pavement.

"Richard, get up, come on!" Ted didn't wait for him as he took the front seat. "Let's get out of here!" He slammed the van door behind him.

Richard gulped air and stood up on uncertain feet. The wight's glassy and unblinking eyes stayed focused on him until he stood, and then it got into the back of the van. Richard hobbled forward and collapsed halfway inside the open door just as Ted turned the key, bringing the van to life. The wight stretched out its long arm to drag Richard in the rest of the way.

The van roared to life and screeched into reverse. Ted threw it into drive and gunned it. Richard slid around hazardously in the back. He grabbed onto one of the seats and took the chance to look out the window at more of the creatures jumping from the library windows and breaking their legs on the ground, while others rounded the building. Their short legs couldn't carry them fast enough to keep up with the van. An angry mob of childlike beings chased them only a short distance.

"That certainly could have gone better." Ted sighed. "I lost my damn camera and our video!"

Richard closed his eyes and put his head back. He decided not to respond to Ted; instead, his mind drifted. He sat, at a loss for the next step in their game. What was there to do? What was left?

I don't want to do anything. Maybe I can just sleep until this all goes away...

The van drove on in silence and Ted eased off the gas. He glanced at Beth in the front seat and then the others in the back. "What? Am I going to be the first to say it? Okay, fine." His voice filled with anger. "*What do we do now*?"

"Let's catch our breath and plan our next move." Beth was still breathing hard.

"What?" Ted shot her an angry glance. "Are you kidding? We barely survived that. We're out of our damn league here. I think I broke my ankle, you probably have a concussion, and it was made painfully clear back there that Richard's not the fount of wisdom that we thought he might be." There was silence for a few moments as no one responded.

"Nothing? Anyone?" Ted's voice was still angry. "Richard, can you tell me what the hell those were? Can you?"

Richard gulped air. He took three heavy breaths before he finally spoke. "No."

"Exactly. *We don't know what we're dealing with.* And guess what? I'm out of bullets! And—" More words were spilling out of Ted's mouth as Richard cut him off.

"But I've got a guess." Looking up into the mirror, he caught Ted's eyes staring back at him. "Sankai—that's what the Japanese call it. A woman gave birth to it. The father or mother was something unnatural, and the baby is that manifested, or it was worked that way by the warlock. A hateful creature that doesn't age past childhood." He didn't break his gaze from the mirror; any lack of confidence might end him. "You want to know how you kill those, Ted? You already do. You beat them to death. There are no magic words to turn them off, no prayer that sends them back. They're half-animal spirit creatures. And I don't know about you, but they seemed pretty damn corrupted to me." Richard's tone was getting faster, angrier. "Their heads were soft. They were aggressive to the point of near suicide. Faces looked like they were melting off. And did you see the way they burned? Like they were barely being held together by magicks. Now, I don't know what the hell the rural small-town version of a Sankai is, but that's what I think was trying to bite chunks off of us." Richard let the anger breathe out and he deflated. "I think we were right on the money. It's a blight warlock, a corruption witch, with corrupted servants. I think we're getting closer. *But what do I know*?"

When no one else spoke, the wight interjected, "Their flesh tasted horrid." It had a look of pain on its face; hundreds of tiny bites and claw marks littered its body. "Their meat was rotted."

"Fine," Ted relented. "You were right, we're dealing with a blight witch." Ted let out a labored breath. "The only thing worse than you being wrong is that you might be right."

"I think you're both missing the big picture here," Beth cut in with a nervous smile. "How did they know we were there, and how do we know more won't follow?"

12

"A FIRE AT THE LIBRARY, EH? YOU WANT A MATCHING PAIR OF arson felonies tonight or something? Boy, do you know that library was the pride of Bridgedale? That library had been there since this was a booming coal town. It's got history."

"Oh, seriously?" said Richard without a hint of sarcasm.

With a roll of his eyes, the lawyer's speech was painfully slow. "The P.D. here ask you about a fire in the library? No? No one mentioned that? Strange. Now Richard, don't you think something like a library fire would have drawn a little attention? A house, deep in the woods as you said, may go up in flames unnoticed, so long as it don't go catching up the forest around it. But you do think there'd be a little concern passed over something like a library, don't you?"

"Yeah," Richard agreed, admitting his own confusion. "Haven't quite worked out that part yet." Still on edge, his hands shook as he came down from his earlier surge of anger. He finished his can of cola and sat in silence.

"I'm sayin' your story don't necessarily fit the facts. Ya'll were getting your asses beat pretty good from what you were saying, right? Broken ribs maybe, broken ankles, concussions? Not to mention all them little bastards biting everyone. How're you still up and walking after all that?"

"Actually, no one got it too bad. Ted maybe, but he's a tough guy, he pulled through. He might have cracked a rib or something, I really don't know much about it. I was fine though, mostly just shook up. Few scratches and what not."

"But you said them lil pig-babies was biting you all up, yeah? Something like your neck, arms? Maybe one of the legs too, yeah? Let's see those little bites."

"Yeah, sure." Richard said confidently, as if he thought Minges was playing games with him. He rolled his sleeve up to show his arm, but it was clean—no bites. "What?" he moved quickly to pull up his pant leg—no bites there either. "No, no, they bit me!"

Am I going insane?

"Right." Minges smiled and nodded before he fell into another fit of coughing. After several loud, hacking coughs, something in his throat came loose. Minges picked up Richard's empty cup and spit into it. He set it back down in front of Richard. "Sorry about that son, no trash cans in here."

I would really like to punch this guy in the head.

"Listen, son, if you admit you're not well, we can start to work our angles and get this goin' in a better direction, yeah? Don't you think it's time we start thinking about step two?"

"That mean you're done listening to me?" Richard wasn't giving up just yet. "If you're done listening, then I'm done talking. About *everything*."

Minges scoffed. "Come on now, old boy. I'm on your side for this, ain't I?" He huffed. "Don't go all puffing your chest up on me, we're the same team, yeah?"

Are we?

Something stirred in Richard; he wasn't sure he could be on the "same team" as a half-drunk attorney who thought he was insane. Staring into Minges's blue-gray eyes for the hundredth time that night, Richard wondered what a man like Minges could do to help him when Minges didn't believe.

Richard's eyes grew wet with tears. "Honestly, I don't know what I'm doing. Everyone was counting on me, and they're all dead now. They're all dead." Trying to hold it back was futile; the tears came heavier and rolled down his cheeks. "I've been a useless waste my entire life, and now I find some people that need me, that *really* need me, and where are they now? Where am I? They're dead and I'm in an interrogation room. I don't even know how I got here."

I've lost my mind. The witch won. He took my mind and made me kill Beth.

"There, there, son," Minges said with lines of sadness stretched across his face. "Don't you go stressing too much. Best of us can crack under the right circumstances, yeah?" He set his hat upon his head, which seemed to make him more professional all at once. "Ain't nothing new, just you rolling the dice and getting snake eyes, yeah? But let's not get hung up here feeling sorry for ourselves. Let's hear what happened next, after that library. Y'all were hell-fire and burning rubber on the way outta there. What happened next?"

"Why do you even want to hear this? You're not taking any notes. What's it matter?"

"Don't you go worrying about that, old boy." He tapped his head. "I gotta head like a tank. Ain't nothing getting loose."

Richard started to nod. "Wait, what do you mean, head like a tank? Are you talking about like a water tank or an army tank, because neither really have anything to do with that."

"There you go again!" Minges jumped up and pointed at him. "There you go, worrying about how I'm saying something more than what I'm saying. Come on now, we're burning good time talking about water tanks and whatnot."

"Well, with what we had, I had determined to do the best that I could, given that we were dealing with a blight warlock. So that meant finding the right thing to fight 'em with. But we were also getting tracked. There was a little debate, and we decided to go on the defensive. We needed to mask our auras, try and do whatever we could to cover our scent, to make it harder for him to find us."

"Interesting." Minges nodded. "So you think this witch is watching you move around? He sent the pig-babies into the library to go get your ass?"

"Yeah, it sounds stupid, right? I don't care."

"No, just making sure we're on the same page here. Not any more stupid than anything else, right? How'd a witch find ya'll anyhow? Can they do that sort of thing really easy? Then, hell, why don't he just send some pig-babies right on in here and get you?"

Richard's shoulders slumped. "He still might." The thought had certainly occurred to him. "But we did what we could do to hide ourselves from him, shield our auras."

Minges fell into another fit of hacking coughs and pulled out a tissue to dab his mouth. "How exactly did you do that? Hide yourself from 'em, that is? You whip up some doohickey to keep this all goin'? This one ain't gonna end with you lighting the place up again, right? Fire certainly seems like a common theme with these events."

"No, no fire. As for hiding yourself, though, anything is possible with the right incantations and components. Some of it does require innate ability or force of will. But that's just the *really* powerful stuff. So it was just a matter of looking through my book and finding the right passage."

"Where's that book anyways? I'd be curious to take a glance at that old thing. Might be a good little prop for the jury, add a little flavor to your plea of insanity." Minges's fat lips smiled with self-satisfaction.

"I don't know where it's at, I told you. Maybe it's still in the van? It's still a little hazy."

"Good ol' head injury will do that, son."

"Well, things are coming back in pieces. I remember heading to the gas station." His eyes darted to the now-blank television screen.

"Hold up there, son. Maybe we're getting ahead of ourselves. Let's take it back a minute. What'd you do after you left the library? Curl up into a lil ball? Sounded like you was pretty hard-hit from that last one. Something like that can break a man's mind, even if it's already broke."

"No, I can't explain it. I mean, I *was* afraid, but I got through it. We all bounced back quickly. We had to. There just wasn't enough time to process all of this; I mean this kind of shit flips your life around. People build religions on stuff like this. It's hard to believe God isn't real when you see the devil's eyes."

Minges gave him a lazy smirk. "Suppose so. What happened next?"

Richard gritted his teeth and tried his best to sound tough. "Well, we knew the son of a bitch was following us somehow..."

"We know this son of a bitch is following us somehow." Ted

groaned and squeezed the steering wheel.

The wight had fallen asleep, or so Richard thought. He wasn't sure if wights even slept.

"I think we need to have a serious discussion here, though, before we go another step farther," Ted said from behind the wheel. "And that is the why."

"The why for what?" Richard asked, leaning up to the front seats.

Ted took a deep breath and pulled to the side of the road. "Why is it we're doing this? Richard, this has to be a talk between me and Beth. I'm sure you understand," he said, dismissing Richard.

"Sure, yeah I guess." Richard leaned back and folded his arms.

"Beth, what are we doing here? What is our goal here? Are we here for this story? Because the camera is gone."

The color had returned to Beth's face. She was still splattered with flecks of blood, and she wiped them away as she spoke. "The camera might be gone, but the story isn't, Ted." She pulled away from the mirror to meet Ted's eyes and cleared her throat. "You know, there was a British reporter who went into Africa to report on the Liberian civil war. He was there as an observer, following the rebels and writing his report. He went in as a third party, a non-participant. He saw atrocities there, he saw men tortured and killed. You know what he came to realize, though? They were torturing people for his benefit. For him to see. Him being there had an active effect on that situation, on people's lives. He had control of what was happening, even if he didn't know it at first."

Her hair had come loose in the fight and now fluttered as she shook her head. "We're not on the outside, Ted. We're not here to watch or report on. We're engaged."

"Exactly. We're engaged, Beth. That isn't our job—it's his." He thumbed back at Richard, who had remained quiet. "Are we some damn witch hunters? Is he?"

Richard's gut twisted. Ted was right, they were woefully unqualified.

Beth ignored him and turned back to Richard. "Why are you here, Richard? You wanted to leave before; do you still want to go now? If you do, we'll end this."

Do I want this to end?

Richard sat in silence a moment, reflecting. Without a doubt, he wanted the night to end. He wanted the witch gone and for everything to go back to the way it was, back when none of it was real.

Or do I? I don't know what this is, but I'm good at it. I know what I'm doing. I'm scared, but in a different way. In what way?

A moment ticked by as the gears in his brain turned.

I'm afraid of dying, but I'm more afraid of being useless.

"No. I want to finish this. I don't want this city to be hurt by him anymore. I want to stop him. I want to stop the witch." Beth smiled at him, her eyes sending his heart into a flutter.

"I'm a reporter and I'm going to tell this story, but I do this because I want to help people. I want to do good in this world." She looked at Ted and laughed. "I'm going to tell this story Ted, but no one is going to believe it. Would you?"

Ted sighed. "No. Don't think I would. I think if we're not dead by morning, we'll be locked up."

"Maybe. But I don't want to walk away from this knowing I could have done something. I couldn't live with myself. I want to help people—that's what I've always wanted. We're going to get this story and we're going to make people listen."

Ted said, "Grandma always told me that if you don't find

your way to God, He'll find His way to you. I remember the crucifix, Richard. What do you think about all that?"

"I have no idea. I don't know what God could have to do with any of this, but I have to believe that if there is God, that He's here with us tonight."

"So that's the why, then," Ted said, gripping the steering wheel tight. "We're here to kill a witch. So we're back to asking the question, what the hell do we do now that he can follow us?"

Beth sat up in her seat, dug through her purse, and came out with a tape recorder. "Hold on, guys. We're going to need to get this all recorded now that we don't have the video. Okay." Beth flipped on the tape recorder and spoke into it. "It's currently 3:16 a.m. We've just left the library and Ted has parked us alongside the road. We lost our video camera, our only documentation of what's been happening. We're going to start using my tape recorder from here on out. I'm going to question our resident witch hunter, Richard Fitcher."

Richard stiffened his back and did his best to let the fear roll off him. "Hello! That's me. I'm Richard Fitcher. I'm the witch hunter. Yeah. We're hunting a witch." The words spilled out. Despite the blood in his mouth, the cuts and bruises on his body, or the fear that sat beneath the surface, Richard felt excited.

Don't screw up, don't screw up.

Somehow, the idea of disappointing Beth was even worse than fighting a witch that could eat his face and rip his arms off. "*It's a lovely night for a witching.*" Richard said it without even thinking.

Shit, did I say that again! Dammit, dammit!

Beth giggled, and Richard hoped that he wasn't blushing too much.

"Richard, what is your expert opinion of what just happened to us? Could you explain in your own words what we've experienced?" Her thin, manicured hands held the recorder just below his mouth.

"We, uh, we went to the library. We were looking for clues on what exactly we're dealing with, and we did. We got it!" He couldn't contain the excitement from growing. "But, uh, I'm not *really* sure what happened next. Some creatures came after us. I think they were Sankai, creatures from Japanese folklore. But I don't know why Japanese monsters would be here. And, uh—Wait, can you edit out that part where I said I wasn't sure? Maybe I can do it again and try to sound more confident or something? I mean, I think they were more like the hillbilly version of Sankai anyway."

Beth silently mouthed the words *It's okay* and then spoke herself. "These creatures, they came after us, and we had to fight them for our lives." Beth took to explaining on her own. "But Richard, *why* did they come? *How* did they come? Why didn't the witch come himself?"

"That part is, uh..." The truth was, Richard had no idea. Why a witch would do anything at all was still a little beyond his own understanding. Richard snapped his fingers. "Well, we weakened the... *the son of a bitch.*"

That sounded pretty sweet I bet. Wait...

"Wait, can I say 'bitch' on here or should I try and keep that kind of thing off? We can redo it with 'son of a gun' if you want?" Beth motioned for him to just keep going. "Anyway, we destroyed his name and ward. He's sending what he has after us. He's probably holed up somewhere licking his wounds. As for *how* he found us... Honestly, I don't really know. It can be from knowing our names or—"

"What!?" Ted yelled from the front seat. "You think he knows our names? How could he know our names?"

"Well, yeah, man. You were freaking *possessed.* The ghost was inside your head. Isn't that obvious?"

Ted grumbled for a few moments on his own before Beth spoke again. "Richard, we've tracked down information about the witch, and according to what you've said, we've weakened him, correct? So what's our next step?"

What's our next step? That's the million-dollar question.

The thought perplexed Richard, and he knew that sitting there silently wasn't lending too much confidence to his "expertise."

"We feast?" The wight cut in as it stirred awake. "Perhaps bovine flesh would help nurture a strategic mind?"

"Feast?" Ted shot back, "Didn't you eat like, *dozens* of little Japanese child monsters back there? How could you *possibly* be hungry?"

"You have been told, male! My hunger is eternal! My desire unquenchable! Which of these concepts needs elaboration?"

"I'm hungry too, but it'll have to wait," Richard said tiredly. "We have to make sure he can't track us down again. We'll have to obscure ourselves."

"How do we do that, Richard?" asked Beth. "How can we hide ourselves?"

"Just give me a minute." He looked down at the gore and mess smeared across his shirt, which leaked a rancid smell. "Let me change my shirt first." He started to dig through his satchel.

"You keep an extra shirt in your purse?" Ted asked with a snort.

"It's not a purse, it's a satchel!" Richard shot back. "And I sweat a lot. Uh, can you guys turn around while I change my shirt?" He started to pull the shirt off, careful not to touch any more of the slick gore than he needed to.

Ted rolled his eyes. "Yeah, you look like the type to break a sweat on a flight of stairs."

Richard pulled on his clean shirt. "And you look like the type that keeps a picture of himself in his wallet."

"Ha!" Ted laughed at that. "You still need a little work, but you're getting there, Richard."

Richard whisked the thought off. "Well, we need to do a few things."

I've got an idea.

Richard went through his tome while Beth watched from the front seat and asked the occasional question. Ted had stepped out to pace in the grass, while the wight idly watched him through the window. The rain had sputtered out again.

"I think I've got it." Richard pressed his finger onto one of the old pages of the tome. "I think he's a scryer. Yeah, that dick has been scrying in on us. Has to be it! Classic douche move." Richard was standing up and opening the door to step out, Beth was coming out right behind him.

"What's that, Richard?" Beth asked curiously, and crossed her arms from the chill.

"A scryer can see where we are. Sometimes they can glimpse future or past events. I think he saw us going into that library and sent the Sankai after us."

Beth's eyes widened. "If he sees the future, would he have seen us get past them? Would he know that we're here right now?"

Richard licked his lips, not completely certain, but shook his head anyway. "Not necessarily. He saw us going there and then he reacted. There is a new outcome from what he saw before, and divination magic is draining, especially if he's weakened. But I get your point. We should get moving."

"Then what do we do?" She turned her gaze to the pages of the book. "How can we stop him from seeing where we're going?"

Richard nodded and pulled a small plastic sheet from his satchel. He had pencils, pens, and chalk. "We're going to have to ward the van." He slid the van's side door open and stepped out onto the slick wet grass. He took the chalk and glanced at his book, then traced the same patterns he saw in the sketches of the book, large circles with smaller lines and circles inscribed between them. In fifteen minutes, he had a spiraling web of lines and shapes across the side.

"What the hell are you doing to my van?" Ted finally made his way over to him, more curious than annoyed. Beth only sat back to watch.

"I'm warding the van to keep prying eyes out. He's been watching us. Maybe not our present selves, but our future whereabouts in brief pieces. He's trying to counter us."

Ted groaned. "Well, I hope he saw me taking a piss over there at least."

Richard slid his fingers onto the sanctified jewelry that still hung from his neck. "I don't think he can see me." He held it up for the others to see. "It blocks me from a lot, but he could be tracking either or both of you. It's best if you stay inside the van as much as possible."

"Where did you get that?" Ted reached out to touch it.

"I was told that the iron bits wrapped with silver you see here were once nails used to crucify saints. It's really old. It repulses almost anything they can throw at you. It keeps your mind clear. I didn't believe that until today. I didn't believe any of this. How could any of it be real?" The admission nearly made Richard slip back to his former, less confident self. "Until today, it wasn't real. *I* wasn't real."

"But look what you've done, Richard!" Stepping forward,

Beth took his arm. "You've saved us several times over, and you're still here with us. We believe in you."

He nodded his head, and though exhausted, he felt a surge of pride. "You two better get in the van." He did his best to hide his feelings. The idea that someone was glad that he was around made Richard ready to take on the worst the witch had to offer.

Richard finished marking, leaving the gray news van now with wide, strange symbols scribbled across it. When inside, he pulled some pouches from his bag. "I can mix up something too that will help obscure you from magicks. It's not a complete failsafe, but it'll at least make it more difficult for him to find us."

Richard worked with what he had, which happened to be two old coffee cups Beth and Ted had from the morning. They dumped the leftover coffee out the window and Richard mixed things there—a sprinkling of holy water, a taste of Chamomile, a sprinkle of Devil's Shoestring, a thin-sliced Galangal root. Then he poured something from the unlabeled vial—a thick, black substance, that didn't pour so much as ooze out.

"Is that Chamomile? I drink that before I go to sleep every day. You're saying some witch's brew has things you can buy at a grocery store?"

Richard finished pouring and stirred everything together. "You'd be surprised what you can do with everyday items. You know, with duct tape and a little salt, I could make a barrier that even a friggin' zombie couldn't cross." He offered the drinks to Beth and Ted.

Ted was hesitant; he just stared into the thick, green liquid. "Now, this does what exactly? It's not going to give me the shits, is it?"

"No, it's just for protection. It will only last for the rest of the night, though. It doesn't eliminate his ability to see you so much as camouflage your aura. It'll make it much harder for him to find you."

Beth methodically described the contents of her drink before downing it in a single gulp, and Ted followed suit shortly after. Wincing heavily, they both began to cough and hack.

"Richard, it tastes terrible!" Beth barely choked the words out.

"So I've heard." He grimaced.

"You've never even tried it yourself?" Ted looked annoyed as he turned to spit out the window; a sludge of black tar-like spit hit the ground. "You better be right about this!"

"Well, we should be fine for a while to plan our next move." Richard shrugged his shoulders.

"Which is what?" Beth said. "Gathering something to fight with? You talked about needing something 'pure.' I guess components for another incantation?"

"Yeah, but that's the hard part." Richard tapped his chin. "I don't have anything like that with me, and I don't know where we can get it."

"Can't we oil your knife up with puppy blood and call it a day?" Ted asked earnestly.

"Gross," Beth slapped his arm with the back of her hand.

Richard sighed. "Yeah, I don't think that'd work anyways." Richard turned to stare at the inside of the van, his mind working out the puzzle.

What can we use to fight it?

"Well, maybe the wight was right." Ted shrugged. "Who is up for food?"

"Really, Ted? You want to eat?" Beth looked at him in disbelief.

The wight perked its head up at the suggestion. A horrific-looking expression of joy spread across its face. "Feasting would be the proper course of action, giving you more feeble humans time to rest and deliberate our next undertaking."

"Yeah." Ted nodded and gestured to the wight. "See, he's got it."

"Do we have time?" Beth glanced from them. "Richard said we were on the clock. Are we just burning time?"

"Damn, Beth," Ted said with clear frustration. "There will be plenty of witches to kill after we've had something to eat. Am I the only one that's just completely drained?"

Richard spoke up, "It's not a bad idea. I mean, what else can we do right now? Of course, we couldn't bring you into an all-night diner or anything," he said, pointing his finger at the wight. "We could bring you out a steak or something though."

"We saw an all-night diner off the exit on the way in, right Ted?" Beth asked with a glance at Ted. "How about we get over there, catch something quick, and fill up our tank."

Ted agreed and they set out. Ted pulled the van out from the grass; it wasn't long before they pulled into the diner. The wight had to be convinced to wait in the van. Richard had to explain to the wight several times how upsetting it would be for others if it stepped out, even if it wasn't trying to eat them. In the end, being under Richard's authority, the wounded wight had no choice but to remain in the van.

"There will be ample portions of both the ham dinner and coke of cola as you have described, yes?" The wight had stuck its entire head out the van door to speak. "And a filling of browns well-hashed?"

"Yes, yes. But only if you're quiet!" Richard tried to give it as serious a look as he could.

They hadn't gone far before Ted began to complain. "I hate that guy. I mean I do. I really, *really* do."

"You just hate him because he tried to take a bite out of you." Richard rolled his eyes.

"And that's *not* a good reason?"

Beth cut in. "By that reasoning, though, Ted, we should be pretty pissed with you. You did try to shoot us both."

"It's not the same thing!" Ted shook his head in disbelief.

Just the thought of that made Richard rub the back of his head where Ted had hit him. A lump was forming.

The diner was a dive truck-stop with a half-dead, flashing light to tell everyone it was open twenty-four hours a day. Just behind the dirty windows a crooked sign with plastic letters advertised the best waffles in the state.

A small collection of old men and tired waitresses milled about, and they all looked up to drink them in as they stepped inside. Richard and the others' clothes were roughed up, and there were more than a few bloodstains. Beth's hair had seen better days, and Ted's eyes were turning a shade of red. Despite all this, Richard wore a heavy grin along with his bruises, his matted hair, and the satchel that he refused to part with.

A waitress who was well into her sixties brought them menus once they had found their seats. She hesitated before she spoke. "Rough night?"

With a polite smile, Beth lied. "We're making a documentary on Bigfoot."

"I see. Well, call me when you're ready." She turned and walked quickly back to the counter.

Richard cleared his throat and placed his menu down. "Is anyone going to think badly about me if I get a milkshake with pancakes?"

13

"LET ME STOP YOU RIGHT THERE, SON." MINGES HELD UP A hand. "This is goin' down a sleepy angle here. You don't need to be telling me about milkshakes with your pancakes, I assumed as much anyways."

"I was building up to something! I was trying to cue you in on how close we were all getting, how we started out that day as just *oblivious* to this other world, but now we're planning a witch hunt. Don't you think that shows our emotional state? That's something other people need to know—we can do this, *they* can do this."

"Son, you're laying on that crazy a bit thicker than needed right here." He waved his hand. "Preaching to the choir right now. I think we need to cut to the meat and potatoes, yeah?"

"Like what? You want to know what happened, so I told you."

"Well for one, you didn't elaborate too well on that 'black unlabeled liquid' you fed out to everyone. Come on now, let's hear it, you were dosing everyone up on some funny juice, yeah?" He slapped the table, rattling it against the ground. "No need to be hiding it right? Told you before, they're gonna get you a toxicity test. We'll see it. Lemme hear the name."

"I don't know what it is—part of the kit they gave me when I headed out." Richard shook his head. "Really, I don't know."

"I see. Them pupils don't look too bad neither, so's I can tell. Maybe you was just eating a little tar then. You certainly wouldn't be the first junkie to go eating some tar thinking it'll get 'em high." He shook his tired head and fanned himself with his hat. "Well, what happened next? Anything exciting or just ya'll sittin' around eating pancakes?"

"Well..." Richard let that trail off and didn't pick it up again.

"Well?" Minges prompted him.

"Well, I was at a bit of a loss for what to do next. If you want to fight a witch, you have to be ready for it. Especially if it's powerful."

"Mmhmm?" Was all the lawyer responded with.

"They can be brought down just like anyone else, but they have protections, enchantments, and wards. If the legends are true, and at this point I've got no reason to suspect they aren't, you can't break through them so easily. You need precise ingredients, components, to cut through their barriers. You need something unblemished, something uncorrupted. I guess that's where the stories of the virgin sacrifices come from." He trailed off to look at the wall.

"That so?" Minges raised an eyebrow and leaned in.

"What?"

Minges cleared his throat. "Are you *unblemished*?"

"What?" Richard said again.

"You have many lady friends?" He winked. "I think you're gettin' what I'm layin' down."

"What!" Richard shook his head. "No! I'm not a virgin. I've had *tons* of sex."

"Really?" Minges said, ever the skeptic.

"Well, at least twice!"

"At least twi—" Minges shook off the confusion. "You know what, it's of no mind." He rubbed his temples and gave an exhausted sigh.

"No, no. We were thinking more toward flowers or other herbs, but the ones that work are impossible to get here. Really rare stuff—Ghost Orchid, Parrot's Beak, Middlemist Red." He nodded. "That last one only grows in two areas of the world, and one of those is a greenhouse in England. They used to grow it there to supply the witch hunters of old Europe, you know? Before they all went kind of, uh, crazy and killed a lot of normal people." A nervous laugh bubbled from his throat.

Oh man, I'm not building a good case, am I?

"Yeah, yeah, I see." Minges nodded, hurrying things along and seemingly not interested in a history lesson. "So, what then? You drive over to the gas station then and start beating people's brains in?"

Richard scoffed and shook his head. "I didn't kill anyone! And no, we didn't go to the gas station yet. We didn't leave. And I came up with an idea."

"Oh yeah, eh?" With casual interest, Minges asked, "What's that, son?"

Richard looked like he wanted to hold something back. He took a deep breath and puffed out his cheeks. "Well, we needed a bit of advice, so I *might* have called for a little suggestion."

Be careful. Be careful.

"Quit being so damn vague, son. Let's hear it."

Richard nodded and the words spilled out as if a dam had finally broke. "I found a passage in the book that lets you contact something from The Outside, the place where spirits dwell. I called in a spirit to hopefully get some hints. I didn't know what would happen. I mean kids try and do it all the time with Ouija boards and things don't always answer! You can't compel something to speak with you. All you can do is knock. How the heck would I know what would happen? How could I possibly know that something would *actually listen*?"

"What did you do?" Minges leaned in with anticipation and licked his fat lips.

"You don't just get to talk with the things in The Outside. It doesn't work that way. I thought it did, but you're not just knocking on their door, you're opening your own."

"YEAH, don't worry. It's not a big deal. It's not like you're letting them into our world or anything." Richard snickered as he stuffed another forkful of pancakes into his mouth. He only halfway finished chewing before he spoke again, "Trust me, my fourteenth-level wizard uses a similar spell all the time. Basically, you ask a question and you get an answer. That way we can ask what we should be using, right? So we can get an edge."

This'll be cake. If it even works at all.

Beth swallowed a piece of egg before she spoke in hushed tones over the tape recorder. "Is it really that simple, though? We just call it in here and then ask it a question?"

"I'm a little concerned here too." Ted cut in. "What does it get out of this trade?"

"Not sure, honestly. We can't be sure it will answer us. Most the time they don't. Worth a shot though, right?"

Definitely worth a shot.

"Richard, this thing isn't going to potentially try and eat us, is it? I've already had two occasions where things tried to eat me today, and I'm not looking for a third," Ted said, staring and holding up two fingers. He shot a glance at Beth. "I'm pretty sure it's going to try to eat us."

"No, nothing like that! It's not anything like that. It's like..." Richard rubbed his chin. "It's like a squirrel, yeah, like a squirrel that is disembodied, answers your questions, and lives in The Outside."

"Richard, that just..." Ted closed his tired red eyes and shook his head, clearly exhausted. "That doesn't sound like a squirrel at all. Does this thing at least have a tail or something? Squirrels eat nuts and live in trees. They don't float around or answer questions."

"I said *like* a squirrel!"

"Wait," Beth jumped in. "What's The Outside?"

"Oh, I'm no expert or anything." Richard searched the table for some way to illustrate his thoughts. Finally, he held one hand out flat over the surface of the table. "See this?" He asked with a shake of his hand. "This is us, this is where we live. This is our realm, or dimension, Earth, whatever you want to call it." He held out his other hand, an inch above and parallel to the first hand. "This is The Outside. Things exist here, not quite in our world, but looking in. A lot of religions have names for it; we just call it The Outside, though."

"Well, see." Ted snapped his fingers. "See, that might be

like a squirrel then, it's outside the window. You should have led with that."

"Oh, yeah," Richard agreed. "That does make it sound more like a squirrel."

"Okay, so we call this disembodied squirrel and ask it where we can get a weapon to fight the plague warlock?" Beth lifted her shoulder as if to ask if that was all. "I guess it's as strange as anything else we've run into tonight."

"This can't be that easy, Richard." Ted scoffed at the idea. "Nothing tonight has been easy."

Richard squinted his eyes and wiped some dirt from them. "No, really, it's not that hard. I think." He slid his fingers into the worn satchel and pulled out the leather-covered tome and opened it with care. He pointed a finger at a section. "See? You say a few words and that's it. If the sprite, or spirit, or whatever, wants to answer, then it does. Nothing big. Probably won't even work."

"No." Ted shook his head. "No, you're wrong. It won't be that easy, there's no way." He banged a hand against the table, jarring the napkin dispenser and saltshaker. "That squirrel is going to try to eat us, I know it."

Richard gave him a blank look and a shrug. "You have a better idea?"

"Ted, are you our expert now?" Beth smirked before she forked another piece of egg.

"Well, I've got an idea or two." Ted licked his lips and leaned in to the table. He held silent for a moment, adding emphasis to what he was about to say. "See, we're going to go find a priest, right? We're going to have him bless some bullets or a knife or whatever, you know, whatever that kind of shit is that they do. Like the thing they do to kill vampires, right? But let's be honest, shooting something is easy, but who wants to *actually* get into something's face and stab it? Anyways, we bless some bullets. Then we find Mister Plague-Face and, well, that's that, right? I'm sure that's in your book somewhere." He snapped his fingers and pointed at the book. "Find the part about shooting things in the face."

"No, Ted. It doesn't work like that," Richard said shaking his head. "You can't just get a priest to bless something, that just sounds fake. You need a weapon carved from sacred wood, forged under a particular phase of the moon, or cooled in faery blood."

"Oh, and *that* doesn't sound fake, right?"

"It also brings up a good question." Beth's eyes darted between the two of them. "Even if Richard thinks he can find the warlock easily, and everything goes great, are we just going to walk up to this old man and shoot him? That's the safest way to do things, right? But can we *actually* do that? What if we're wrong?"

Richard wasn't sure what to say to that. She was right, of course, and from the best he could tell, Ted thought so too.

Who would actually do it? I can't kill someone. I almost lost it choking the life out of one of those monsters back at the library. I don't think I have it in me to kill something like that.

"I'll do it." Ted finally spoke up. "Maybe our buddy out in the van can do it, but if he can't, I will. If we can get close enough, I'll do it." He avoided eye contact as he started shoveling more food into his mouth.

Richard's heart had been beating fast, threatening to burst inside his chest, and he had only just realized it. So quickly had his mood shifted, so quickly had the dead come back into his thoughts. His mind drifted back to the library.

I strangled one of those things. I crushed another. But it was only because I had to do it.

He told himself that over and over again, each time less convincing than the last.

It was only because I had to do it. I had to.

The look in its eyes as it died filled Richard's mind, making it hard to consider anything else. He was sure those dying eyes, monster or not, would follow him to the grave. He had never killed anything in his life. He remembered then the sticky mousetrap his mom had laid out so long ago, how she so carelessly told him about the trap, that it was something the mouse would step in and then not be able to get out of.

What a horrible thought that had been for him; that this thing would be frozen there, terrified and stuck until eventually it succumbed to death. But that was wrong too. He hadn't slept that night thinking about it, and he heard squeaking in the kitchen. He thought about waking his mother, about asking her to take care of it. Instead, he brought it outside and got a hammer, intending to finish it with mercy.

But he didn't.

It kept on squeaking as he sat there, crying, trying to force himself to finish it. Instead, he dropped it into the trashcan and went back to bed. Decades later, he still thinks about that mouse, about how he left it. It died either way, but it was a lot more painful because of him.

Why is this all coming back?

"Richard?" Beth patted his arm. "You okay?"

He shook away those confusing thoughts. "Nothing that a milkshake won't fix." He slurped some down.

"Let's get back on task. You say the only way we can do this is by asking these questions? Well let's do it. Let's do it right here." Ted rapped his knuckles against the table.

"We can't do it right here!" Richard could hardly contain

his surprise, but was thankful to talk about something else. "Everyone would see us."

"Really? Because I think being safe in a crowd sounds like a pretty damn good idea." Ted leaned back in his chair and crossed his arms. "I think we should do it *right* here. Hell, we're doing it for all these people, right? We could have just left town."

"And by *crowd* you mean two waitresses and three half-asleep truck drivers that didn't sign up for this?" Beth shot back at him.

Ted continued to saw through his steak and took a bite, chewing it only halfway before he pointed the fork at Richard. "He's the one that said it'd be safe."

Richard nodded. "Yeah, I guess he's right." He glanced over his shoulder at the waitress, now preoccupied with one of the truckers that had walked in. "All right, I think we can do this." He picked up one of the saltshakers and unscrewed the top. He winced when the metal squeaked against the glass. "Oh, I hate that noise!" He continued to wince for a few moments longer as he poured the salt out in a small circle. He spied over his shoulder as if he were committing a crime. With the tip of his fingers, he smoothed the salt in front of him into an almost flat canvas. "I'm going to request that the spirit write what we need here in the salt. I think that should work."

"All this time with a 'cabal of witch hunters' and you never saw any of them do something overtly supernatural like this?" The cameraman's voice was filled with disbelief.

"Well, we tried something like this one time in the sand." He peered nervously at the other two. "Didn't get a bite, though."

"Well, hopefully, we don't get a bite now either." Ted knocked on wood.

"Let's figure out what we're going to ask first, right?" Beth said. "We're going to ask it where we can find the materials we need to kill this witch, but what if it tells us Canada? We need to be more precise."

Richard nodded, "Yeah that's a good point..."

"So, let's ask where the *closest* thing is that we can use to fight the witch. How's that sound?"

When they all agreed, they quietly joined hands and Richard said the incantations, "...et offer salis. Die obsecro me..." The lights of the diner flickered once. It brought confusion and grumbling from those eating.

Ted's gaze searched the table, then across the diner. "That it?"

They all looked at the salt, but nothing happened. "Yeah, well, like I said, there's no way to force it to—" Richard stopped midsentence as the salt began to part, as if an invisible fingernail was being dragged through it. A thin straight line appeared, then a curve. Just as quickly as it began, it stopped.

A full minute passed in silence. Richard focused on the salt, willing it to form something coherent, something intelligible, but nothing came. He knew there wouldn't be, he knew because he had that same itch he had before—the same one he had in the house and the library. That itch that was just beneath the skin and that spoke to him without words, telling him that something bad was about to happen. Something wicked was on its way. But he tried to ignore it. He only stared and waited for something to move.

When nothing did, Beth finally spoke. "That was weird. What does it mean?"

"I... Uh. I have no idea? Is that some other language maybe?" Richard squinted his eyes and turned his head. His hand shook beneath the table and his stomach twisted into knots.

"Are you kidding me?" Ted huffed. "You have to specify the language it uses?"

"I don't know! I said I never did this before!" Richard shot back. His foot beat a rhythmic tune against the floor.

Please, please, don't tell me Ted was right.

Like it was kicked by a mule, the front door blasted open, shaking the glass, and a voice rang out: "Well hello there, good people!" A figure strolled inside, a slippery wet smile on his face, and left dark, muddy footprints without the slightest concern. A long, dirty, brown coat trailed behind him, looking as if it had served as burial attire in some hole dug in the woods. Despite the hour, a large-framed pair of sunglasses sat on his nose, sending mirrored reflections of everyone who turned to look at him. A thick, blonde handlebar mustache hung just below his nose, and greasy hair peeked out from beneath his wide-brimmed cowboy hat. His skin looked as if he had once been dark, but had paled to a deathly muted tone.

"Such a fine establishment!"

The waitress, who had jumped when the door burst open, now looked irritated. Her voice was flat. "Sir? Maybe just take a seat in one of the back booths and I'll be right with you." She hadn't bothered to fake a smile.

"No need for a booth." He took a few muddy steps toward Richard's table. "My friends here have a seat for me." He picked up speed as he strode confidently to them. In one smooth motion, he slid into the seat alongside them.

He took a moment to let his gaze cross each member of the table, the mirrored lenses sending their own bewildered looks back at them. "So, I got your call." He pinched the end of his sunglasses and slid them off his slender nose, showing vibrant purple eyes with bright specs that ebbed and flowed as they caught the glare of the light. He kicked up his mud-covered boots as he leaned back, slinging off black-brown sludge onto the table.

"We, uh..." Richard's mind was a blank slate. His stomach twisted even more painfully now, and his throat went dry. He couldn't stop his hands from shaking, so he kept them below the table.

This isn't what was supposed to happen!

Beth was the first to speak. "Who are you? *What* are you?" Though startled, she remained persistent, ever the investigator.

"Your pudgy buddy here threw a hook out into the abyss and I took the bait. So here I am." With a wave he presented himself, caped in his dusty old clothes that looked a century out of fashion, save for those new sunglasses now sitting on the table. "Well, perhaps it was more like opening the front door and turning the light on than a hook with bait. But you can call me '*You*' or '*That guy*' if you want. No need for names between friends, eh?" He sat there; a moment's silence passed before he seemed to grow bored. "I'm something of a spirit, more to it than that, sure, but why complicate things?"

Richard peeked behind him, but, oddly, no one seemed to be paying much attention to his table. They all went about their business, eating and talking, reading the newspaper, nothing beyond the ordinary.

"Don't worry your ears off there, sweetie," the stranger with the purple eyes said. "They're dosing on my glamour, beautiful thing that it is."

"I uh..." Ted was nervously trying to form a sentence. "I thought we were getting a squirrel? I was okay with a squirrel. This isn't a fucking squirrel, Richard!"

"A squirrel? You mean this?" The stranger's jaw stretched down farther than it should have been capable of—nearly a foot wide from jaw to jaw—revealing several rows of teeth. He reached his dusty hand in, not bothering to pull up his sleeve, and slid it down his throat, elbow-deep. He pulled his arm back, his sleeve now slick with a white liquid that slowly burned off as the light touched it. His untrimmed and yellowed fingernails held a ghostly gray tail connected to a small sprite with three sets of legs that worked furiously to free itself from his grasp.

The small frenzied creature squealed as its half-dozen squat legs whipped fruitlessly around. The stranger held it before him, examining the sprite with its eyes full of panic, then stuffed it back into his mouth. The sprite gave one final futile squawk as he closed his mouth. The purple-eyed demon brought his hand up to his mouth and burped. "Excuse me. I saw that little buddy answering your call, but I figured I'd take over. Could do for a snack anyways."

"Yeah..." Ted nodded his head. "That looked kind of like a squirrel."

Beth braved forward. "What are you going to do to us?"

"Didn't you want some damn answers?" He scowled at them. "You chumps call me in here then act confused? This is a pretty shitty séance, I must say."

"I didn't." Richard said, repeatedly shaking his head. "I didn't call you."

"Oh, but you did..." The man brought his face inches from Richard's and stared into his eyes. His smile slid away, only to return a moment later. "You turned the light on and opened the path, my friend. Maybe I'm not what you were expecting, but I'm what you got."

"I've never, *never* heard of anything like this." Lines of

fear were forming across Richard's face; he couldn't stop them.

"Is... Is this goddamned guy the plague witch?" Ted was inching from the table.

"No, he's not. He's something else," answered Richard.

The stranger scoffed and swayed his head from side to side. "Swindlers, I tell you. You've already asked me several questions and no one's even offered me a drink?" He dipped his fingers into the salt and then, with a brush of his hand, violently swept it from the table. "The salt might have appeased your squirrel, but it won't me. No sir. I'm into things a little more solid, things that might bleed just a *tad* more than salt does."

"No." Richard shook in fear but refused to bend. He bit his lip hard enough to draw blood, hoping that'd be enough to steel his resolve. "We won't give you anything. I know what you are."

A false god, a trickster. A spirit of nature.

"I know what you do to men, the people who follow you. *You're a daeva.*"

The thing that played in the flesh of man curled its lip into a sneer. The gaps in the daeva's teeth revealed the shark-like rows behind, sawing back and forth, growing in anticipation. It held its face in that way for several long moments before something more sinister slipped across its face—a smile. Somehow, that was worse for Richard. "I can smell something on you, can taste it in the wind. You're not like these two." It waved its dusty hand, disregarding them, and focused on Richard. "They're not made of your salt." The daeva stared, not into, but through Richard's eyes and into the pit of his soul. Richard felt its gaze slither in and down his insides, licking and assailing them. But Richard gripped his hand tightly and stared back with as menacing a look as his feeble gaze could construct.

Don't be afraid. This is a game. Don't be afraid and make a bad move.

The daeva snorted a single grunt that might have been a laugh. "I can eyeball a novice when I see one. You're entering into a dangerous game little *witch*." A jackal's laugh ripped from its throat. "But you know what? Whether you wanted me or not, it doesn't matter. That's not how it works. We'll do business just the same, or I'll find something else a little bigger than that sprite to drag back with me to make it worth the trip." The daeva dragged its nail across the table, leaving a dark groove. Its eyes tipped toward Beth and then Ted with the threat.

Richard's skin crawled and squirmed beneath his clothes. The daeva's hot breath, its bright and vibrant eyes, the old clothes, it was all a construct that told Richard he should be scared of this thing that came calling from The Outside. The lizard brain in Richard told him to be scared, but his training told him to hold.

Richard drew in a breath; he knew that if he made a request or formed a poorly worded question, it could mean the end of his life or one of the others. He had to think carefully—there was so much to lose and so much to gain. Several moments passed as his mind worked, the gears turning in his brain, calling up old words from his books and the words of his mentors, while sifting through useless knowledge for what might save or condemn his life.

Think, Richard, think.

But there was something else nagging him. Something else that told him there was more here than he could see.

The daeva sniggered again as those eyes, so cold but still so bright held on to him, its gaze worked across Richard, who felt as if it was running fingers across every inch of his face. "I feel like we've gotten off on the wrong foot." It smiled kindly and drummed its fingers on the table. "I'll do a little more explaining then, hmm? Give you a little something for free? A devil's mix is in the air, powerful energies are shaking loose. Was it you? Did you stumble into something and make a mess of things?" It waved a slender finger in the air. "You shake things up like that, and bigger things than squirrels come looking. But there's no need to be afraid." It reached out and touched the tips of its fingers to Beth's warm hand; she pulled back quickly and shuddered. "The daevas aren't *inherently* evil, friends. Perhaps your buddy here doesn't know, but once invited in..." It drew a circle in the air; a light purple trail of energy followed behind the finger. "I can stay here until business is concluded. So ask what you will, or I'll be on my way until you're ready."

Tightness formed in Richard's stomach, a lump that told him not to speak, to shut his mouth, and to let someone else take over. But Beth's eyes met his, asking him to help without so much as a word. So he tried. The words came out before he even willed them. "There's a warlock here in town, a plague witch. We want to kill him, and we want to know the closest tool we can use to do it."

The daeva threw its head back into a hearty laugh. "Is that all?" Its head rolled as if on a hinge to look at Richard once more. "Well, it's going to cost you."

"I don't have anything to pay with," Richard said, unsure.

The daeva's tongue licked out to rub the front of its teeth, or taste the air—Richard didn't know. "You've got two friends here. Do you really need both?" There was innocence in the daeva's question.

"No!" Richard shot back. "We won't give you anyone!"

"Relax! Relax! It was a *joke*! I'm trying to break the

tension here, get me? But you're going to need to give me something."

"How about the wight?" Ted butted in.

"You have a wight?" its curiosity was palpable. "Perhaps that'd work."

"No, Ted!" Beth blurted. "He saved you, how could you do that?"

"He also bit my arm and threatened to eat both of you." Fire burned behind Ted's eyes. "He's a damn monster!"

"No, we can't do that." Richard shook his head, and rolled his words out as stiffly as he could. "We are not turning him in, Ted."

"Really?" Ted's face contorted in anger as he spat the words out. "Because I'm pretty damn sure he'd eat any one of us if given the chance!"

"We can't do it! I'm not giving anyone away!" Richard shouted and rose to his feet.

Ted immediately stood up to challenge the smaller man, his face turning red and veins popping in his neck. This was Ted; he would get what he wanted through intimidation. Richard knew, and he was afraid of this. He was more afraid of men like Ted than anything else. Still, he refused to stand down.

Their commotion drew no attention from the rest of the diner. Ted's gaze, sharp as a dagger, stabbed into Richard. "We're done listening to you, Richard. You've fucked up one too many times. Sit down."

The daeva watched in amusement.

I'm not sitting down.

"Take a walk, Ted. Go home. We're not doing this your way." This was the first time Richard ever stood up for himself. His nostrils flared and he gulped for air, but he was in control—angry and afraid, but in control.

"Girls," the daeva mocked without rising from its chair. "You're both pretty. Take a breath and calm down. A wight would certainly work, but you have something else that'd work too." It pointed its pale finger at the protective jewelry hanging from Richard's neck.

The words snapped them into focus. Ted and his anger were no longer a concern. The necklace suddenly felt warm against Richard's chest, as if thinking about it was enough to heat it. Richard's hands rose to clench it as he took his seat.

I can't. This has save me so many times already.

"No, I can't give this up."

"So then we're back to the wight, right?" Ted shot from across the table.

"No." It broke Richard's heart to say it. He'd had the necklace for years and loved it before he even knew there was power in it. "It's fine." He wavered, rubbing his fingers over the metal cross before he reached back to undo the clasp. He held it in his hand for a few long moments before he spoke; his words were slow and his voice was uneasy. "The legends say you can't lie." Not a question, but a statement.

The stranger had fixated upon the necklace as Richard gathered it. Its gaze traced up to meet Richard's. "Clever of you to form your questions into statements. Yes, it's true, we cannot lie when in a bargain."

"Then I don't think this buys me one question." His hands tightened around the cross, hard enough that he felt the sharp metal edges cut into his skin and a wetness fill his grasp. "I think it buys me at least three."

"Three?" A laugh spurted out from its lips. "Your friends here have asked me that many already." It waved a hand toward Beth.

"You might not be able to lie, but you can deceive. I'm

the one that called you. I'm the one that pays. They don't. You answered those for free." Richard glared. "We don't owe you anything for that."

The stranger threw its head back and barked out laughter, each laugh more frightening and inhuman than the last. Its head rolled from side to side on its neck until it turned its piercing eyes onto the others. "*See*?" It looked at both Ted and Beth. "He's smarter than either of you. He's a damn *scoundrel*. He pushes a hard deal, but he won't get three answers. I'd be willing to part with two, though." It finally turned back to look at Richard. "Two answers, no more. And it's only because I like you." Its wicked, curled lips did nothing to hide its annoyance.

"You'll answer everything as best you know it, sparing no detail or otherwise deceiving us with an unclear answer." Blood had pooled in Richard's hand and started to leak between his fingers to the floor, but he didn't care.

"A bargain well made. Deal."

Richard reached over and set the powerful, bloody artifact down in front of the daeva. At first, his fingers refused to drop it, but after a deep breath, Richard let it drop from his hand, clattering to the table. The false god sucked in the air, clearly enjoying the aroma of freshly spilled blood. Its long tongue stretched out of its mouth, farther than Richard would have imagined it could, and tasted the blood specks on the necklace.

"Quite a thing you had there, buddy." Its hand slammed down, hard enough to shake the table, as it grabbed hold of the artifact and drew the bloody necklace in. "Now that we have that unpleasantness out of the way, let's hear that question again. Make it all official-like."

Richard let out a deep sigh and clenched his eyes. The moment the cross left his neck, he felt like a lesser person—

his shield stripped away as if it had been a piece of himself. He knew what he had lost. He was naked now.

No, I'm more than that. I can do this. I can do it.

He lied to himself. He finally opened his eyes and spoke, steeling his voice from quivering. "We want to kill the plague witch here in Bridgedale. We want to know what weapon we can use to do it, one that we can get and use tonight. What will work?"

The stranger leaned in close enough that its stale breath assaulted Richard. The witch hunter wanted to draw back, but instead forced himself not to show weakness. The daeva drew a finger up and pointed at Richard's satchel. "Can I see your purse there, sweetheart?" The stranger's purple eyes burned. Richard felt like its gaze was digging into him, lighting his blood on fire.

Richard gripped the bag tightly and kept the monster's stare, feeling a primal instinct that told him not to ever turn his back on the daeva.

Something is not right here. We're being played.

"Come on, you're being a baby. I'm not going to steal your stupid knife." Richard still refused. "Fine. *You* open that bag and take it out."

Carefully, he opened his bag and pulled out the blade, the same he'd used to find the witch's name. That same etched wooden handle carved from a tree where a witch was hanged, and that same blade that was forged in a church by a priest.

"*You* take *that* blade and you plunge it into the bastard's heart. He'll die as good as anything would." He opened his arms, "Now, wasn't that worth the price of admission? I just saved you a whole mess of trouble!"

Richard turned it over in his hand. "We had it the whole time..." He gripped the worn handle tightly in disbelief.

Did I lose the necklace for nothing? No, something is not right.

"The means to kill the witch has been with you the whole time." The stranger said joyfully, delighting in Richard's loss and misery. "But that's a good thing, right? Don't look so glum. You'd rather go running around out in the woods or raiding some poor gypsy's workshop? You know how hard gypsies are to come by these days? They are quite delicious though, so let me know if you do happen by one."

"So that's it? We've got it then. We can end this." Ted's eyes filled with hope.

"Cool your horses there, Red," The stranger said with a toothy grin. "Pudgy here still has one more question. A deal was made and it cannot be broken." It spread its arms open wide. "Think carefully, friend, you don't get many choices like this in your life. So what is it? Divination, location, truth?" Its gaze cut deep, peeling away the layers, and touching the fear in each part of Richard's being.

Be smart. There's something here you don't see.

"You want to know the best way to kill that witch? Where he's weakest?"

Richard's eyes focused on the daeva's mouth, the sharp white teeth hid below his curled lip, and the sawing row of fangs hid behind them. The slick, knowing expression it had, the arrogance and pure attitude that oozed from the daeva's grin.

Think, think carefully.

"No? Want to know which stock is going to jump five thousand percent in the next few years? Maybe you can die a rich man." Its eyes, its smile—sharp as a blade.

Don't jump. It's a game. It's trying to make you move.

The stranger's words now came out like nails on a chalkboard. "How about the next great tragedy that would befall your country here? You want to know where the bomb is? Who it's going to kill? You could stop it. They'd write your name in history books. You never did like being a nobody, did you?"

No, no there's more. There's more. I can feel it.

"Or how about where you die?" The daeva persisted. Each word was drawn out to torture Richard. "I could tell you when, tell you how. Could tell you how it feels when *she* pulls your head back and the blade goes in."

She?

His mind danced and cried out.

No! It's bait. Don't bite! Don't give in!

"No? What about love? You look the lonely type. You want to know of the woman that you would fall in love with? You want to know what's happening to her right now? I'll give you a hint, *maybe* she's had a little too much to drink, *maybe* you could tell her not to get into that car."

It's hiding something. It's planned this. Nothing this powerful would just show up, not with such a meager ritual. Not unless it wanted to. There's a game here that I don't see.

Richard let out a breath and filled his lungs again. He looked up from the table and met the daeva's gaze. Richard's eyes didn't burn like fire, nor did they reek of horror and pain like the daeva's. Richard's eyes were simply stone.

"What are all the reasons as to why you came here?"

The daeva's joy slowly faded away. All pretext of kindness or humor melted away; all the fabricated smiles and gestures were gone. But the rage in his eyes was still there, burning as hot as hellfire.

"I'll ask you only once to withdraw that question and step back onto the safer path, the one that *everyone* else walks. Ask me how you die, or how you can become rich. Ask me which woman will lay with you, or how you could be king." The words were stiff. "Dance like a mortal, a thing of soft flesh and bone that breaks easily. *Ask me something else.*"

This time Richard leaned in, and he did not avert his gaze nor stammer.

"No."

The daeva's head rolled back and shook in an unnatural blur. It swung loose on its neck from side to side before it pulled level again. "Then so it is. Well done; I've underestimated you." The daeva didn't pretend to enjoy this; there was no mock enjoyment in its voice. "I'm here for *you.* You are here because of my making. When you cast your lot with the stupid knife-in-the-bowl trick, I was the one that grabbed the blade and aimed it at your warlock. Did you think such a novice trick would expose such a power? Did you not stop to wonder why such a deceptive creature as the warlock would be open to such magicks?" It scolded Richard and drew its hand up, exposing its sharp nails. "I stuck my hand through from the abyss and turned your blade. I burned what was left of my essence to force your blade through the ether and aim it at that bastard's name. The witch has shackled me to him, *me, a god of men*, to his purposes. I grabbed onto your witching spell and set you upon him as a distraction, an annoyance, but you've been doing quite well, haven't you? I tried to pierce your mind in the house—did you feel it? Did you feel how I worked my fingers across your memories, pulling them away? I couldn't, though. I couldn't get anything out of you because of this." It held up the bloodied cross.

I remember him. I remember the itch inside my mind.

"You're a fool, a fucking fool, but you had this. You tore down his name, his source of power. And now, with this cross on me, that motherfucker won't bind me again. Now

I'm free to walk these planes, free to once more be worshipped and draw from the lives of men." Again, it twisted its profane lips into its deceptive embrace of a smile. "And if you do manage to slay the witch, I'll snatch him in the afterlife and eat his soul. If you die, I am none the worse." It pulled off its hat and slipped the metal treasure, the cross that had once been Richard's shield, around its neck. "But perhaps a great deal better than before."

"So we've been played?" Ted rattled from across the table. "This *thing* is using us in its own vendetta? Screw this shit. Let's go home. Let the diva here fight its own war."

"Well damn, Slick, ain't you the smartest of the pack?" The daeva's greasy, stiff hair hardly waved as it shook its head. "You'll play your part, lest you worry about a pissed off witch on your ass for the rest of your days. He's got ways of finding you, ways beyond what you can understand."

"Then help us!" Beth's eyes were filled with desperation. "Tell us more, where he's at, what he can do. Tell us everything!"

"It can't." Richard said, in a weak voice. "It doesn't work that way. It doesn't know the future. It can only use its energy to look to it, to answer a question. But it's running on empty. Why else would a false god be looking to three novice witch hunters for help? It's not nearly as scary as it wants us to think it is."

We're in too deep to stop now.

Calling the daeva a false god clearly struck it. Its eyes confronted Richard and drew him in. Richard couldn't look away, couldn't possibly break whatever struggle they had here. "Pudgy here is right. I'm running low on juice, and I don't live here. I don't know where the hell he is in the fat, disgusting physical sense. But I did do you a favor. Your stupid trick wouldn't have worked without me, and if it did at all, it would have sent you full tilt at a plague witch. He's hundreds of years old; he would have consumed you in moments. You wouldn't have been a threat, only a mild annoyance."

The daeva shook its head in disgust. "I can tell you, however, that he's weak enough with his name destroyed that you can track him again another way. You try the Witch's Dance with him, and you'll get a bead on him. It's not much, but it's the best your sorry lot has got. Hit him while he's weak. Kill him for me, and for yourselves. Hell, kill him for everyone he's tormented, and everyone he will destroy if you don't. Or just kill him because you don't have a choice. I don't really give a shit what reason you come up with."

A Witch's Dance?

"What's that?" Richard said, confused. "A Witch's Dance? I've never heard of it."

"That's the problem with you damn mortals, each of you comes up with your own stupid name for something. Nothing is ever uniform. In The Outside, like you called it, things don't have names that can be changed; it's not something you can dally with. Things are or they are not. They cannot be altered."

"What in the hell are you talking about?" Ted finally spat out.

"He's saying that language isn't a construct where he's from like it is here." Beth said. "Is that right?"

"Sure. Whatever. I don't expect your soft brains to understand such things."

"Then what do we do then? What's the Witch's Dance?" Richard leaned forward in his chair.

"That would be telling, wouldn't it? And you've only paid me for two questions. Besides, I think a slick little witch burner like you could figure it out. It'll be a walk in the park, I'm sure."

Carelessly, it waved a hand. "Well, it's been fun. But our business is concluded here. Try not to take too long, though. I might just get hungry enough to try and snag a bite here, might be worth what trouble I'd stir up, eh?" Its wet tongue snaked out and licked its lips as its horrible eyes turned to the others in the restaurant. Not another word crept from its mouth, only a low and playful whistle as it spun on its heels and strolled from the diner.

Beth let a moment pass before she broke the silence at the table. "What in the hell just happened? What did we just see exactly, Richard?"

Richard cleared his throat. "I don't know *exactly*, but it *was* a daeva. They're beings, outsiders, whatever you want to call them, that people used to worship as gods. The priests and clergy used to hunt them or expose them as demons. Now they're angry, vengeful shells of what they once were. And the daeva was right. We don't have a choice. We're a threat that the witch will deal with, sooner or later."

"Then this doesn't change anything." Beth's hair fluttered as she shook her head. "We're still going forward, we still have to finish this. Now we just have more of an incentive."

"The sooner we get this done, the better." Ted scooted forward in his chair and pointed a finger down at the dagger Richard was gripping. "Give me the blade. When the time comes, I'll do it quick and we can get the hell out of here. You just figure out where the hell he is Richard, and I'll do what we need to do. Can you do that?" Ted asked with irritation, like Richard had failed him again. But Richard didn't mind.

Thank God.

Richard didn't want to kill anything, even something pure evil. He handed the knife over to Ted without any of the hesitation he had shown with the daeva.

I'll get them there, Ted will do it, and we're done. Everyone can go home. Everyone will go home. Everyone will go home.

He repeated the thought over and over to himself. But despite how many times he said it, he couldn't make himself believe the words. He felt the change in the wind and the itch on his neck.

Now what the hell is a Witch's Dance?

14

"Mmhmm." Minges patted the sweat that was beading on his head with a hanky. "So, you believe you let that son of a bitch out, eh? What'd you say its name was?"

"I didn't." Richard said. "It was a daeva, if that's what you're asking, but it wouldn't give us its name. Like I told you before, names hold power."

"Yeah, yeah, you said that for sure." Minges nodded and took a deep breath, fanning himself with his hat. "Getting hot as all hell in here. So you said that this fella took your charm bracelet, right?"

"Sanctified necklace." Richard corrected him and sank deep into his seat. "It was my protection, and with it gone," he hesitated, "I can't be sure of what I've done."

Did he make me kill Beth?

The thought sank deep into him and rubbed sharp edges on his insides. It made him want to throw up. He took in a breath to keep it all down and wondered where it all went wrong.

When the daeva took the necklace, that's when it all started to go to hell. It's all clear now that I say it. He took my necklace and the witch got into my mind.

Minges had been momentarily content to suck in air and fan himself, leaving Richard to his own thoughts. "You sayin' that losing that necklace is why you caved that poor girl's head in, yeah?"

"I couldn't do that. I wouldn't do that." Richard bit his lip. "No, it's all a lie. I didn't kill her. There's no way." If his eyes hadn't been so dry at this point, fat tears might have started again. "But maybe he made me do it." Conflicted, unsure, his head sagged in defeat.

"Well, then." Minges perked up, clearly excited by the change in direction. "What happened to ya'll next?" Joy crept back onto his face.

"What else was there to do? We finished eating and made a call to The Kord. After that, we went out to the van. I made the same drink that I gave Ted and Beth." He smiled slightly, remembering the moment. "They were right. It tasted terrible."

"Yeah, yeah. You know it ain't gonna look too good in court when they ask what ya'll were drinking and your best answer is 'some black tar shit I put in there.' " He gave a sarcastic snort under his breath.

"I'd tell you if I knew."

"I'm sure you would," the lawyer agreed. "But I got another question for you, son. If you thought this was all true, everything, this witch, this demon, them pig babies... Why didn't you just *go home*? Call the damn police? Anything? I hear what you're saying. He's chasing you, he's on your ass. But it just don't make sense. How are you going to go up against something that's doing all the shit you're saying it can?"

"I told you before. I've never been good at anything." He

gave a shy, sheepish smile. "When my dad walked out on me and my mom, she shut down. I could never really get to her." He looked up to meet his lawyer's tired eyes. "But this —I was afraid—but I could do this. I could do it. I could help in this." His gaze fell to the floor again. "But if Beth really is dead, then I guess I couldn't. I guess I can't do anything."

Minges took in a deep breath and stopped fanning himself. "Don't worry there son, we're gonna get this all sorted out, and get you what you need, yeah? Let's hear it, what happened next?"

The hooks of doubt were there now. Beth was dead and maybe Richard had done it. He told himself it wasn't him, but part of him was afraid it was true.

The tears began streaming down his face. "I got the book out, and Beth and I started to go through it..."

RICHARD SIGHED and flipped through the pages again. "I don't see anything like *Witch's Dance* in here."

With the false god gone, life continued as normal in the small diner in the quiet town of Bridgedale. None of the occupants seemed concerned with what had happened or even aware that the daeva had come at all now, no one was any the wiser that devils walked among them. Richard envied them and their ignorance. Some part of him wished he could turn the clock back and just never get out of bed this morning. But there was another side, a side that told him this was who he always was, even if he didn't know it. Though afraid, he felt sharper than he ever had, and that was the part of him that was enjoying the ride.

He turned another of the yellowed pages, pages he had

read a dozen or more times before but never with such focus. Beth sat alongside him, reading what little of it she could.

Ted leaned back in his chair, occasionally offering unhelpful advice. "It is probably something like a rain dance, right? You could do that to summon the witch. You guys do weird kinds of shit like that, right?"

"You can't summon witches." Richard glanced from the book to Ted. "You can summon spirits, demons, and other things that exist outside our plane of existence, but you can't summon something that's already here. I told you that already."

Ted scoffed. "This isn't like some stupid dance-off, is it? Like the song where the devil offers Johnny a fiddle of gold against his soul, and they had a fiddle-off?" Ted's eyes rolled at the absurdity of it. "Hell, I hope it's not a dance-off."

"A dance-off!" Richard snapped his fingers together.

"What? Are you serious? I was joking. Man, this occult shit is really stupid."

"Yeah, what are you saying, Richard?" Beth said, ignoring Ted.

"Well, I don't mean it's an *actual* dance-off, but that gives me an idea. I think I know what it might be, but it's not in my book. I remember my group back home talking about something like it; they called it a *Mind Brace,* or something. The witch is trying to scry us. He's got his eye out there searching, looking for us. There's a way to try and find that, grab onto it, and look back through it at him. I don't know much about witches fighting each other, but it sounds like something they might do in a *Witch's Dance*. We could find his consciousness out there, and then find out where he is physically."

"Great." Ted slapped his hands together. "So we call your buddy Kord—"

"The Kord."

"Right. We call your buddy, *The Kord,* ask him how you do this, then you shoot your brain out there and get us a lock. Is that what you're saying?"

"No, no." Richard shook his head furiously. "No, not me. I mean, we'll call The Kord, and he'll do it and tell us where the witch is. I'm not really qualified for that level of ritual. I mean, what happens if I open my brain up and some spirit jumps in, or some dick ghast tries to possess me or something? Man, what if a goblin tries to wreck my brain with illusions?"

Beth furrowed her brow. "Can that happen? Are you opening yourself up for something like that?"

"I don't know! I mean..." Richard absent-mindedly rubbed at his chest where the necklace had been. "I didn't think that daeva would show up either, but he did! I didn't know any of this was real this morning! What if goblins are real? What if minotaurs or mermaids are real?" A sudden realization poured over Richard. "Oh crap guys, what if aliens are real?"

"Dude has a point." Ted nodded. "I mean, not about the aliens or anything, but I figured as much about the rest of it. I think it's becoming painfully clear that Richard doesn't *actually* know what the hell is going on. He was thinking that the witch was fifty years old, but the daeva told us he's hundreds of years old. The best Richard has is an educated guess. He's opened a lot of this up himself. Hell, we could be staring down alien mermaids here in the next twenty minutes for all we know."

"Alien mermaids don't exist!" Richard shot back.

"Are you sure? Are you *sure* they don't exist, Richard? I don't want to take the risk. God only knows what an alien mermaid would do to you."

"No, that's not true, Ted." Beth shot back, standing up for Richard. "The daeva told us as much. It's been behind things, manipulating the outcome. It's not Richard's fault. This whole thing got started because of us. Richard wanted to turn away, and you and I pushed him into it."

"Oh yeah? And you missed the part where he said that if Richard's plan actually worked how he expected that the damn witch would have eaten all our faces off, right? You missed that part?"

Beth took a deep breath, but Richard butted in. "He's right, Beth." His gut twisted with guilt; it hurt him to admit it. "I'm out of my fishbowl here—this is the deep end for me. I've read this stuff, I know it, but I never knew I had to take it so seriously. I don't have any practical experience with any of this."

"Richard, I'm not saying that we shouldn't call The Kord. We should. But none of this is your fault. You've done better than any of us could have hoped for. You're the reason we're still alive."

Her words were like coffee for his soul, it perked him up and gave him strength to keep going. As long as Beth was with him, he had hope. She was strong and confident—everything he wasn't.

Ted breathed out a sigh and crossed his arms. "Yeah, well, you're not wrong, Beth." It was the best Ted would do.

"All right, Richard," said Beth, "so here's what we'll do. You call The Kord again, see where he's at and see what we can do before he gets here. Find out what this *Mind Brace, Witch's Dance* thing is, and see if he can help us out with that." She smiled and rubbed his shoulder. "Either way, we're with you."

"Yeah, we're with you, bud." Ted nodded. "Until I can stick that witch and we're done."

Richard nodded and sucked in a breath. So many people were counting on him. So much of what happened had been dependent on him making the right choices. There was a witch loose in Bridgedale, and he was the hunter on its trail.

I have to be careful. I have to be smart. I can't let anyone get hurt.

After they finished eating and paid their bill, Beth asked the waitress if they could use their phone.

"None of ya'll Bigfoot hunters carry a cellphone?" The waitress asked with a stiff face.

"Left them with the monkey suit," Beth said with a full grin of perfect white teeth. "We won't be long."

The waitress, her face still drooping like hot wax, finally relented. "Don't you take too long. Owner'll have a conniption fit if'n you run the bill up."

"We'll make it quick," Beth said, her smile still as bright as ever.

Richard glanced once at the waitress and then at Beth. The waitress groaned and walked off. Stepping in then, he got The Kord's number from a note in his book and punched it in. The phone rang several times.

Finally, The Kord answered. "Hello?"

"The Kord? It's me Richard again."

"Richard? Good. Did you figure out what it is we're dealing with? I want you guys to stay put after you do. No need to go mixing anything up until we get there. We're still a few hours out. I just got Cherrytop, Severin and Ripsaw up, but we're still waiting on Deezenutz. His mom said he spent the night at his girlfriend's house, so we're on our way over there right now." He spoke a million words a minute.

"Yeah, yeah. Gotcha." Richard said, struggling to keep up. "But yeah, we think we know what it is. We think it's a plague witch."

"Got ourselves a plague witch!" The Kord said. A hoot of cheers followed.

"Plague witch! Yes! YES!" A muffled cheer came from the other end of the phone.

"Where are you, exactly?" Richard asked a little nervously as he twined the phone cord with his finger.

"I told you, we're on our way. We're in the Silver Bullet." The Silver Bullet was Ripsaw's name for his silver station wagon. "Cherrytop, look up the chapter on cast bindings!"

Another muffled reply came: "Got it!"

"By the way, Richard, we've all been talking and we think Rich-sword would be a better name for you. How's that fit?"

Richard smiled at Beth, who was patiently waiting. "Yeah, that sounds great, but I actually have another question for you. What's a *Witch's Dance*? Is that the same thing as a *Mind Brace*?"

"Wait, what?" Richard was about to speak before The Kord cut in. The others were talking in the background. "No, wait a second, Rich-sword. Guys, guys, shut the hell up for a second okay? He's talking about a damn *Mind Brace*."

"Well, I just wanted to know if it's the same thing as a *Witch's Dance*."

Richard could hear the muffled chatting from somewhere else in the car; he thought it was probably Severin. "A Mind Brace? Yes! *Hell yeah*!" There was a round of hooting.

"Guys! I said shut up a second! Yeah, Rich-sword?

Maybe. A Witch's Dance might be the same thing, but hell, man, that's dangerous stuff. I can't say for sure either way, I've never heard of it."

"Yeah, well, we think this douche is scrying us. We were ambushed. We think he's out there getting ready to run or hit us again."

"Hell, you were ambushed? What's going on there now?"

"Well there was a daeva—"

"There was a friggin' daeva?!" The Kord shouted into the phone. The background started their muffled chanting of the word *daeva*.

"Yes," Richard whispered. "I just talked with him. He was kind of a dick. He said he grabbed my ritual and aimed it for me, and the witch had him enslaved before, but after we destroyed the name's placement, the witch was weakened and the daeva was able to get loose and come talk with us. He said the witch is vulnerable right now, but could still shrug off the dagger ritual, and that he couldn't help me again. And if someone performs a Witch's Dance, we could try and get a lock on the witch. So I was thinking maybe you could, you know, do the ritual?" Richard trailed off and listened to nothing but silence on the other end.

The Kord finally cleared his voice and spoke. "Sure thing, Rich-sword. I mean, yeah. I'd totally roll with that son of a bitch, no doubt. Plague witch, I mean, for me? What's that, like the fifth or sixth I've beaten the shit out of. No doubt." The Kord laughed on the other end. "But I can't really do it from here. You're going to have to do it."

"Me? The Kord, I really can't. I don't even know how!" Richard's voice started to rise with panic. "Seriously, man, can't you, like, pull over for fifteen minutes and get it done?"

"No can do, buddy. We're working double time, quick as

we can. We didn't even stop to eat, just got drive-through. Hell, we even skipped Wendy's when we saw there was a line. Had to settle for Furger Burger." Richard heard him slurp from a straw as if to emphasize his point. "But listen, man, you've got this. Seriously, you have his name and broke its placement? You talked with a friggin' *daeva* for shit's sake. Dude, you got this." Richard could hear the slick smile on the other end somehow. "Besides man, it's impossible here. You need connections here. I've never been to Bridgedale. You've got an emotional connection with this witch. He's totally your bitch, dude."

"How about we just wait?" Richard glanced up to a clock on the wall. "You guys will be here soon. Can you do it then?"

"Well, we'll be there soon, for sure. But I think you can do this, Rich-sword. The bastard is weak. You locate him for us, all right? It's not that bad. You have your manual, right?"

Richard nodded. A moment passed before he realized The Kord wouldn't know he nodded. "Yeah, yeah I've got it here."

"Take it easy, man. How about we just skip the Mind Brace for now. If the bastard is so weak, let's just go for straight scrying. You have his name, yeah? Get into your book and find the section on scrying. You're going to use that witch's name and perform the ritual. You're going to find him, and if not, then no harm, no foul, right? It's cake and you've got fork in hand, yo."

"Really? You think so?" Richard asked uneasily.

"Absolutely," The Kord said with stark, glowing confidence.

"O-okay." Richard nodded. "But isn't it like the same thing? If we're both scrying for each other, doesn't that force a Mind Brace?"

"Dude, you're worrying too much and you're kicking ass. Think about that. You've destroyed an ancient witch's placement, you've stood against a wight, and you've traded barbs with a damn daeva. Scrying? That part is cake; eat that shit man. *Eat it.* Have I ever lied to you?"

I did. I did confront a wight, and negotiated with a daeva.

"Yeah, you know what? You're right." Richard nodded again. "We did do that. There were even some monster Sankai too. We got past them too! Scrying is cake; you're totally right. Seriously." The Kord always knew how to get him up.

Yeah. He's right. This will be the easy part. We can get this damn night over soon.

"Sankai? Tell me all about that later, all right?" Someone else in the car echoed the word 'Sankai?' and Richard heard more muffled speaking. He heard scratchy noise as The Kord covered the receiver and said something incoherent before he spoke to Richard again. "So you're set? Find a quiet place, get to scrying, and we're good to go, right? You're going to need to find some place that can help you focus those energies of yours."

"Hell yes!" Richard pounded his hand against the table. He glanced up to see the waitress giving him an irritated glance. "I mean, yeah. I'm on it. We'll get this done."

"It's time for a witch burning, Rich-sword. I'm out." The Kord hung up the phone.

Man, that guy gets me pumped up.

Richard stuck his chest out and hung up the phone. "I know what we're going to do next. We're going to go scry this bastard. See where the son of a bitch is nesting for when The Kord brings the fire to burn his ass." Richard grinned to himself and nodded to Ted and Beth.

Man, this is big. We're finally doing something. We're going on the offensive.

"We need to go somewhere private, somewhere I can go into a trance and try and scry him. I've never done it before, but it should be cake." Richard bobbed his head up and down. "I think."

Should be easy, right? Yeah, easy. I think.

15

"YOU'RE ALL PIDDLE-PATTING AROUND AND WASTING TIME, IT sounds like." Minges slurped on a fresh cup of coffee. "What's this scrying hoo-ha you're talking about now?"

"It's casting your mind out, to see a window of another. Find out where someone is, see what they're doing, all that." Richard scratched his finger idly against the table. "I'm not a powerful practitioner, though."

"And this is another one of those things you've never done before?" Minges scoured him with a skeptical look. "Some powerful hoodoo that you seem to be able to call up as needed?"

"I mean... I guess?" Richard shrugged his tired shoulders. "I've gone through the rituals before, but I didn't really trust them. Trust is a powerful component to magic—you need to believe it'll work. Besides, like the daeva had said, there were powerful energies in the air then, things you can grab onto. I could feel it all night, like an electric buzz under my skin. Maybe it was his name breaking, or just the fact that there were so many potent creatures running about.

Whatever it was, magic just seemed to come a little bit more easily."

"And you're drinking the Kool-Aid now, like you said." Minges smiled. "You get all this tied up in your head and it becomes a lot easier to fall into the dreams. Not to mention that tar you were eating before."

Is this all a dream?

Richard wanted to curse at Minges, tell him he was wrong, but, instead, all he could do was clench his fist, and wonder. Something itched beneath his skull, a feeling that told him it wasn't all quite real.

Is he right? Is this all a dream? Am I insane? No.

He took a deep breath and pushed the nagging dread deeper. He couldn't doubt himself now, not after all he'd been through. He had to stop the witch. He had to do what he could to make it all mean something.

Maybe I can't do it now, but I need to make sure that someone else can, that someone else can pick up where we left off.

"I'm not insane." Richard shot a defiant look at Minges. "There's a witch loose in Bridgedale and I'm the only hope there is against him now. I might not live out the night, but another will come after me."

Minges sighed and nodded. "Probably will do our defense better if you keep spouting it all anyways. So, what happened next?"

"This uh... this shouldn't be too hard. I think." Richard struggled to keep his teeth from chittering as he laid down in the cold van. He had removed his coat as part of the ritual, which called for him to bare himself to the world. Richard was pretty sure that meant to be naked, but he was hoping that taking off his jacket would be enough. Ted had driven them down one of the old roads and parked off to the side, hoping for some privacy.

The wight was hunched over him, struggling to fit into the small space of the van. "How frail a thing man is, that the elements can harm you so. Is it possible you may die?"

"What, from just a few minutes without my jacket? Come on, I'm not that bad!" His skin prickled, but it was important he have as much skin exposed as possible. Something to do with the meditation phase.

"Well, this is as quiet as it's gonna get," Ted said, looking out from the front seat. "Sure you don't want me to leave the heat running?"

"N-no. It's okay. But man oh man, it's getting cold fast."

They had pulled the seats out of the van and set them on the side of the road. Richard had placed a few candles around and drawn some shapes inside a circle. He laid between them in the cramped news van, thankful that it was big enough and he didn't have to do it outside.

"We can't do anything else, Richard? Only watch?" Beth asked from the passenger's seat.

"Just make sure nothing bothers me while I do it, all right? I'd *really* hate to wake up to find something chewing on my toe or something." He rubbed his hands together. "I just need to lay here and focus." He crushed some herbs he had taken from his kit, rubbed them between his hands, and dragged them across his forehead. "Jeez, I hope I'm doing this right."

"We'll watch you, buddy, don't worry." Ted said without so much as a glance back. He kept his gaze scouring the outside.

Richard nodded and lay back. "Just try and stay quiet so I can focus."

"Let's just step outside, Ted," Beth said with a smile to Richard. "Good luck."

"I will watch over my human," the wight said as he thumped down on his hindquarters, causing the van to shake.

"Just don't eat him." Ted said before closing the door behind him.

Richard closed his eyes and laid out his hands. The chill of the van seeped into his skin and burrowed into his bones; he clenched his fists in an effort to bite back the cold. Inside, he could hear the heavy breathing of the wight, and through the thin metal walls of the van, the muffled talking of Ted and Beth. Richard drew in deep breaths, filling his lungs from bottom to top. He rubbed the herbs between his fingers and focused on a name, drawing the letters like ink on paper in his mind. He exhaled and etched the letters, one by one.

Erlend Boberg

His friends were right. That name had power, and something more. It sent a buzz through his veins that seemed to stretch out around him. The buzz extended from him like his own flesh and he felt it touch the wight and the van around him.

Erlend Boberg

More than just a name, it was a target. A weakness. A wound left from the days of mortality. Richard focused on it and a creature took form in his mind—a beaked thing with dark feathers that fluttered for a moment in his mind's eye.

Am I just imaging that? Was that the witch? Am I doing this right?

He tried harder to focus, drawing up mental walls around the witch's name so that nothing else could come in. He worked the herbs through his fingers until he was sure they would leave a dark brown stain across his palms. What did he expect? He didn't know. He didn't know what success would look like.

Maybe it will look like some kind of hazy puddle, like in the cartoons?

"You think it's going to work?" Ted asked, in what might have been a shout for the way it pierced the van.

"I don't know. We have to give him a chance, though." Beth responded with equal volume. "Richard is sticking his neck out for the rest of us."

Damn, they are getting loud.

"We're only in this mess because he *doesn't* know what he's talking about. What we need to do is go sit our asses down and wait for his buddies to roll in here. Then you and me can just get on out, let the professionals wrap this up."

"You act like we haven't talked about this, Ted. The witch could be gone if we just sit on our hands. Are you willing to do that?" The frustration in Beth's voice was clear.

The beaked figure fluttered through his mind once more. A trail of feathers floated behind it.

Was that the witch?

Whatever it was, he couldn't hold it. It faded from his mind's eye along with the name and the walls. He licked his lips and opened his eyes. "Guys, I don't think I can do it."

The wight didn't look at him; instead, it was leaning into the front seat and staring through the window, as if it had seen something.

"It didn't work." Richard leaned up and rubbed his hands together. He was warm now, maybe too warm. Clearly the van wasn't the best location. "I guess I have to go outside." The wight ignored him still, its head shifting slightly from side to side as if to focus.

Richard grunted and turned to grab the latch on the

van, but found it impossible. His hand sifted through it and went straight through the door of the van. He lost himself in panic and fell through the van door, colliding with the ground. His head shot up to see the van door unopened.

He jolted up and saw Beth and Ted talking undisturbed. Richard started taking short, shallow breaths and looked at his own hands—they seemed pale compared to what they were before and the chill was gone.

I'm inside the void. The place between. I'm in The Outside.

Everything was pale. The words were no longer muffled by the van; the trees stretched impossibly high and at strange angles. Snow came down in small flakes and collected on the ground, despite this, he no longer felt a chill. He didn't feel anything at all.

"There you are, little witch," a voice said from up in the trees, behind him and in front of him all at once.

Richard struggled to his feet and shouted, "Who's there? Tell me!"

It's not supposed to be like this. I'm not supposed to be out of my body.

A black mass of charcoal feathers jumped from the trees and glided down to the ground, landing silently. It rose to stand as tall as a man, but it was no man at all. A large curved beak came from its face, and two small, beady, black eyes glared at Richard, with a third in the center of its forehead. It pulled in its long, black wings, even as more feathers shed from it and burned away when they hit the ground.

"I'm the herald, The Crooked King, The Walker between the here and the there." Its clawed feet stretched out as it slowly closed the distance between them.

Richard stumbled back, putting another foot between

them for each one the beast took. "You are the herald? For the plague witch?"

"I am," it responded, and kept its slow prowl forward. "Are you surprised, little witch? Are you confused? I think you're new here, little witch." It squawked what might have been a laugh. "I don't think you know what you're doing."

"Did you bring me here? What do you want?" Richard clenched his fists and tried to sound strong. He glanced once at Ted and Beth, still talking amongst themselves, unaware of the conflict.

"Why? Because it amuses me to do so." It leapt into the air and flapped its wings only twice, gravity no constraint, before it came down ten feet on the other side of Richard. More feathers fluttered down, most sizzling away before they met the ground. "This age sees few that walk the planes or hunt. Few that offer challenge. Few that can play the game as did those of the old ages. What little we see are those that stumble upon this place. Long dead are the orders of the slayers that may have provided challenge, now only the likes of you, the few and accidental. Such a bore, this is. Do what you can for me, little witch, run for me. Run for me so that I may enjoy this a moment longer." It stomped a single claw forward and fully spread its black wings, from tip to tip, farther than Richard's height. "Run!"

The fear caught him, and Richard ran to the woods as fast as his legs could carry him. He shot one glance back to see The Crooked King leap mightily into the air and flap his powerful wings over Richard.

Oh God, oh God! Run faster, run faster!

Richard's mind spun into a panic, unable to draw up any thoughts but *run* and *faster*.

Above, the herald squawked, a laugh that echoed through the world he was trapped in. It swept down like a bird of prey and cut across Richard's shoulder before taking to the air again. Richard cried out and shot his hand to the wound, his fingers drew back, wet with bright red blood. Real blood.

That hurt! Oh my God! It can cut me here!

It came to a perch far above in the trees, which didn't seem to move despite the size of the thing. "I've been watching you, little witch. I've been following you from here to there and here again. Such a curious thing you are, to have such power and to know such things. Do you know the words you speak, or do you mock them? Are you like a fool with fire?"

Richard clenched his hand around the wound. "I'm not a witch!" He yelled up. "I didn't mean to be here! I didn't mean to get into any of this!"

"And yet, here you are. You stir your finger into arts that you don't know, failing as often as you succeed. You challenge a thing that is the scourge of men, a thing no longer chained to a mortal coil. You dance with it like your blood runs as red as a god's. But I've seen your blood. I've tasted it, and I find it as bland and tasteless as every other man of this age." It jumped to another branch, flapping its wings but once. "Perhaps you can have a purpose. Perhaps he'll let me keep you, little witch. You are fun to chase and I enjoy your screams. Audacity is amusing in its own way. In time, you may find a way to serve."

"I, uh..." He let the pain help him focus. "Maybe, sure, but I've never really been much for servitude." He saw red slip down his arm and drip from his fingers; it fell to the snow but left no marks. He looked back to see that there were no footprints in the snow. This wasn't his world. This was a different game, and one he didn't know how to play.

Think, Richard. You're not scrying. He pulled you in here

somehow. Or stopped you here, or maybe this is the Mind Brace or Witch's Dance. It doesn't matter. You can't win here. What can you do? You can get back. That's all you can do. Black leaf and ephemeral salt can pull something out.

The cogs turned in his mind, drawing his thoughts to his satchel and the ingredients inside.

"Well I... Yeah maybe though? I mean, you seem pretty cool," Richard said to the crow.

"Eh?" it said as its head cocked to one side.

He took several steps back. "What exactly would the servitude entail?" Richard raised his eyebrows to feign as much interest as possible.

"Nothing you would enjoy, I am sure, little witch. But your consideration is of little concern." It leapt to a closer branch.

"Of course, of course." He took two more steps back in the direction of the van. "That's obvious. But isn't it lonely, being stuck out here? Why are you called The Crooked King, anyway?"

"I am king of this domain, little witch. Ruler of where you walk." There might have been some pride in its words.

"Oh yeah? And this place is lovely, obviously. I mean, seriously, I get the crooked part. That's your beak, right?" Richard laughed nervously. "But really, are you a king of anything if you are a servant to the plague witch? Wouldn't a better title be The Crooked Duke or something?"

"Fool!" In a blur, the crow leapt from the branch to the ground. "Your tongue lashes out at your betters! You will not need it to scream, so I will tear it from you!"

Richard didn't wait. He turned to run, while the thing squawked behind him. He looked back over his shoulder to see it launch itself into the air.

"Oh shit, oh shit!" he swore to himself as he dashed through the ethereal world.

"Run!" It shrieked from above. "Run!"

Richard caught sight of the van again, Beth and Ted still casually talking to the side. "Beth!" Richard yelled, but she didn't notice. He stumbled over his own feet and hit the ground face-first. He slid across the ground like it was ice, turning over on end and gliding across the surface, straight through the van. When he came to a stop just beneath the van, he sat up, his head pressing through the bottom, and gasped when he saw his own body.

The crow shot through the back end of the van, sticking its head through the doors and lashing its hooked talons out at Richard. The wight turned to them—its ears perked and its tongue licked out to taste the air. Its eyes turned to focus on the blood leaking from Richard's shoulder.

Richard shoved the thought to the back of his mind and grasped for his bag, but his hands slid through it as easily as they did the van. "Oh no!"

"Was that your plan?" The crow stepped from the outside into the van, pulling itself in and using this world in ways Richard didn't know were possible. "Is that black leaf and salt I smell? A pity. That would have been quite useful to you. You are excellently supplied. But I am the king of this domain, and you can use nothing here that I would not have you use."

"Help me!" Richard yelled in desperation. The wight's ears shifted.

Can it hear me? Maybe it can—it's from The Outside, after all.

"Ah, the wight. Worry not for it. The master will have it bound again soon."

"Wight!" Richard yelled again, causing it to snap its head

and shake the van. "Black leaf and salt! Get the black leaf and salt!"

The crow's eyes focused, curious for a moment. "What are you doing?"

"Get the friggin' black leaf and salt!" Richard screamed as loud as he could. The wight shot to his satchel and began to sniff at the pouches.

"No!" The crow jumped forward and ripped at Richard with its claws.

The crow's body was whole, and Richard grabbed at its wings, holding its claws back. "The black leaf! The salt!" He screamed again. The crow's beak came down onto his head, digging into his scalp with a piercing blow. Richard screamed again, not sure if it had gotten through his skull.

Then he gasped in air, real air, just as the cold was on him once more. The wight's hand was up, throwing the black leaf into the air. Richard's eyes shot from side to side, dazed and confused. A ghastly hand yanked him from behind, smashing him against the back of the van and pulling him up until he cracked into the roof. "And the salt! And the salt!" He yelled again and again. He was free for a moment before another yank pulled him hard and the van's back doors opened. He slammed into Ted.

"What the hell is going on, Richard?" Ted yelled from the ground.

"The salt, the salt!" Richard was dragged across the ground by something unseen. The wight stretched its long legs and arms from the van and hurled a handful of salt at Richard. It hit him and brought the crow into their world.

The monstrous crow, a disjointed mockery of man and bird, shrieked and tried to pull Richard up. It found the winds of the real world heavier than those of its domain and couldn't get into the air. The wight leaped from the van and collided with the crow as Richard was thrown in the scuffle.

Richard bashed into the ground, but he laughed—the pain was no consequence to him. He laughed as it faltered, as it flailed against the wight.

You're not the king here, crow. This isn't your world. This is ours.

The wight found no need to exert itself against the much weaker creature and its hollow bones. Instead, it wrapped its long fingers around an arm-wing and ripped it loose with ease, creating a gush of blood. The wight thrashed it against the ground with heavy blows.

Richard shook off the daze and stood up. "Hold it! Don't kill it!" Richard shouted through squinting eyes. The wound on his head was bleeding as fast as he could rub it away. He rubbed the tip of his sleeve over his forehead, staining it red in the process.

The wight roared in anger, but obeyed. It turned and thumped the bird against the ground. Feathers fell off but no longer burned.

Richard turned to spit up a gob of blood onto the dirt. "Listen here!"

"No!" The herald chirped. "I am The Crooked King! I am The Lord of the Between! I won't be held to your submission!"

"Oh yeah?" Ice water seemed to shoot into Richard's veins and his fists clenched. "You're about to become Lord of the Wight's Lower Intestine if you don't shut up and listen!" Richard paused and looked at Beth. "The lower intestine is the one before it becomes poo, right?" He turned back to the crow. "And you were only a duke anyway! A duke at *best*."

"Shall I begin the feast?" An eager, fanged smile crept across the wight's face.

"No!" The crow squawked. "Unhand me!"

The wight slid its large hand around the beak and pinched it shut.

Richard's hand shook. He hadn't been able to scry the witch and they were no closer to the end of this night. Instead, he had a head wound and several fewer components to work with. He was as close to death then as he had been at any other point in the night. This thing would have played with him, would have enjoyed enslaving him, or pulling pieces of him apart—and now he had the opportunity to do to it what it might have done to him. Anger growled inside of him.

"Richard, what is this?" Beth closed the distance, with Ted right behind her. "Is it the witch?"

"No." Richard shook his head and wiped away more blood. He grunted from the pain now as he was coming down from the adrenaline. "This friggin' asshole was clawing me up!" Richard bit his lip and did his best to resist kicking dirt into the crow's eyes.

Beth pulled a napkin out of her bag and started to wipe Richard's bloody forehead. He grunted from the pain as she touched the injured spots on his head.

Why the hell do I keep doing this? I don't know what I'm doing.

"You're coming out a little worse for wear, Richard. Thank God you know what you're doing." Beth said, patting away the grime. "Not sure what we'd do if we lost you." Beth gave him another smile that warmed his soul, cooling the fire in his blood.

Richard's shoulders slumped and he smiled back, letting her wipe the rest of the blood away.

Because I'm the only one that can.

The wight cleared its throat. "Previously, we mentioned a feast?"

Richard sat, silently considering for a moment. Thoughts of the bird ripped into pieces definitely seemed satisfying, but they needed answers. They still needed to find the witch.

I'd love to see that thing get ripped up right now.

"Well?" The wight prompted again.

"I'm thinking!" Richard shouted back.

16

"You're kidding me, boy," Minges snorted. "You just happened to figure out what it was to take that big fella outta a dream and into reality, eh? Must have a whole host of things in that purse of yours."

Richard ignored his condescending tone. "I didn't know for sure it'd work. I just had to guess. I didn't even know how to get back into my body. It was the wight—he has a foot in our world and a foot in the other it seems." Richard bobbed his head. "He did seem spooked the moment I began the ritual."

Minges rubbed his fingers over his graying beard, coolly inspecting Richard. "Yeah, he just went on ahead and saved your ass, eh?"

"Yeah, he did. I don't know what I could have done without him. Black leaf and salt will force you awake, throw the soul back into the body, but someone else had to do it. I didn't even know I was going to be in a projection." Richard's eyes flicked away for a moment. "Hey, by the way, you can't be a king if someone else is controlling you, right?

Wouldn't it be a duke or something? Pretty sure he should be The Crooked Duke."

"And you just knew that this would pull the crow out too?"

"Well, I don't really *know* anything. I have suspicions and I can guess. If he would have stayed in there and not followed me out, that'd have been just as fine." Richard sighed. "I suspect the crow is made of the same stuff the wight is, half here and half not. I think, when he had hold of me, I pulled him partly into this world. I don't really know though, it's only a theory. I think that whole place was a visual representation of what is happening here. It was snowing there, and it's getting bitterly cold here. And the trees just looked wrong. It's the corruption—it's more obvious there than it is here."

"Yeah, I bet." Minges looked askance at Richard. "Or maybe you were still coming down from that tar."

Richard sighed. "Well, I had to tell Beth and Ted what happened. That I wasn't able to see the witch, but, instead, got chased by that damn thing. Beth said she thought she remembered seeing a crow following us back at the house, in the woods. I don't know if that was him or not. Would he even need to follow us physically like that?"

"What'd you do with this ol' 'king' that you had wrapped up and bleeding? You beat his brains in too?"

"No!" Richard shot back. "I mean, sure, we didn't just let him go. How could we? But we didn't *beat* him to death or anything."

"Why am I thinking you are avoiding telling me you did something else just as bad? Is it because you *did* do something else just as bad?"

"Well, I mean, I had used up a lot of my components at that point. And you know what's something else I noticed?

Those feathers weren't burning up here in our world like they were in his. I think there's something there, so I asked Ted to pick them all up. I got dozens of them, seriously. And we weren't really worried about the guy bleeding out. I mean, those kinds of things?" Richard snorted a laugh. "We're not so lucky. You need some weirdo magic to mess around with those kinds of things; they don't die as easily as just bleeding out." Richard plastered a smile on his face.

Minges just gave him a dull stare. "Yeah? And?"

"Well." Richard folded his hands in front of him, lacing his fingers together to appear as diplomatic as possible. "I *might* have let the wight eat his arm."

The lawyer's eyes went wide. "You people were eating pieces off of something?" He scooted his chair a foot back. "You were eating people?"

"No, no! I wasn't eating anyone! The wight was!" Richard nodded as if that made it better. "Besides, the arm was already torn off anyway. But seriously, though? He was a total dick!"

"By God, son! What'd you do with the rest of him?"

"Well, we still needed to find the witch, and we wanted to milk what we could from the crow."

"Now see, I'm not sure when I should be taking you figuratively or literally with the way you're spouting shit. So when you say milk him..." Minges trailed off and tipped his chin down.

"What? No! You can't milk a crow! Wait, you can't milk a crow, right?"

"Wouldn't have put it past you to try." Minges let out a breath. "Glad we got that behind us, though. So we got us a one-armed, one-winged, six-foot crow-man writhing on a dirt road right now as your monster buddy has 'em gagged, that right?"

Richard considered and nodded his head. "Yeah, pretty much, I guess."

"Okay, so here's my next question: What the hell do you ask a one-armed, one-winged, six-foot crow-man that's gagged by a monster? What use could something like that have to you?"

"The witch, of course! He's his damn herald, right? He should know more than a bit about him. And Beth got him ready to pour it all out."

TED MOUTHED some curse words as he picked up feathers from the ground. A trail of them led toward the front of the van, while several of them laid around the torn arm-wing that sat a few feet away.

"Hmmm." Ted picked up a stick he found in the ditch at the side of the road. He prodded the torn limb. "Is that thing going to bleed out with only one arm?"

Beth had wiped away nearly all the blood from Richard's head. The wound wasn't as bad as he thought. He might need stitches later, but the bleeding in his scalp had stopped after several minutes of Beth's attention.

"I don't think so, right, Richard?" Beth said with a half-glance to the wing and then to the bird. "These things don't seem to bleed out ever. It looks like it's already stopping."

True enough, the bird seemed to be relatively fine under the wight's grasp; its stump had even stopped bleeding.

"Yeah. I guess so," said Richard.

"These things are total shits," Ted said with a shake of his head. "Won't even die like normal people."

The crow fought weakly against the hold, but the wight's powerful form had little trouble keeping it pinned. "Do we have need of this prisoner or should the feast begin?" The wight was growing impatient.

"Hold on, I'm still thinking." Richard bit his lip. "This guy was going to rip my tongue out and enslave me or something!" Richard shuddered. "Man, I freaking knew guys like him back in high school."

"You knew guys that were trying to enslave you back in high school?" Ted snorted before he turned his attention back to the wing. "This damn thing is nasty. Look at that." Ted pushed the feathers away from its arm and revealed a clawed hand. "Looks almost human, except for that demon-skin and those claws. Hey, thanks for taking this one alone, buddy. This thing looks... shit!" The dismembered arm's hand began to open and close into a fist. Ted instinctively hit it with the stick until it stopped moving. "What are we going to do with this nasty thing?"

The wight's eyes perked wide again in anticipation.

"Ow!" Richard grunted as Beth wiped some dried blood away. "Well, if he can stop being such a dick, we can try talking to him." He scowled at the crow, who motioned for the wight to let him speak.

The monster groaned but eased his grip around the crow's beak. The moment he did, it began to squawk curses at the wight. "Unhand me! You are beneath me, apostate! You—"

"Gag him," Richard said. The wight closed its hands around the beak again, clenching it tight enough that the crow couldn't move. "Eat his arm too, but save me the feathers."

A sickening smile ripped across the wight's face. It pinned the crow's face to the ground with its knee and stretched its long arm out to grab the meat.

The crow tried to hiss and fight back, but it didn't have

the strength to put up any resistance. The wight snatched the limb and shoveled the meat into its mouth. This close, and in the headlights of the van, it was clear how cruel and hideous a thing the wight's mouth was. Each tooth seemed to move on its own, each sawing away pieces of meat as it came in. The wight ate loudly, sucking away the flesh with selfish desire. Richard had to look away before it turned his stomach.

"For fuck's sake!" Ted turned around and looked like he might gag.

"Could you at least keep your mouth closed while you chew?" Beth shot at the wight. "What was the point of that, Richard?"

Richard swallowed what might have been a bit of vomit. "Well, I think it could have reattached the arm, but I wanted it to know I was serious. I didn't think he'd eat the whole thing in a few seconds!"

"For shit's sake, Richard, he ate *dozens* of those pig monsters even when he thought they tasted terrible!" Ted spat. "He'd probably eat that entire crow too and then want to find out if it had a brother."

Beth stepped closer to look at the crow. "You hear what they're saying? He'll eat you as sickeningly as he ate that arm. Did you see the way his teeth cut through it? Looked pretty painful, though it'd be over quick. So I think you need to be a bit more easygoing with our friend here, especially after what you tried to do to him."

Richard snorted a laugh. "Yeah, you'll be King of the Lower Intestine!"

"You already made that joke." Ted said as he rubbed his nose.

The lids on the crow's eyes had stretched wide enough that it looked like the black pearls might fall out. With the crow's beak pinched shut, it couldn't say anything, but it didn't have to—its eyes said the world.

Ted was focused on the bird-man, visibly on edge. His hands were curled into fists, and his jaw was tightly shut. Likewise, Beth seemed to have a cooler head, but it seemed like there was something beneath it. Richard could tell by the way one foot was pulled back and her body angled just slightly, as if she was ready to draw back if she had to. She was scared, but she was there to face it and talk with it, this thing from the abyss, that for all she knew could eat her very essence.

Richard was scared too, but it wasn't the same. He knew that, somehow. It wasn't that this spirit-walking, man-sized crow frightened him, it was just that it had claws and things that cut. This new world, new realm of existence, didn't frighten him. Richard was scared of a lot of things, but not this. Bugs made his skin crawl and if a woman gave him a second glance, he'd go mute. But he felt oddly at peace with where he was now.

"Now listen, crow." Beth planted her foot forward and leaned down to look it in the eyes. "We've been cut, chased, bludgeoned, and nearly eaten enough times today. You can keep quiet and fill the wight's belly, or you can answer our questions and go back into your world to leave us alone. You get me?"

Richard limped to stand next to Beth, the ache in his leg growing. He motioned for the wight to ease its grip. "Let's hear what he has to say."

The wight's long fingers curled away and the crow's beak stretched for a moment—the wight had probably been holding it too tight. Its black, scaly tongue whipped about its mouth as it spoke. "How can I know you won't eat me anyway? I can't get back into my world without magic, and it'll take a long time for my arm to grow back."

"The fucking arm can grow back?" Ted scoffed behind them. "Of course the damn thing grows back. Obviously."

"We've got the wight with us." Beth said, taking the initiative again. "Did you know that we traded with a daeva for information? Why would we bother with you? If you really have been watching us, you'd know we'd just leave you alone. You can be off to do whatever it is a crow would do."

The black pearls shifted in the crow's sockets, its gaze tracing a line between each of them, weighing them. "I was not a slave like the wight or the daeva. I served one more powerful than I because it was my pleasure to be in his servitude and I received ample rewards and freedoms for my service." The black orbs came to a rest on Richard, and pierced him with its gaze. "I would sooner fill this one than betray my lord. I would cast down my life to inflict upon you what harm I would. But I won't." It gasped as the wight tightened its grip.

"No wait, let's hear what he has to say," said Richard.

It groaned weakly as the wight's grip eased. "I'll tell you how to find him. I'll tell you where to look because my master would want it." A caw scratched from its throat as it shifted its head to the side to stare at Richard with one eye. "He knows your blood. He knows your name and he knows you have struck him. You will not rejoice for this wound, but cry because of it. For, with it, you roused his anger. He is an ageless thing! His power is dark and strong!"

Another caw ripped from its throat and echoed through the trees. It reminded Richard that there were things in the woods, things in the dark that he should fear.

Is it doing something?

"Just tell us how to find him then!" Richard yelled.

"My wings were true in my world; my feathers gave me flight there and guided me. There are not many places in that world, but one. You ran there as if you could go from here to there, but there is nothing in between this and that —there is only the between. A shade of my blood and a feather to finish will guide you to him. Wait for him if you would. Seek refuge in your shelters, arm yourselves for war. It means nothing! He hunts you now, little witch. He beckons you!"

"Cries of the defeated!" the wight said though a pointed grin.

Richard wished that the wight were correct, but something told him otherwise. A creep in his bones that spoke, instincts from the lizard brain, or a sixth sense he never knew he had before this night. There was something in the air, eyes that were watching him, even as the herald was imprisoned in front of him, like invisible fingers that ran up his back and down his arm to pull at his fingertips, welcoming him in.

"Your irritations have lasted long enough. But seek him if you would, for my master has no fear of you! Be quick, so that this night may finish. Be quick, so that—"

The feeling had pulled Richard too close to his captive. The crow whipped its hand free and slashed a claw at him, catching him across the cheek. The tip of it was enough to cut his flesh and draw blood, but not enough to end him. The wight shoved down with its arms, pushing the bird and its frail body against the ground. Richard heard its hollow bones crack and break nearly all at once. Like a starved wolf, the wight lurched upon the broken mess and ripped bloody chunks to gorge upon.

The crow tried to caw again—perhaps one fleeting

defiant laugh in the face of death—but whatever it had intended, it turned quickly into a horrible, suffering cry. Richard froze in place, and it wasn't until Beth pulled at him that he could look away. Another memory from the night, more fuel for the nightmares that were sure to come.

The screams didn't last long after that.

17

"The hell you say?" Minges spat. "You said you didn't eat him!"

"No, no, no." Richard rubbed a sore spot on his head. "I said, *I* didn't eat him!"

Rising to his feet, Minges scoffed. His thick fingers snatched up his paper cup as he paced back and forth, turning on his heels. "No, this won't do. There's someone out there that your people ate. Who the hell do you think that actually was? My God, did you people snatch someone out of their truck?" He ran a hand over his bald scalp and shook his head. "You got us right up a shitter, son."

Richard gulped down the lump in his throat just as the doubt crept in. He had been fighting the idea the whole time, but then where was that witch? It should have come for him by now, but it'd been several hours and there was still no sign of it. Hadn't he been attacked at every turn? Hadn't he been assailed with each step by the wicked things that had a taste for men? What if Minges was right and it was all a figment of his imagination? What if there is real blood on his hands...

No. He's wrong. God, I can't crack. I can't break. I can't let it win. God, oh please God, let it all not have been fake.

Something flicked within his mind's eye and horror crept in. Beth's face, broken and bleeding, a child dead at the library, the shriek of a dying cat as he clubbed it with hands that could be no one's but his own. Suddenly, his own thoughts were suspect, and only one thing was certain:

Beth is dead.

His lungs labored for breath. He didn't know what was true; there had been too many lies, too many illusions. He couldn't be sure. But, just as the ghost had taken Ted, the witch might have taken him. Might have made him kill.

If Beth is dead, then it's still out there. Even if I'm sitting here, I need to do what I can. I need to clear my head and get my story out there. Beth wouldn't want this to be in vain.

"God, I'm feeling so damn foggy right now." Richard clenched his eyelids shut hard enough that it hurt. "I just need you to listen to me. I need you to listen and stop telling me it was my fault. I need this all to have been for something."

"Lord," Minges's lip curled in disgust as he continued to pace. "*Witches.*" He spat the word out.

Richard's eyes popped open wide. "I don't give a damn if you believe me or not. I don't care. But I want you to listen and I want there to be someone else to tell the story. There has to be something. My friends will be here soon, and someone needs to tell them what happened if I can't."

"I'd *love* to talk with your friends. In fact, I'm certain that I will before this is all done."

"Listen." Richard struggled to keep the desperation out of his voice. "If you listen to me, get everything down and tell it to my friends later, I'll do whatever you want." He gripped the edge of the table. "I'll say or do whatever you want, just please, listen to me."

Minges turned squarely back to Richard. "Hell, you think I'm listening to all this because it's fun?" With a loud thump, he sat back into the chair. "All right, then. We're gonna hear the rest of that story, then we're gonna start talking about what to do about your murders."

A chill crept across Richard's skin, making it prickle. "Well. The crow told me that his feathers would help me find the witch, so with a dab of his blood I was off again."

"I GUESS it's The Outside? I don't really know. My best guess is that it's like a room of the supernatural world, The Outside."

"Like a room?" Ted crossed his arms and leaned against the van.

Richard exhaled liked a deflated balloon. "Well, like I said, I'm no expert. The Outside doesn't have to look like our world, but sometimes it does. Sometimes a mockery of this place, sometimes not. It's whoever is controlling it or influencing it."

"Who is influencing this area, Richard?" The soft sound of a tape recorder buzzed between them.

"I don't know. The witch, that crow maybe? I don't know. When it comes to their world..." He gestured to the wight; it was crawling across the ground and licking the bloody slop from the dirt. "I have no idea."

"Do you have to go back, Richard?" Beth asked and took his hand. "Isn't there another way? I hate to say it, but maybe we should wait for the others. You only barely made it out before—what if you can't get out this time?"

It was true—Richard had no desire to go back into a world that he didn't understand and didn't know the rules of. That whole place itched. Just as he went in, he felt its warm tips on his flesh.

But it wasn't my body, was it? I don't have a body there, I don't breathe air there. I don't even know how in the hell I bled there.

He shook, and not just from the cold. "I know. I'm scared to go back in again."

Beth took his cold hands into hers. Richard had no idea how she could stay warm through all this. "Richard, you're the bravest person I know. You don't have to do this, though. We don't know what to expect. What will you even do when you get there? What makes you think you can find him this time? It wasn't at all how you imagined before."

She's right. I could just wait. I should. When the others get here, they'll know what to do.

Richard wanted to leave it to someone else. He wanted to hand this whole thing off to someone more experienced, someone better equipped, someone who could finish it. But he knew better.

He's vulnerable now. That doesn't mean he's not still dangerous, but this might be the only chance.

"No. I have to go. We can't wait anymore. We have to do it now."

"Why?" Beth shook her head. "Why can't we wait anymore? Maybe Ted's right, maybe we just need to get the hell out of here."

"Finally, someone other than me is making some damn sense," Ted agreed.

There was a pain when Richard shook his head, a wound that he had sustained from the crow or from something else. "No. I just..." He struggled to explain it, but he didn't know how to put into words the feeling in his gut, the feeling that told him it was now or never. He imagined soldiers might feel it, or a hunter moving in with bow in hand.

But that's what I am now, aren't I? I'm a hunter. I don't have a bow or a sword, but a book and a dagger. This is me. I'm the only one that can do this.

"You have to trust me." He looked at each of them. "I have to do this. I don't know why, but I have to. I just have to."

"All right, Richard, we'll trust you." She gripped his hands in hers.

Ted huffed. "Not like we have much of a choice to begin with, but we're with you, buddy." He clapped Richard on the back.

Air filled his lungs as Richard breathed deeply. He wished then—and not for the first time—that he had his cross to rub, to gain some comfort from. Instead, his hand absently grasped where it had been.

"All right. Give me some room." Richard prepared the ritual again and laid once more against the cold van floor.

"We'll be here, buddy," Ted said from inside the van this time, with the black leaf and salt within arm's reach.

Following a guidance ritual, he took the crow's feather, now dabbed with the crow's blood, and laid it on his chest. It wasn't long until The Outside opened its doors once again. This time, he knew the instant it touched him. His eyes popped open, but instead of the illusion of the van and coldless snow upon the ground, now there was nothing. A black emptiness surrounded him. He would have looked at his hands, but there was nothing there. No hands to see, nor eyes to see them with. He would have tried to call out, but there was no air in his lungs, nor even a mouth to shout, only a spirit and mind to think.

What the hell is going on? There's nothing here!

Was it all a cruel game? Was he stuck in nothingness now? He didn't know. Maybe the crow would have its revenge with him locked away forever.

The crow, the feather!

It came, the feather, appearing out of nothing. It floated in front of him, continuously drifting from side to side without actually falling. With his will, he grew fingers and reached for the feather. And as his fingers touched the soft black of the feather, he knew the truth of this world: *your will controls it.*

He held the feather between two fingers because he decided there was a hand to hold it. Then, he stepped forward onto ground, because he made ground to step on. It was hazy at first, like a dream that he had leashed. But he wasn't done, now he would play the name in his mind, the name that instilled fear and held power.

Erlend Boberg

"Ah, little witch, there you are." The voice came from everywhere and nowhere. There was no sound here, so there was no voice, only thought and belief.

"Is that you, Boberg?" There was nowhere to look for the voice; there was nowhere to hide. A thing was or it wasn't.

"That is a name you are foolish to use. A name for a thing long dead and remade."

"Where are you, Boberg?"

No sooner had the words been thought than a place took shape: a gas station on a lonely stretch of road without a house to be seen in any direction, devoid of the woods that filled the rest of the town. No, here there was only the station, the road, and empty hills.

He couldn't tell the name of the road it was on, or if it was north or south of where he was, but he now knew it just the same. A connection was made with it that would lead him as easily as a hound's nose along a trail of blood.

"Are you looking for me, little witch? Do you suggest that I hide from you? Come to me quickly, and I will take only the necessary amount of suffering from you. You are an annoyance that can be dealt with; you may waste no more of my time and flee with what you still have."

"No," Richard said and heard thunder boom behind the words. "You're scared of me. I know you. I know people like you. You're terrified that I'll stop being scared of you. I'm not scared of you! I'm not afraid of you anymore!"

"Oh, but you should be." Gnashing teeth formed. "I've sucked the marrow from the bones of many greater than you." A claw appeared and drew a line in the air that bled, as if a mind could bleed.

"You can't hurt me here," Richard said, but he was still unsure. "There's nobody here. This is what we make it, and I won't let you hurt me here."

The face appeared from the black ink of the darkness, shaking the darkness off like drips of water. "It is only flesh that can be hurt, only blood that can be spilled? Where do you think you are, little witch? Whose manor do you think this is?"

Fire caught against the black ink and thousands of hands reached from it, each crying out pleas for mercy. "A mind is a fragile thing—it breaks as easily as glass." A rush of brown sludge filled the void. It moved and breathed, and patches of hair grew on it.

A being strode across it, one unafraid to touch the darkness—or it simply was the darkness. "I could show you things here, things that would cut you more deeply than a blade. They would scar you, for they are not illusions of fiction but of things that do exist, places where you can go, places where I may send you should the desire strike me." His skin was pale and putrid looking. Diseased.

Oh my God, this is the Witch's Dance, the Mind Brace.

"I'm not... I'm not scared of you!" Richard repeated, but this time with much less confidence. He tried to force his order and sanity across the world, but failed. What spots of light blossomed from the sludge and the abyss burned away like wildfire.

A thing with two heads—one short-necked and still, the other long-necked and waving—strode out from the dark. Another creature—without eyes to see, but with a mouth that filled its head—scratched its way across the ground. Dozens of little fingers peeked out from the black soup and pulled with them giddy snouted horrors. Still more drew from the unknown until Richard could not tell one from the other.

"There is no sun here lest I will it. There is no life unless I demand it. The light doesn't touch the abyss, and it won't touch here. Wake now and seek me, or flee if you would. But go now, little witch. Stay here any longer and you may not know yourself."

Though he had no body, Richard trembled.

Wake up.

A scream pierced the air, and it was several long moments before Richard realized it was his own. His hand clutched at his chest, where his heart thumped like a drum and cool air filled his lungs.

"Richard! Are you okay?" Beth jumped back into the van with him and grabbed his hand.

"Oh my God, I saw it all. I know what it is, I know what it looks like."

"Saw what?" Ted asked from the base of the van.

"Hell."

18

"Hell!" A throaty grunt erupted from Minges's throat. "You ain't got nothing if not a flare for the dramatic, son. Snort'n the funny juice will get you into all kinds of nightmares."

"What are you talking about? Why would anyone snort a juice anyway?"

The lawyer rubbed a fat finger back and forth beneath his nose. "You know what I'm talking about, I'm sure."

Richard shook him off. "It was Hell. Those things walked out, and you could feel the hate seething off of them. Those things were impossible—there's no way something like that would exist in nature. Those huge mouths, and claws, and hooks. Just everything geared toward pain and suffering." Richard shuddered. "My God, just seeing it, even for those few seconds, it could have stopped my heart."

"Yeah well," Minges said. "You learn anything from the trip?"

"Yeah. I learned where the witch was."

"Seeing a lonely place on a stretch of road was enough to tell you where he was?"

"It wasn't like that, it was like my body knew where he was even if my mind didn't. I couldn't have given you directions, or drawn a map, but I felt pulled toward it, like a dowsing rod." Richard nodded. "And I also knew him."

"Eh?" Minges puckered his lips and furrowed his brow. "Who?"

"The witch. Erlend Boberg."

A dread filled the room. Minges fell into a fit of coughing again; he doubled over and had to place his hand against the table. His face came up, red and choking, to stare at the wall for a few moments. After some time, he stopped and sucked in air.

Richard gasped. "Did you see something?" He felt the itch on his skin, the buzz that the name always had. He hadn't meant to say it—it just slipped out somehow.

"No, suppose not," Minges said, fanning himself with his hat. Despite the chill that was clawing across the windows from the outside, the room stayed just as warm as it had been the entire night. "What do you mean, you know about him?"

"I don't know exactly how, just like everything else, but we touched minds. I *saw* him, pieces of him anyway. He used to be a regular guy, a long time ago. Not sure when, it's blurry. He was just some guy though, and he got into all this. Started with some book and, little by little, he unmade himself."

"Okay. So why is any of that important?"

"Don't you get it? Why should we be afraid of him? He's not a demon. He's a thing that's afraid to die like anything else. He can be killed."

"Eh." Minges started to wave Richard off and glanced toward the door. "Let's stray away from that line of thought, eh?"

More than ever before, the fog was starting to pull away from Richard's mind. As things became clearer, they became more real and frightening. "It's all becoming a lot clearer now. What we did and what happened next."

Minges popped his hat atop his head. "Talking about things will do that. Helps get the memory banks working and the gears turning. We play it all out like this, even the fantasies—it'll all start to cut out the deadwood."

It wasn't like before, but now Richard watched himself through a movie of memories. His hands weren't his own, even though he could feel through them. But just as clarity came, so did the truth, the truth of what he had done and the blood now on his hands. A sickening feeling slithered into the room and up his back.

"Oh my God." Something cracked in Richard's mind as he started to remember, as pieces came back together, but he still wasn't quite sure. Despite how dry his eyes felt, the tears dripped once again. "It was right before Beth..." He couldn't force himself to say it, that she was gone. Instead, he absentmindedly felt for his chest, where the necklace had been. Just like Ted when he was possessed, he couldn't remember exactly what had happened, but it started to come back now. Richard's heart pounded in his throat. Slowly the pieces came together.

"I remember where she died."

RICHARD CLENCHED HIS JAW, ready to move. He was sure, *sure* that the witch was scared and *sure* that they needed to move, now, while the witch was at his weakest. There was no one else; there was no one to wait for. It was now or never.

They came to a fork in the road. "This way."

The wight greedily tore at the food they still had for him, only bothering to chew once or twice before swallowing and discarding whatever container it had come in. "It is important to properly prepare for war." It didn't bother to look up as it spoke.

"Yeah," Ted said from the driver's seat as he took the van down the road toward the witch. "I think you guys are right. Better to have the wight step in and take the licks before I try and shiv the warlock."

The wight looked up as jelly from a piece of pie dribbled down its face. "Take the licks?"

This was the first time Richard had seen any of these back roads, but he knew them all the same. Every curve and every tree that hung above was etched into his mind. Soon, they were coming to the empty roads where the trees had long since been cleared on the flattened hills.

"Are you ready, Richard?" Beth asked with a hand on his shoulder.

"Yes, I'm ready. This will all be over soon."

I'm scared, but so is the witch. When was the last time he feared anything? When was the last time he knew what it was like to be afraid?

"What should we expect when we come up on him, Richard?" A soft light glowed on the tape recorder as Beth held it up between her and Richard.

"Well, we can expect he's scrambling to get out of town. We've disrupted his haven, so he'll want to get some distance from here, rest up, and establish himself somewhere else."

"Yeah, maybe," Ted cut in. "Or maybe he's going to have another thing walking around with him like Igor back there." He pointed a thumb at the wight. "You were way the hell off with that thing in the diner, Richard."

"This isn't typical!" Richard yelled back. "Nothing here is like how it's supposed to be! You heard the daeva talk, it was messing with us the entire time, but it's done now. It's only us and him."

"Somehow, I think hunting witches requires some skill in improvisation." Ted's gaze caught Richard's in the rearview mirror. "We can't get caught with our pants down again, Richard. You asked the stupid daeva what it was here for and what it was doing rather than what kind of defenses the damn witch had."

"You could have said something, Ted, you could have offered a suggestion instead of sitting there ready to shit your pants!" A well of anger burst open and surged out of his mouth. "You've been riding my ass all night, but what the hell good have any of your suggestions been?"

Calm down.

Richard shook his head and spoke again before Ted could counter. "There's a lot of energy up in the air. It's turning things on end. Letting these very powerful entities move between The Outside and here, it's disrupting the power of this warlock, and it's giving us a chance here. I'm making this up as I go along, I *am* improvising."

Ted scoffed. "Well, what was the point of learning about the daeva thing then? Why'd you want to know?"

"Ted." Richard shook his head. "You don't get it, do you? That is something that used to have a *religion* around it. Why the hell would it be making house calls? And we did learn more from it."

"What's that?" Beth finally interjected, more interested in the story than the argument.

"Well, if he was under the control of the warlock, but able to get loose to come to us, we know we must have hurt the warlock pretty badly. Maybe even more than I thought, since his leash on the daeva snapped or at least got a hell of a lot looser. We also had to know what his hand was to play in all of this, why he was here."

"You rolled the dice and they came back snake eyes. Fine. I can at least understand why you rolled 'em." Ted kept his gaze forward this time. "Just tell me if I need to turn off this road."

"Fine." Richard felt a burning sensation growing in the back of his head, but he tucked the feeling away. Ted was making his skin crawl, so he took a deep breath and tried to let it go. His mind started to wander at what Ted had said, if he really did ask the wrong question, but he stopped it. There was no point in wishing he was somewhere else. He was here, now, and if he wasn't focused he could get them all killed.

"We're getting close." Beth's eyes widened as she turned to look out the window. "Am I the only one that feels it?" She looked down at her arm to see the hair standing on end.

"I'm getting it too." Richard looked up from the bowl. "This is where he's at."

Ted took them through another section of old roads with thick woods on either side. The moon was still high in the sky, but the thought that in just a few hours the sun would be rising brought a little comfort to Richard, as if the sun was all they needed to kill what lay in the dark.

They turned onto a more trafficked road and breezed past some old-looking farms that had fences with thick-wrapped barbed wire. They stayed on the road, silent as they drove, with less and less evidence of the people that lived in the town appearing outside the windows.

And then they were there.

They saw the light from the old gas station. It was far down from the highway, something set for just the people in town. It looked aged, like something built in the '60s or '70s, and they didn't seem to have even bothered changing their sign that simply read "Petrol." Richard was sure now; there were no further conflicts, no more ambiguities. It was clear.

This is where the evil lies.

"It's here." The hair on Richard's neck stood on end.

Ted stopped some ways down and let the van idle. He took in a deep breath. "Well, the lights are still on, after-hour lights anyway. Are we going to run into anyone else?"

"I don't see any other cars." Beth leaned forward and stared out the windshield. "I don't see anyone at all, actually."

Ted turned back to look at Richard. "Well, are we going to do this?" For all the talk of killing witches before, only the van's motor felt a need to fight back the silence now. It idled on as Richard worked up his courage.

"Man is such a fickle thing." The wight finally blurted, cutting away the silence. It turned to briefly gobble down a powdered donut. "Ride your carriage to the tavern there and we shall fall upon the weakened warlock. It is not such a thing that needs further discussion." As it spoke, pieces of the donut fell from his mouth. "We shall finish our tormentor quickly, in the same haste he would have for our party."

Ted scoffed. "You just get those creepy fingers of yours warmed up back there, Stretch. When we get there, you tear ass out of here and sniff him out, you hold him down, and I'll finish it, all right? Don't be too worried if a finger or two finds its way into his eye either, we're cool with it."

"What is 'tear ass?'" the wight asked, intrigued.

Richard cut in. "Just be ready."

The van pulled into the gravel parking lot as Richard reached into his bag and plucked out the blade. He gripped its wooden handle tightly and inspected the grooves in it, grooves in wood older than he was. He had to wonder about its history.

Has this blade ever killed a witch before?

"Let me have it." Ted snapped his fingers and held his hand out to Richard.

It's good that Ted wants it. It's the right thing to do. He can do it, you can't. He's stronger than you.

With some reluctance, Richard handed the blade over to Ted. They all filed out of the van. Richard breathed in the cold night air and searched the length of the road, making sure there was no one else who might interrupt. "I guess it's now or never, right?" He swallowed his fear and tried to lock it away somewhere else. He didn't feel much else—neither nervous nor excited—only numb. His legs felt like they weren't his own, and his body seemed to move forward without him commanding it. He felt as if he were only watching it all play out.

"Stay close to me, Richard." Beth warmed his arm with her own, entwining them together.

He was happy for it; Beth had been with him every step of the way. She'd been the one that fueled his confidence, helped him understand that he could do it all. He was glad that she was still here with him.

With his free arm, he gripped his satchel close, almost by instinct. He already had his hand deep inside, resting on his book. The pages gave him some comfort, as if they held the answers to everything.

I'm ready.

The wight stretched when it climbed out from the car, making it a good deal taller than the rest of them. A moment later, it hunched forward into its natural curved shape and used its knuckles to touch the ground for support. It didn't even hold the illusion of humanity when it scampered forward this way. Ted, clearly reluctant, followed behind it with the blade held tightly by his side.

There was a faint orange light outside the gas station, but with no lights on inside it was nearly impossible to see into the pitch dark. The wight swept forward, galloping on its knuckles, the calluses on its hands and feet providing ample protection against the gravel.

The wight pressed its long face to the window of the station, leaving a smeared mess as it jolted toward the door. It held its nose a few inches from the handle and drew in a breath, drinking the scent. "The warlock dwells inside." Its flat lips curled up into a sneer.

Richard couldn't help but think of just how the wight had been a servant to the warlock only hours ago, but now was eager to rip him apart.

What if Ted was right? What if it turns on me just as easily?

He stuffed the thoughts away with the fear—any more doubt and he wouldn't be able to take another step forward. He had to trust the wight now. He had no choice.

Ted stared through the glass door and into the darkness behind it. He bent from side to side, trying to get a better view, though none was available, then cautiously grabbed the handle, as if it too could be a threat that could sink its teeth into him.

We're crossing the Rubicon. The point of no return.

"*Wait,*" Beth said, her voice low. "Is that safe? To go directly in like that, as a group?"

"I'm open to a better idea if you've got one; we're not exactly a SWAT team," Ted whispered back.

When no one else had anything to offer, Ted turned again to the door. It stuck, but with a little force, he pulled it open. "Not locked—that's good, right?"

Or maybe he wants us to come inside.

A bell at the top of the door jingled when the door opened, forcing Ted to wince. He froze in place, studying the dark, but when nothing lurched from it, he continued forward.

Richard trailed in behind him. Faded lime-green tiles covered the floor and an old, dusty register sat at the clerk's counter. Soft lights glowed behind the coolers, which were filled with drinks that had old labels and promotions that ended decades ago. Most of the shelves were filled with products that looked like they had lain untouched for years.

The wight took a few steps forward and stopped to sniff the air. "A thing of decay, putrid smell." It took another whiff. "He's soiled himself."

"He shit himself?" Ted asked with wide eyes and a nod of his head. "Well, that's definitely a good sign, right? You don't usually shit yourself out of confidence."

Richard's calm was starting to break and he shook with anticipation, his muscles ready to jump or run. He whispered, "Where, though? Let's finish this quick."

The wight fell farther to the floor and sniffed as its tongue slithered out. It stepped forward to lick a brown stain on the floor before it skittered toward the back, with the group following closely behind. The wight's pace slowed as it came to a door and reached out a three-fingered hand to softly push it open.

Richard held his breath as the door creaked open, the smell inside immediately assaulting their senses. Richard coughed as the thick stench came over them and the wight pushed into the room with no clear regard to the odor. Beth reached in to hit the light, illuminating the room.

Nothing.

The small room was empty, save for an old bed with

dark brown and black stains, but nothing of particular strangeness. Richard sniffed the air but drew back again, covering his nose with his arm. He wasn't even sure where the smell was coming from.

Is it the stains? Something soaked into the mattress? Is this where I was supposed to go?

He was suddenly no longer confident, no longer sure of that gut feeling, of anything.

Beth let her arm pull away from Richard's as she stepped inside. The smell didn't seem to bother her, but her lip curled up and he could see the disgust behind her eyes. "He's not here, Richard. He's gone! You idiot."

Did she just say that?

His stomach was tied in knots again, and his mouth went dry. The witch was loose, and apparently Richard didn't know where. He failed.

The witch is ancient. It's dealt with things like this before—of course I couldn't find it so easily. There's no way I could have overwhelmed it in The Outside and known where it was.

"I think maybe it tricked me," Richard said sheepishly.

He watched as Beth scoffed and walked out. Her confidence had lifted him and her trust had given him resolve. He couldn't hear Ted's curses; they fell on deaf ears as he focused on Beth storming out.

"Fucking useless," Beth said as she walked down the hallway.

His heart broke.

19

"That it? You get there and there's nothing?" Minges shrugged his heavy shoulders. "Kind of a letdown, yeah? All that just to get to an empty room? Didn't find nothing there? Besides that brown stain that you felt like mentioning—thanks for that, by the way." He rolled his eyes. "The girlie got a little pissed at you, though, right? But that's probably right around when things begun to unwind."

Something clicked in Richard's brain. The little haze that was left fell away. "Beth was really mad at me, I remember that. Wait, there was something else." More unraveled, like boney, ghastly fingers reaching into his mind. The thin fingers grabbed at the curtain his consciousness had constructed and pulled it open.

The blood...

"Yeah? What's that, son?"

Richard's eyes mindlessly searched the scratches and grooves in the table in front of him as his mind worked. He dragged his finger over the web-like patterns. "We looked over the rest of the place. We found the crawl space, we looked through the register, everything. There wasn't any trace of him." He squinted his eyes in confusion, trying to remember. Drips of memory began to take color and form, but they came in cloudy and disjointed. The thoughts mutated and changed like water—no, like blood—in his mind.

"Then what? You keep telling me the same thing. I got that part; you didn't find anything."

His thoughts played out like a black and white picture with color leaking in, painting a horrid image of blood and broken bones. "Oh my God..." His voice cracked and then he bellowed when the color painted a twisted, dead grin on Beth's face. "I killed her!" Richard threw his head back and cried in frustration. Blood rushed to his face, making it warm and bright red. "I killed her! No! No, God, please!" The color formed blood spatters across the floors of his memory. There was no curtain anymore, no lie to hide behind.

I killed her. I cracked her skull. I broke her body. I beat her to death.

Minges leaned back in his chair and said nothing; he only brought his hanky up to dab the sweat from his face.

"No, Beth, no!" Richard wailed. He brought his hand down onto the table, beating against it until his knuckles felt like they might break. "Please, God, no!"

"There's nothing here, Richard." The frustration in her voice cut away at him. "You kept saying everything would work, but now what?"

"Yeah, there's nothing. We're shit out of luck." Ted batted

away a piece of trash. "Got something else there in your stupid book or what?"

"I... No," Richard was taken aback by their cruelty. "I told you guys, I haven't done this before! I don't know what I'm doing. I'm trying my best!"

"Your best isn't good enough. What the hell use are you anyway?" Beth turned to leave.

"Me and Stretch here are going to step outside, see if we can find anything." Ted glared. "Try to do *something* useful, all right?" He slapped the wight on the shoulder. Richard heard the bell on the front door ring twice as the two left.

"Beth, I'm sorry." Richard scrambled back to her. "There might be some interference here. I don't know what's happened exactly. It's not my fault, though. We just have to keep looking. If we can't find him, The Kord will be here soon and he'll know what to do."

"The Kord." There was a chill in her voice. "He sounds just as stupid as you. This is all just some game for you. You guys all stumbled into it and then dragged us with you. I almost died tonight, Richard. I almost died because *you* said *you* knew what you were doing."

"That was back when I didn't know it was real! I believe in it now. I know it's all true now. I just... I've never done this before!"

"Yeah, you keep saying that." She mocked Richard's voice. "*I've never done this before.* So what, Richard? If you're no help for us, then just leave. We'll do it by ourselves. You're useless."

What the hell is wrong with her!

"I'm not useless! I was the one that saved you at the house!" He felt an ember of anger start to grow in his chest. "*I'm* the one that got you out of there!"

"Yeah?" She stepped over to one of the coolers and took

out a can, cracked open the seal, and took a drink. "You're also the one that pointed us here! Everything, *everything* that has happened tonight has been because of your incompetence. You're supposed to be a professional, but you can't even do this. What can you do, Richard? What can you do?"

The ember burned hotter and spread to his shoulders and down his arms. "I didn't want to come here, dammit! I wanted to leave! You guys dragged me into the house! You wanted your damn story and you got it! I came along to help you, to protect you!"

"Great job you're doing, right?" She took another sip. "Look where we're at. The sun is nearly up and the witch is almost gone, and then what, Richard? *Then what*?"

"Shut up!" The fire in his chest burned hot, sending the flames up his neck and down his legs, a fire that burned just beneath his skin now. He stomped over and slapped the drink from her hands, sending it crashing to the green tile floor. "Shut the hell up!" Something in his mind cried out for him to stop, but the fire burned it to a weak whisper.

She responded with a slap across his mouth. "You're pathetic."

The heat touched that bare skin where she struck him. He glared into her brown eyes, those same eyes that had warmed him before; now they only made him burn. "Get the hell out then! Go write your damn story and leave me alone!" He shoved away a shelf of goods as he made his way out, but then he caught sight of it—an axe resting in the corner behind the counter. It looked new, with a *For Sale* sticker still on it, maybe the only thing in the entire store that wasn't coated in a layer of dust. Richard felt a cool breeze riding across his back; he couldn't pull himself from it. The power was there, locked within the axe's handle and sharp edge. He brought the axe up closer to his eyes to inspect it, not realizing he had even gone to pick it up.

The fire took control of him then, the heat surging into his arms and legs. He felt the adrenaline as the chase began, now hunter and not prey, for the first time that night. It came in a blur with only flashes of things that caught his eyes, things like the dull side of the axe catching the glass of the front door as he burst through it. There was a screech as the axe came up and a flash with a red streak as it fell. The screech turned into a gurgle as the axe rose and then fell again, a crack of bone to accompany it.

The anger drove him and controlled him, but it was the collapsed, bloody mess that had been Beth that brought him back to his senses. A strange, satisfied grin rode across her mangled head. His hand opened and the wooden handle slid away and clattered against the pavement. The fire breathed out all at once, replaced with the cold air of the night, the cold night that had been with him as much as anything else.

What did I do?

Beth lay there; her brown leather jacket was torn and bloodied. There was a huge gouge in her chest and several across her scalp. It had caved in like a rotten pumpkin. Her body shook and jolted violently in the throes of death—but the grin stayed there, unflinching, as if the reaper's own fingers held it in place.

Richard brought his hands up and into his hair, smearing the blood across his face and hands. His stomach jumped, and he felt as if his mouth would fill with the evening's pancakes.

The blood, there's so much of it, so much blood.

Where Ted or the wight were, he didn't know. He could hear the sirens now. How the police had been called or arrived so fast, he had no idea, nor did he care. Nothing mattered now, and he collapsed to his knees. He wailed loudly. The blood from the piled mess in front of him leaked toward him, drenching his knees. But something came in the thickness of it; a maze of lines and webs began to form cleanly in the blood. It cut away into a single word:

Lies.

20

"Lies," Richard repeated. He started to bring his head up from the table. "Lies." He looked down at his bloodless hands. He felt the dry leg of his jeans. Where were the cuffs that Minges thought he wore? Where was the heat that Minges fanned? Why did Minges not see the window in the room?

"What's that there, son?" Minges's interest was piqued again.

Richard didn't respond; he only looked to the spider-web grooves in the table, cut deeper now than they were only seconds ago. *Lies, lies, lies.* The word was scratched there over and over again, like a living thing that demanded to be seen. He burst to his feet and sent his chair clattering to the floor. His gaze raced across the wall, drinking in the bleakness of it all. The word was scratching itself everywhere in the room, and more kept forming. *Lies, lies, lies.* He turned to stare at Minges, still not completely sure of what was happening.

Minges too rose to his feet and held his hand up cautiously to Richard. "Now listen, son, take a seat there.

You're losing your damn mind. Don't you go doing nothing you shouldn't be doing, okay?"

"*Who are you*?" Richard demanded.

"I'm your salvation here Richard, I'm the only one that's going to get you out of this mess, but you need to listen to me." Minges's accent had melted away, while an uneasy smile slithered across his face. "You need to listen to me. Sit down, and let's talk about what happened after you killed her."

"I didn't kill her. I wouldn't." Something strong took hold of Richard. "You're lying to me."

Whispers filled the room then, seemingly from a thousand different voices speaking all at once, with only one thing to say: *Lies, lies, lies.* Their dull repetition continued and blurred out anything Minges tried to say. But he did try. Minges screamed at the top of his lungs, but Richard heard nothing—he didn't want to hear any more from him, so he didn't.

The voices stopped only when Richard decided to speak. "You're a damn liar, and I've heard enough from you." Richard moved over to the door. Without looking, he knew that the walls and windows behind him were melting away, along with Minges, who no longer bothered to resist. Richard knew what this was now, knew that he was trapped in the recesses of his own mind, and he would no longer be a slave to their control.

Wake up.

He stepped closer to the heavy door in front of him, but each step seemed to make it stretch farther away. He saw dark, demonic images fill the window in the door. He saw their razor-sharp teeth and their frightful smiles, as if they were waiting for him to open the door and let them in. Another threat from the dark, from the unseen, a reason to be afraid of the unknown, a reason to cower and submit.

I won't be afraid of you anymore.

Lies, he repeated to himself. *It's all a lie.* The door stopped stretching away as Richard took control of his mind, no longer a toy to be played with. He grabbed the handle on the door and ripped it open, frightened, but ready for what came next, ready for the monsters that hid in the dark.

RICHARD GASPED. He thrashed from side to side, dazed and confused as to where he was. The peace and serenity he felt only moments before while trapped in his own mind were gone. The very real, cold, and cruel world set on him. The aches of the night assailed him; a pounding headache told him this world was real.

The Witch's Dance, the Mind Brace, he had me. He was winning.

He moved to stand up, but instead rolled off a bed and fell to the ground, sending a gust of dust up into the air that filled his lungs and coated his face. He coughed hard and wiped at his eyes. The room was dim and choked by darkness; a single lantern near his bed was the only source of light. He heard something hiss in the corner.

Richard scrambled to his feet. "Wha—Who are you?" He was still dazed and half-blinded.

An eerie form took shape in the dark corner. The dark image sat in a woven chair that creaked as it started to move. The thing slid out of its seat and slapped the floor like a soaked towel dropped on a hard floor. A thin hand stretched into the light of the lantern and it started to drag its way toward Richard.

It crawled into the light of the candle, revealing its bald head and burnt, dark-brown skin with deep black scars scattered across it. Its limbs looked thin, starved even. Though hideous, its torso resembled a person with its head, ears, and arms; its lower half did not. Where a man would have legs, it only narrowed off to a thick, squat tail that dragged behind it uselessly.

It struggled across the ground, inching closer to him. Richard caught its gaze and recognized its blue-gray eyes.

This thing was Minges.

He knew the creature had been trying to control him, corrupt his mind. "Get away from me!" Richard stomped his heel down on its weak fingers. It wailed in pain as the bones crunched beneath Richard's shoe, but it kept dragging forward in its desperate attempt to end Richard.

It latched its weak, broken fingers onto Richard's pant leg and pulled itself up. It snapped its mouth open and shut in rapid movements. Richard smashed the bottom of his hand down across its soft skull and, as it connected, he felt something slide away beneath the creature's flesh and knocked it loose. It had no strength to stop him as he kicked it hard, again and again. Its brittle bones and cartilage cracked and shattered beneath his blows. "Get the hell off me!"

It moaned weakly as Richard turned around and rushed out of the room, only hesitating long enough to grab the lantern. Richard threw his shoulder into the wooden door, busting it open. He turned back to see the creature still weakly reaching for him with its other arm cradled to its side. He slammed the door shut and scrambled into the hallway, leaving the horrors of that room behind him.

The shadows from the lantern's flame danced across the carved, uneven stone floors and walls as tunnels stretched off to the left and right of his room. Something screeched from deep within the tunnel that went left, which was enough to send Richard in the other direction. His hand fumbled at his side as he quickly realized his book and satchel were gone.

Oh, God.

Naked. He had no tools, no friends, no weapons—he was useless once more. After taking a bend in the tunnel, a strange light shone at the end. The stone was slick from water that leaked down the damp walls and formed small pools on the floor. He moved as quickly as he could manage, while still avoiding the puddles. He barely noticed a door dug into the side of the stone tunnel; he gave it a single glance and hurried past it toward the light. But thoughts of death and pain clouded his mind, along with a promise made, a promise that could be relied on.

Where are Ted and Beth?

It would have been easy to forget that door. But his thoughts drove him back to it, away from the light at the end of the tunnel, and back to the dark and the unknown. There was only a moment's hesitation before he grabbed the handle and pulled it open.

Ted was strapped down and splayed across a wooden table. Rough, frayed ropes were knotted around his wrists and feet, holding him prisoner, tied to the operating table. An old air tank rested at the side of the table with a clear plastic hose connecting it to a brown leather hood that was strapped to Ted's face. Richard instinctively looked at the corners of the room, praying that there was not a horrid creature like Minges. He was relieved to find it otherwise empty.

He was next.

"Ted!" Richard set the lantern down, and with a quivering hand pulled the mask off Ted. "Ted! Ted are you okay?" He shook the larger man, only to see his head roll from side to side.

Another violent shake and Ted's eyes slowly began to open. He mumbled several words before he became coherent. "Where are we?"

"Hold on buddy, I'm going to get you out of there!" Richard's fingers worked at the frayed ropes.

"Richard? Oh shit, where the hell are we?" Ted was regaining himself more quickly than Richard expected.

"I don't know, but we need to find Beth and get out of here! What do you remember?" The rough rope cut Richard's fingers as he worked at it, but it didn't slow him down. Soon, the last of the knots came undone.

"I can't..." Ted blinked hard, trying to force himself to think. "Wait, I remember! We were inside the gas station; he came out of the walls! He hit us! Don't you remember?"

"They were doing something to me, they were in my mind," Richard said, blinking rapidly. "I don't remember much after getting to the gas station."

Ted stood up on shaky legs and nearly collapsed after his first step. His eyes returned to the gas mask. "What the hell were they giving me?"

"I don't know." Richard shouldered Ted's arm to prop him up, but he was too heavy for Richard's weak arms. He groaned and did his best to hold Ted up. "Come on, Ted, you have to work with me here."

"Oh, man." Ted retched a spray of yellow and orange onto the ground, partly soaking his leg.

"Just a little ahead! We're almost out. Just hold it together, man! There's a light at the end—we'll get to it and get out!" Richard grabbed the lantern with one hand and provided the crutch for Ted as they started to move out.

The two struggled to the end of the tunnel, which turned sharply to the left and merged into stone steps. They climbed up and entered the gas station through a hidden door set in the floor. There was a sharp contrast between the ancient-looking stone tunnels and the white walls and green tiles of the gas station. Without hesitation, Richard shot up the steps first and set the lantern aside as he reached down to help pull Ted out.

"I'm okay, I'm okay. It's wearing off." Ted shook him off and instead grabbed onto the edge of the hole to pull himself up. Climbing to his feet, Ted quickly jolted past Richard and to the door.

Richard left the lantern at the base of the tunnel and followed Ted, glad to allow someone else to lead. Ted, who seemed to have completely worked off the effects of the drug by the time he got to the front door of the gas station, ripped the glass door open, sending the bell into a fury of commotion. It was already starting to swing closed when Richard grabbed it and pulled it open.

Ted slapped his jean pockets, then pulled out the keys before he hit the van door. "Let's get the hell out of here!"

Richard glanced at the front passenger seat, and then something struck him and broke him away from his panic and instinct to run. That was where Beth had been seated.

We're leaving Beth.

"Wait!" Richard's eyes went wide as the full realization came to him. "Wait, Ted, we can't leave. What about Beth?"

"What about her, Richard? We can't do anything for her." Ted threw the door open and was ready to jump in. "Dammit, Richard! Get in!"

We're going to leave her.

"The witch has her..." The words choked out and he started to shake.

She's as good as dead.

"I know he has her, and *we can't do anything.*" Ted threw a cautious glance back at the gas station before he came out and rounded the van. "Come on, man!" He opened the van door and tried to stuff Richard inside, while Richard half-heartedly went with him.

She's as good as dead.

Richard wanted to go. There was nothing he could do now. He knew that she was beyond saving. If Minges was with Richard, and Ted was on his own, then the witch must have Beth. He couldn't fight it. She was probably already dead.

Ted is right.

Richard was halfway in before he froze, and something deep inside him stirred. He felt terrified for his life, for what he could lose. But, he felt even worse for Beth. "I can't leave her, Ted." His eyes grew wet.

What's my life worth?

"Richard, Richard!" Ted yelled and slammed a hand into the side of the van. "The damn knife is gone! It's gone! I don't know where it is or how to find it! We're going to get the hell out of here and let your buddy Kord roll in here later, all right man? He'll find her, he'll save Beth. You and I can't do anything."

The knife is gone. The book is gone. Beth is gone.

Richard simply shook his head. "I can't." He held firm in the door of the van. "He could be hurting her right now, Ted."

"Dammit, Richard!" He banged his hand hard against the frame of the van again. "This isn't a story! This isn't a damn fairy tale! *You're not the hero!*"

That shook him. He wasn't the hero. He never was. Richard never finished anything, was never good at anything. And now Beth was going to die. He might also die, but he wasn't going to run. He wasn't going to run anymore.

"Maybe." A cold defiance took him as he pushed away and closed the door. "I might not be the hero, but I'm not going to leave Beth down there." He shoved past Ted and started moving forward.

"Richard!" Ted yelled behind him. "Come back here, man! You're going to get yourself killed! Richard! It won't save Beth to die with her!"

Beth didn't leave Ted. Beth didn't give up when she found out that there was a witch hurting people. Beth never turned on us, never wavered. Beth held my hand when I was going to break, and whispered to me when I froze. I'll die for Beth if I have to.

With every ounce of his will, he forced each step forward, despite the instinct that told him to run. He beat back the whispers of fear that told him he was useless, that he should go with Ted. Richard wasn't a hero. He wasn't strong and he wasn't brave. He was a coward, afraid of everything. Now he was afraid for Beth, and would rather die trying to save her than live knowing that he left her to save his own worthless life. Beth was something special. She was someone worth dying for.

The last thing he heard before opening the gas station door was Ted's van bursting out from the parking lot. Richard had one last fleeting glimpse of Ted tearing down the road before he set himself to the hatch in the floor. He picked up his lantern and held steady for a moment, then looked at the hole in the floor, set in darkness and holding horrors beneath the green tile and white walls.

He held the lantern before him and let its light push back the darkness that threatened, even now, to overtake him. He moved toward where he had been, toward the tunnel where he had heard the scream. Every few feet, he stopped to listen, but over the sound of his own heavy breathing, and the beating of his heart, he wasn't sure if he was missing anything. With the lantern held high, he set his feet the stone steps. He held his breath as much as he could, commanding his senses to tell him all they could.

There was a dripping sound he hadn't heard before, which sent an echo through the chambers. The same smell of decay as the house and the monstrous children was in the air; it was the smell of a plague witch, this much Richard was now sure of.

The lone beam from his lantern cut through the dark as he made his way back to the room he had awoken in, back to where he had made that first choice to run from the scream.

He found the door of the room. He could hear the soft whimpers of pain coming from the inside, but he didn't open it. He didn't want to see that horrible face again, that thing that called itself Minges.

That wasn't the witch. Just another of his servants.

He started down the other way, farther into the tunnels. His hand shook, causing the beam to jump from side to side.

Another inhuman screech echoed through the tunnel; it lasted for a few moments and Richard had to close his eyes tight and stand still until it finished. Pictures of Beth in agonizing pain raced through his head. He tried his best to shut them out as he started pushing forward again. The hallway bent and twisted before it wrapped its way back around the foundation of the gas station.

The stagnant smell grew stronger and threatened to overwhelm Richard as he came to the end of the hallway. He pulled the collar of his jacket over his nose and breathed through his mouth as he closed in. There was a door there that looked much the same as the one he had left, and a soft light glowed between the cracks of the boards.

I need my knife. I need the book.

He hesitated. Would it help Beth to run in unprepared? Unready for what would come next? Or should he try to find his tools first?

A cry of pain erupted again from behind the door and the choice became clear: he couldn't leave Beth to another moment of that pain by herself. He grabbed the brass handle of the door and, with what remained of his resolve, he threw his shoulder into the door.

Tied to the chair with the same frayed rope and wearing a hood similar to Ted's, Beth sat in a corner, unconscious. Her jacket was torn and Richard could see scratches that trailed from beneath the hood toward her ears. The wight was there too, strung up on the stone wall with thick heavy chains and a small metal cage around its face. It shrieked in pain with its inhuman voice while a small creature, one of the Sankai, sawed off bits of the wight, leaving bloody, black wounds. The Sankai turned to Richard, an old, serrated butcher's blade held tightly in its hand.

But something darker had been watching from the corner of the room. A man with a black cloak shifted his head toward the intrusion, and Richard could see him clearly. His skin was a pasty white, as if the sun had not touched it in years. It was his eyes, or lack thereof, that drew Richard in. His soft, pink eyelids were sewed shut. It looked as if a bad infection had taken root there, stemming from the wire but not spreading to the rest of his face.

The cloaked man rose to his feet and dread rolled off him in waves. His presence gripped Richard, who froze in panic. Terror made him want to turn away, but he couldn't take his eyes from the monster in front of him. This was the blight witch, the plague warlock, the evil that had been corrupting him this entire night. This was the monster that ate souls and lurked in shadows. This was the reason men fear the dark.

The warlock's head tilted only slightly. "So good to see you up and walking." Each word dripped venom, every syllable a curse and a threat. "You've been so bothersome all evening, and why should that stop now? But you will be an annoyance no more. We will have oh so much fun together now." His thin lips tightened into a smile.

"L-let them go," Richard stuttered. "We're le-leaving."

The wight's desperate eyes found Richard and focused on him. It roared again, as the child-like monster began to saw once more at the muscle on its leg, no longer concerned with Richard so long as its master had him.

"But you've just arrived?" The witch glided smoothly toward Richard, despite how frail and old he looked. "I relish the opportunity to study someone such as you." A black, oily hand slapped against the wall; slime-covered tendrils sprouted from his fingertips and raced across the wall to slam the door shut. "Take a seat; you won't be going anywhere. I have many questions for you, and I had hoped to take it from you in a more pleasant way without wasting even more of my time. I have to assume that your presence here means my servant is dead?"

Richard jumped at the door slamming shut. Tears streamed down his cheeks as he spoke. "We just want to go home."

"No, no you don't." There was only bleakness on his face. "You wanted to kill me. You had ample opportunity to go home, but you've sought me out and now here I am. Are you some great hunter to wish to face me?" His face twisted into general curiosity. "Are you a paladin trained by the church?

A descendent of the Templar? Does a drop of angel's blood run through your veins? A powerful psionist with abilities yet to be displayed? Or are you simply a foolish bumbler that's outlived his luck? The latter, I suspect. It was rather foolish for you to come here. Now tell me, fool, of the other names that would hunt me. Give me their names now and I will end you quickly; delay further and I will make you watch as I peel the flesh from this woman's bones, and when her screams and pain end, yours will begin."

Richard's eyes darted to Beth; he saw her chest rising and falling with short breaths, taking in whatever concoction the air tank was forcing into her lungs. "Let her go, and I'll tell you whatever you want." He held the lantern up to clearly show his face. "Please, let her go."

"This woman, with whom you've shared my name?" The warlock stretched his other arm out and pointed the tips of his fingers at Richard. "I think not. I think your capacity to bargain is long expired. How interesting it is, though, that someone such as yourself could have come so far. You've killed my minions, stolen my guardian, burned my name to the ground, and now you think to assault me in my den?" A jagged smile scratched across his face. "And imagine my surprise, my utter astonishment to find out that you are *nothing* like what I expected, nothing like what I've prepared for. What twist of fate has been so merciful and kind to you? Did you bargain your soul with a demon for the likes of me? Or is an immortal out there holding your strings while you play out your neurotic dance? No matter—I'll strip my answers from your hide until I have no further use for you." An instant later, black tendrils raced down his arm and over his fingers and stretched sharp tips quickly toward Richard.

Instinct took hold and Richard hurled the lantern forward. It collided with the witch. The lantern spewed its oil and flame in a hail of broken glass, and a blaze caught instantly against the witch. A dozen shrill voices lit into the air, as if every part of the horror before him screamed. The witch's body burned and shot back against the wall, slapping against it like wet tar. The hot tar on the wall oozed and swirled with different faces forming in it, some with gnashing teeth and others crying out. Bubbles of yellow puss inflated and popped, sending sickness to splat against the ground. Wet tentacles thrashed out, trying to find something to punish.

Richard was unable to rip his gaze from the sickening sight. It wasn't until the small pig-like creature roared in its own pathetically small voice that Richard's attention broke. It stopped sawing on the wight and dashed at Richard with the blade, its thick jaw loose and wailing. When it closed in, Richard kicked it hard enough that he felt its jaw break beneath his foot. The force of the blow sent the creature sailing through the air. It rolled around aimlessly in a daze, no longer attempting to get up as it huffed in strained gulps of air.

Richard took one step forward and cried out in pain. He hadn't even noticed the creature's blade until he had tried to move; it was lodged deep in his leg. Choking back another scream of pain, Richard reached down and pulled the serrated blade from his wound, a burst of blood coming with it. He let it drop to the stone floor as he limped across to Beth and pulled the mask off. Her eyes fluttered open and rolled around trying to focus on something.

Even quicker than Ted, she began to refocus. When she spoke, her voice was weak and quivering. "Richard?"

"Beth, Beth, get up!" He slid his hands beneath her arms and tried to pull her up, but the rope was bound tight. He collapsed to a knee and searched for a loose end, but they were too tightly knotted. He pulled against them, but they cut Beth's hand, making her groan in pain.

Oh no! We have to move fast!

The pounding inside his head grew louder than the witch's screams and Beth's groans. He turned around to grab the blade, a simple thing that could be found in any butcher's shop, from the cold stone floor and brought its edge to the rope, sawing it back and forth, careful not to cut Beth. Though he worked carefully, a voice inside his head screamed at him to go faster.

Beth's eyelids continued to flutter rapidly as she struggled awake. "What is that, Richard?" She stared over Richard's shoulder. He spared a glance back to see the black sludge on the wall forming once again into the shape of a man.

Richard didn't answer her as he went back to working harder on the rope. A missed stroke slit his thumb open. "Ah frig!" By instinct, he stuck the thumb in his mouth, and his gaze darted to the witch once more.

There were four writhing faces amongst the sludge, but they slid together into one and began its curse: "*A thousand deaths*!" The voice was bitter, old, and pained. "*You will die a thousand deaths for what you have done to me*."

The head stretched from the wall and poured onto the floor, beginning to take shape.

"Richard, stop, go!" Beth pleaded with dull words. "Leave me, go! Get out of here!"

"No," he grunted. But the blade was not cutting fast enough; the warlock would soon be on him.

"*I will rip every bit of pain I can from you and from her. I will relish every whimper and every tortured cry*." The black sludge now started to turn into a thing of flesh; even the wire restrung itself through his eyes and the diseased pink flesh knitted anew. "*You will know the mistake you have made to think you could kill me. You will beg for the release of death every moment henceforth until I grant it to you, and then I will raise you again to suffer until I have had my fill. And only when your screams become too sickening for my ears to endure will I let you end.*"

There was no hope of survival, no possibility of winning. No magic knife. No powerful artifacts. No satchel with components or book with answers. He could stay and die with Beth, or run to save himself. Richard was born a loser, and he would die as one—he had no doubt of that now.

He gripped the rough handle of the serrated blade as he turned to face the witch, this thing that preyed on men. Nothing in his life had prepared him for this. Nothing about Richard told him he could stay and fight. He had no courage, nor strength of will to overcome. All that remained was a man, a weak man. And in that moment, Richard was content to die that way, but not without one final act.

"*Like an orange, I will peel you. Like glass, I will break you,*" the witch still threatened.

The fire was there again, burning hot in his chest and filling his bones. It wasn't anger or fear, but strength to stand and die on his feet, to die with Beth rather than to leave her in the dark. The fire spun up his spine and into his eyes.

I won't die cowering.

With that final thought of defiance, Richard stepped forward and the butcher's knife came up, even as another curse and promise of pain formed on the witch's lips. The pointed edge came down into the soft sludge of the witch's head. Richard felt it dig deep and strike with such force that the blade only stopped when the handle met the witch's bone.

The warlock's eyes rolled up to the top of his head as he

tried to stare at the blade. Where the flesh had only just taken shape, small black veins slithered out from the wound, like snakes that continued to grow. The warlock said nothing as it started to melt away. Like wax against a candle flame, his face began to drip. Sagging globs of flesh melted from the blade as if it breathed fire. He didn't look pained or scared, only shocked at first. He didn't die quickly, but took several long, confused minutes in his throes of death.

In truth, Richard didn't know why either, why a simple blade like that could kill the witch. Was it carved from enchanted wood? Was it forged in demon blood or cooled in widow's tears? He didn't know, and he didn't care. As the witch melted into a thick black tar, nothing more for the night to fear, Richard thanked God for whatever mercy he had been given. Then he went back to work on Beth's bindings.

EPILOGUE

BETH SAT AT HER COMPUTER, STARING AT THE BLINKING cursor on her screen. That night had been the most traumatic experience of her life, and writing about it was one of the hardest things she'd ever done.

It wasn't the rope burns on her wrists—she'd bandaged those—or the cuts and bruises on her body, or the fact that her notes and the video were lost; she remembered everything very clearly. But nothing felt right. Every word she typed was wrong, every sentence broken.

She'd already finished and deleted the entire article several times over, each time starting from a new beginning, telling a new angle on the story, but each time falling flat.

A Thing of Darkness, one title read. *A Night of Fear* was another. *My Night in Bridgedale* was a more humble choice. Finally, there was *The Plague Witch.* She hated that too.

None of it worked. She couldn't explain it, but none of it seemed right, none of it told the *real* story. No matter how much she tried, her fingers wouldn't tell the story.

Why? Why did it all feel like a lie?

Why did it feel like she turned her back on the truth?

Was it that she didn't expect anyone to believe her? No, that couldn't be it. She knew most wouldn't believe her, that they'd think she was insane, or just a liar. But she had to tell it anyway. It was still truth, no matter who believed it.

So why can't I do it?

She remembered when she was gripped in horror, afraid of what was to come, as she sat strapped to that chair, watching Richard turn to fight the witch.

To save me.

Her eyes were blurred, but she saw that mass of liquid rot cursing Richard as it clung to the wall. She saw that cheap blade in Richard's hand and, as he stepped closer, she knew what he was going to do. She knew he wouldn't leave her.

He was going to die there with her, but some part of her was glad for it. Glad that she wouldn't die alone. She was embarrassed at that thought still. She knew better, though, and screamed at him to run, but he didn't seem to even notice. He intended to die there with her.

Richard was going to die. The same man had trouble looking me in the eyes earlier, but he killed it.

It was startling for them both when that knife killed it. That knife sunk deep into its brain and struck the plague witch dead—that simple knife.

But it wasn't the knife, was it?

Only when its eyes sunk into its head and that low deathly moan finally escaped its mouth did she finally start to hope that they might live. And only when its elongated finger-like tendrils, stretching from its puddled mass, stopped flopping against the ground like fish out of water did she believe they would live. They had survived the impossible: Richard had struck dead an ancient evil, and he did it without artifacts or enchantments. Without holy blades or blessed necklaces.

Richard did it.

When he got her out of those ropes she wanted to go, run with him as quickly as she could, but he refused. He didn't leave with her until after he had found the key and set the wight loose. He told her he had made a promise to that creature, and that he wouldn't leave it behind. He wouldn't leave any of them behind.

I would have left it.

Even after he had freed the wight, Richard wanted to go through the rest of the witch's den. To make sure there were no other hapless victims waiting. He had told Beth to stay with the wight outside, but she insisted on going with him. Together, the three of them uncovered the rest of the rooms, except one that Richard insisted stay closed. She didn't know why, but she did hear something moaning behind it.

They found his artifacts, his book and his blade. They also found tomes collected by the witch. One, a diary detailing bits of his history and his family legacy, along with shelves of other tomes that held a myriad of information. She had looked only long enough to see that some of the early entries dated back hundreds of years to the old world, to Europe. She was still too shaken to look further, and was content to give them to Richard.

It hadn't surprised her that Ted had left. She knew he was only barely holding it together that whole time, and she didn't begrudge him for leaving. What sane person wouldn't have? They were living through a horror story—who wouldn't turn back? But she knew who wouldn't.

Richard wouldn't. He didn't.

Richard had stayed with her until The Kord and his friends showed up at the gas station. With no van, they were forced to stay in that evil place. But the sun was rising, illuminating the darkness, and there was no reason to fear that place anymore.

Beth didn't know how The Kord knew to come to that station; she could only assume they used some type of magic like she'd seen so much of that night. The Kord also didn't fail to meet her expectations, a thin tall man who would look at home at a sci-fi convention, and his friends were just the same. But they were all as amazed as she had been that Richard had killed the blight witch. No one seemed to know how he had been able to do the warlock in, how that knife could have worked.

She hadn't either, not until days later. It wasn't until after they parted ways, until after he told her he wasn't finished. He had told her, in the same casual and unpretentious way that he always had, that he was going to find the daeva that had tricked them. That he wasn't going to let it run loose in our world. That the new books showed him even more, that he was going to learn more, and he was going to go deeper into The Outside if that's what it took.

Richard wasn't finished.

But when he was gone, and as she was typing up her notes, the pieces came together. She burst into laughter at how easily they were tricked. She laughed at how the daeva hadn't lied but led them to believe what they had expected, that only something special, something *pure,* could kill the witch.

Wasn't it so obvious now? Could a blade be pure? A blade made to kill and hunt evil? No, a blade can't. But Richard was pure. More than any blessed blade or sanctified metal. The daeva had told them that the witch couldn't stand against something uncorrupted and pure. "*You* take *that* blade and you can plunge it into the bastard's head. He'll die as good as anything would," the daeva had said.

Any blade would have worked in Richard's hands, but that one was just the closest. Even after all that, he still didn't suspect that it was he who had that power.

The Kord had helped her and Richard fill in the gaps, like the creature that was inside Richard's mind. It had been trying to corrupt him, lie to him. And with his unconscious mind, he refused it. He pushed it out and was able to break free.

Uncorrupted. Pure.

She couldn't find any better words to describe Richard. He was more than the coward he thought he was, or the fumbling nervous man he appeared to be. Richard was proof that we could all become something greater. When faced with the impossible, Richard stood. Richard was the hope of man, and proof that our destinies are unwritten. Richard was proof that our fates are our own.

It was then that Beth knew what was wrong about the article. She erased the article's title, *The Plague Witch,* and changed it.

The Witch Hunter: Into The Outside

She hadn't been there to report on the death of a monster, no matter how cruel and inhumane. She was there to witness something greater than it—the birth of a hunter, a man of hope.

She was there for the Witch Hunter.

THE WITCH HUNTER WILL RETURN

Witch Hunter: Gods and Monsters

Coming soon

ABOUT THE AUTHOR

J.Z. Foster is an Urban Fantasy / Horror writer originally from Ohio. He spent several years in South Korea where he met and married his wife and together they opened an English school.

Now a first-time father, he's returned to the States—and his hometown roots.

He received the writing bug from his mother, NYTimes best-selling author, Lori Foster.

He is writing a growing universe and exploring all the dark corners of it. Check out his other books and let him know how you like them!

NOTE FROM AUTHOR

Did you like this book? Then *please* consider helping me out with a review on *Goodreads*, *Amazon*, or anywhere else!

I am trying to make writing my full time career to give you as many good books as I can, please help me do it!

Reviews help sell books and get the word out for starting authors like me.

Thank you for the help!

FOLLOW THE AUTHOR

Want to know when the next book drops?

You can follow his writing progress on his Facebook page, https://www.facebook.com/JZFosterAuthor/

Want to know what else is going on in JZ Foster's world, or write to him directly?

Send an email to **Boogeymancomes4u@gmail.com** or follow him on *Instagram / Twitter* at **@JZFosterAuthor.**

Sign up for his newsletter here: **https://tinyurl.com/JZFosterAuthor**

ALSO BY J.Z. FOSTER

Look for these titles on Amazon now!

Witch Hunter: Into the Outside

The Wicked Ones: Children of the Lost

Mind Wreck: Shadow Games

 Witch Hunter: Into the Outside / J.Z. Foster -- 1st ed.

J.Z. Foster. Witch Hunter: Into the Outside

Created with Vellum

Made in the USA
Lexington, KY
23 May 2018